P9-EKS-092

JACK WILLIAMSON AND JAMES GUNN

STAR BRIDGE

TOR®

A TOM DOHERTY ASSOCIATES BOOK

STAR BRIDGE

Copyright © 1955 by Jack Williamson and James E. Gunn

Designed by Greg Collins

A Tor Book
Published by Tom Doherty Associates, LLC
175 Fifth Avenue
New York, NY 10010

www.tor-forge.com

Tor® is a registered trademark of Tom Doherty Associates, LLC.

The Library of Congress Cataloging-in-Publication Data is available upon request.

ISBN 978-0-7653-3502-9 (trade paperback)
ISBN 978-1-4668-7045-1 (e-book)

Tor books may be purchased for educational, business, or promotional use. For information on bulk purchases, please contact Macmillan Corporate and Premium Sales Department at 1-800-221-7945, extension 5442, or write specialmarkets@macmillan.com.

First published in the United States by Gnome Press

First Tor Edition: November 2014

Printed in the United States of America

0 9 8 7 6 5 4 3 2 1

CONTENTS

STAR BRIDGE

PROLOGUE

"A historian is not just a chronicler of what has been," the Historian said. "The fruit of his labors is a series of terms from which the future can be extrapolated.

"His significant function is not bookkeeping but prediction."

Swiftly, then, in flowing characters, he began to write:

THE HISTORY

Empire. . . .

The greatest empire of them all, spanning the light years, gathering in the stars like a patient fisherman with a golden net.

Eron. Poor, barren planet, mother of greatness. Name of empire.

World after world. Star after star. Build a model. Scale it: one million miles to the inch. An Earth-size planet would not contain it.

But if you had that model and looked closely—closer yet—you would see the stars joined together by a delicately shimmering golden tracery like an iridescent web.

For an empire is communications, and communications is an empire. The fact of the Eron Empire was the Tubes. Each gleaming strand in the vast web was a Tube, a bridge between the stars, over the wide, dark river of space.

Star bridge. . . .

1

FORBIDDEN GROUND

The flaming wheel of the sun had passed the apogee of its journey across the sky. It had started down toward its resting place behind the looming mesa when the rider stopped to let the tired buckskin pony drink at a gypsum spring. Buckskin once but no longer; sweat and red dust had blended and dried into another coat.

Caked nostrils dipped into the water and jerked back, surprised. Thirst forced the head back down. The pony drank noisily.

The rider was motionless, but his hard, gray eyes were busy. They swept the hot, cloudless blue sky. No tell-tale shimmer disclosed the presence of an Eron cruiser. The only movement was the lazy wheeling of a black-winged buzzard.

The eyes dropped to the horizon, studied the mesa for a moment, and slowly worked their way back through the wavering desert. The rider turned in the saddle and looked back the way they had come. The pony lifted its head nervously; its legs quivered.

The rider patted the pony's sweating shoulder. "We've lost them, boy," he whispered dustily. "I think we've lost them."

He forced the reluctant pony away from the spring and urged it on through the eroded, red-dust desert toward the bare, dead mesa where once the great city of Sunport had raised itself proudly toward the stars.

The rider was tall and deceptively lean. He could move quickly and surely when he had to and his broad, flat shoulders were powerful. From them hung the rags of what had once been a dark-gray uniform. Dust and sweat had stained red the legs of the tattered pants, but the leather boots were still sound.

A canteen hung from the saddlehorn, sloshing musically as the pony plodded toward the mesa, its head low. Around the rider's left shoulder was a cord that hugged a heavy unitron pistol close to his armpit. Its blue barrel was stamped: *Made in Eron.*

No one would have called the rider handsome. His face was thin, hard, and immobile; where a month's bluish growth of beard had not protected it, the face was burned almost black. His name was Alan Horn. He was a soldier of fortune.

In all the inhabited galaxy, there were no more than a hundred men who followed Horn's profession. Their business was trouble and how to profit from it and survive. They were strong men, clever men, skillful men. They had to be. All the others were dead.

The red dust rose under Horn and drifted behind, and his narrowed eyes were never still. They searched the sky and the desert in a long, restless arc that always ended behind him.

An hour before dusk he came to the sign.

The rain that had sluiced away the topsoil had spared the granite boulder. From the rusty metal post set into it, a durex oblong hung askew. The centuries had cracked and faded it, but the bastard Eronian which served as a space lingua was still readable.

WARNING!
Forbidden Ground

This area is hereby declared abandoned. It is prohibited for human occupation. All persons hereon will surrender themselves to the Company Resident at the nearest gate. Failure to comply will forfeit all rights of property and per-

son. Notice is hereby given that this area will be opened
to licensed hunters.
—Posted in this year of the Eron Company 1046,
by order of the General Manager.

Horn spat through sun-blistered lips. For more than two centuries the nomads of this desert had been hunted like wild animals. The desert was wide—the fences of the nearest occupied area were almost 1,000 kilometers eastward toward the Mississippi Valley—but Eron was efficient. Horn had seen one savage on the desert; he had bought the pony from him.

Bought? Well, he had paid for it, although the pistol had been more persuasive than money.

The pony lifted its head and began to shiver. Horn raised himself in the stirrups and looked back. He stood there, silent, unmoving. Then he heard it, too. His back stiffened. He drew in a quick, sharp breath.

The baying of the hounds, distant and terrible. The hunters riding to the music of death.

Horn sank back into the saddle. "They've picked up the scent, boy," he whispered, "but they've been on our trail before. We got away. We'll do it again."

But then the pony had been comparatively fresh. Desert muscles, spurred by terror, had pulled them away. Now the weeks of relentless riding were apparent. The pony was gaunt, spiritless. The distant clamor only made him tremble. And behind him they had fresh mounts now, fresh, bell-throated, slavering mounts.

The thought narrowed Horn's eyes. Why were they after him? As a deserter? As a casual prey? Or as a man with a mission who had been hired three hundred light years away? Horn would have given a great deal to know; it could be the knowledge that would save him. He glanced down at the pistol. That would be a surprise for them.

His hand lifted from the saddlehorn to his waist, to the fat belt that encircled it snugly under the trouser band. Hard money, not company scrip. Money as solid as Eron.

What brings a man three hundred light years across the galaxy? Money? Horn shrugged. To him money was only a means of power over those who valued it. Not everyone did. The nomad would rather have kept the pony. Some things you can't buy.

Horn had told the man that, the man who had whispered in the lightless room on Quarnon Four.

The one altruistic act of Horn's life had just ended in failure, as it was doomed to do. The Cluster had been beaten from the start. But it had fought, and foolishly Horn had volunteered to fight with it. He had shared the fight and the inevitable defeat. Penniless, weaponless, he had gone to meet the man whose message promised money.

The cautious darkness had been a surprise. He had stared into it and decided, suddenly, not to take the job.

"You can't buy a man with money."

"True—in a few cases. And the others won't stay bought. But what I want to buy is a man's death."

"Three hundred light years away?"

"The victim will be there for the dedication of the Victory Monument. All the killer has to do is meet him."

"You make it sound simple. How does the killer do it?"

"That is his problem."

"It might be done. Eron would have to help. . . ."

As the plans tumbled over each other in his mind, Horn had reversed his decision. Why? Had it been the challenge?

It had been impossible from the start, but impossibility depends on acceptance. It is less than absolute when a man refuses to recognize it. The difficulties were great, the odds were greater, but Horn would conquer them. And, having conquered them, be left unsatisfied.

Life holds no kindness for such a man. Any defeat short of death is only a spur; success is empty.

With cold self-analysis, Horn recognized this fact, accepted it, and went on unchanged.

Horn looked back again. The hunters were closer. The baying was clearer. The slanting rays of the sun reddened a cloud of dust.

It was a three-way race with death: Horn, the hunters, and the victim. Horn jabbed his boot-heels sharply into the pony's flanks. It gave a startled leap forward and settled into a tired gallop.

Horn's only chance was to reach the mesa first. Fifteen minutes later, he knew that they would never make it.

He noticed the footprints.

They were fresh in the red dust, close together, uneven. The person had been staggering. With instant decision, Horn turned the pony to follow them.

A few hundred meters farther the dust held the imprint of a man's body. Horn urged the pony forward. The baying behind was loud, but Horn shut it out. Time was growing short. The sun was half a disk sitting on the mesa. Darkness would soon hide the trail, but it wouldn't dull the nostrils that sniffed out the way he had come.

The pony's unshod hooves clattered suddenly on a stretch of rock. The ground had begun to rise. Coming down into the dust again, the pony stumbled. Horn pulled it back to its feet. He strained his eyes through the growing dusk.

There! Horn kicked the pony again. Once more, nobly, it responded. The shadow ahead drew closer, resolved into something forked and weaving. It turned to look behind, opened a mute, shadow mouth, and began to run, stumbling. Close to another stretch of rock, it fell and lay still.

Horn rode well up on the ledge before he let the pony stop. He sat in the saddle for a moment, studying the flat stone table. It was a full hundred meters across. On the mesa side, the table shelved down gently to red dust once more. To the left, it dropped off sharply.

Only then did he look at the man crumpled in the dust. Once he might have been big and strong and proud. Now he was a stick man with blackened skin stretched taut over protruding bones. Nondescript rags hung from his waist.

Horn waited patiently. The man levered himself up on an elbow and raised his head. Red-rimmed eyes, swollen almost shut, peered hopelessly at Horn, blinked, and widened a little. Surprise and relief were in them.

A-roo! The hounds were close.

The man's mouth opened and shut silently. His tongue was black and swollen. His throat tightened and relaxed and tightened again as he tried to speak. At last he forced out a thin thread of sound.

"Water! For mercy's sake, water!"

Horn dropped off the pony and unhooked the canteen from the saddlehorn. He walked to the edge of the rock and held it out to the man in the dust. He shook it. The water tinkled.

The man whimpered. He dragged himself forward on his elbows. Horn shook the canteen again. The man moved faster, but the few meters to the rock diminished with painful slowness.

"Come on, man," Horn said impatiently. He looked over the man's head, back across the desert. The dust cloud was rising higher. "Here's water. Hurry!"

The man hurried. Grunting, grimacing, he crawled toward the canteen, his half-blind eyes fixed on it unmoving. He crawled up on the rock, one hand reaching.

Horn stooped instantly, lifted him, tilted the canteen to his lips. The man's throat worked convulsively. Water spilled over his chin and ran down his chest.

"That's enough," Horn said, taking the canteen away. "Not too much all at once. Better?"

The man nodded with dumb gratitude.

A-Roo!

Horn glanced up. "They're getting closer," he said. "You can't walk, and I can't leave you here for the hounds. We'll have to ride double. Think you can hang on?"

The man nodded eagerly. "Shouldn't—let you—do this," he panted. "Go on. Leave me. Thanks—for drink."

"Forget it!" Horn snapped. He helped the man stand, steadied him by the pony, and lifted the man's left foot into the stirrup. He shoved. Although the body was light, it was all dead weight. Getting it balanced in the saddle was an act of skill.

AROO! Horn could distinguish the different voices blended into the call. He wrapped the man's hands around the saddlehorn. "Hang on!" he said. The hands clenched, whitened.

The man turned his terrified eyes down toward Horn. "Don't—let them—get me," he pleaded in a toneless whisper.

"YI-I-I-I!" Horn yelled shrilly.

SPLAT-T-T! His palm exploded against the pony's rump. The pony jumped forward. The man reeled drunkenly in the saddle. He turned his head and stared back with eyes that were suddenly, bitterly wise. Horn watched the swaying rider. His jaw muscles tightened.

The pony ran down the stone ramp into the dust; the man clung desperately. Horn turned then and reached the rock edge to the left in four giant strides. He dived, lit in the dust doubled up, rolled once, and was still.

A-ROO! A last time, and then no more. They were too close now, too intent upon the prey to break the silence of the kill.

Horn heard the swift, soft padding of dust-muffled paws. He huddled close to the rock, watching the red dust lift over the edge, higher, thicker, nearer. As the hounds reached the rock, the sound became sharper. Nails clicked. Horn closed his eyes and listened.

The rhythm was broken. One hound had slowed. Horn reached toward the pistol.

And then a sharp command. The slowing paws picked up the pace. Dust and distance muffled them again.

Horn risked a quick glimpse over the meter-high ledge. They were gone, their attention all for the fleeing rider ahead.

Horn shivered. There they were, the terrible hunting dogs of Eron. Mutated to the size of horses, they could carry a man for loping hours; their giant jaws could drag down anything that moved. Four-footed terror.

And on their backs, shouting them in to the kill, the golden-skinned merchant princes of Eron, reddish-gold hair gleaming in the dusk. Mutants, also, it was said. More dreadful, certainly, than their mounts.

They closed in. The fleeing man turned in the saddle and clawed at his waist.

The pack was only a hundred meters behind when Horn saw something glint dully. Instinct drew his head down. A muffled sound of impact was followed by a screaming shriek of metal on stone. The bullet whistled far into the desert, propelled by the pistol's miniature unitronic field.

A pistol, Horn thought. *Where did that stick man get a pistol?*

Horn peered over the edge again. One dog was down, a leg crumpled under it, but its mouth was snarling with thwarted desire. Its rider lay stunned in the dust. The rest closed in, undeterred. Their prey, his last strength thrown into the one effort, clung hopelessly to the saddlehorn with both hands, his face turned back to look at death.

There was no sound now. There was only the silent pantomime of death being acted before Horn's eyes. The closest hound tilted its head, jaws gaping. The jaws closed. Within them was the pony's hind quarter.

The pony reared, feet pawing the sky in frantic terror and sudden pain, tossing the rider high into the air. As it reared, its feet were drawn out from under it. As it fell, it was torn apart.

The man never hit the ground. Savage jaws were waiting for him as he came down flailing the air with arms that no amount of fear-spurred desire could turn into wings.

Poor buckskin, Horn thought, and burrowed deeper into the red dust.

THE HISTORY

Toll bridge. . . .

Consider the man who invents a new method of transportation, whose toil shortens the way. Surely he deserves the gratitude and reward of his fellow men.

For centuries the speed of light was an absolute limit for space travel, and even at that speed the stars were years between. Then the Eron Tubeways Power, Transport, and Communications Company introduced the Tube. As soon as a conventional ship carried terminal equipment to a distant world, it could be linked to Eron. The stars drew close.

Three hours to Eron.

Inside the mysterious, golden tubes of energy, space was somehow foreshortened. It was a different kind of energy, and it created a different kind of space.

The Tubes, moreover, transmitted power and messages at the same speed. For the first time, interstellar civilization was possible. There is no doubt—the Company deserved a great reward.

But every bridge led to Eron, and the toll was high. . . .

2

BLOOD MONEY

The night was thick; clouds veiled the stars. Even if there had been a break in the sheer cliff face, Horn might easily have missed it. So, when he first saw the dim, reflected glow against the mesa wall, he shrugged it away as the rebellion of strained eyes against an impossible task.

The darkness had been a comfortable blanket as he had crept from the ledge toward the mesa. Since then it had become a curtain through which he couldn't find his way, a barrier he couldn't climb, an opponent he couldn't fight. It was an enemy, like the three hundred light years, like the arid desert, like the hunters, like the mesa wall.

The darkness would pass, as the others had passed, but the unscalable wall would still be there, tall, straight, bleak—impassable.

Now time was an enemy too, this an enemy escaping, slipping away hour by hour, fleeing minute by minute. The Earth turned, the night whispered by him, and the sun would find him—where? Still searching for a place to scale the unscalable? Or lying in wait for an unsuspecting victim at the scene of Eron's greatest moment? The bullet in his pistol was paid for; the money hung heavy at his waist.

Horn's jaw tightened for a moment—and relaxed. He had

conquered the others; he would conquer these. Destiny had shadowed him from the first, stepping in his tracks as his foot left them. Soon he would hold the moment, fixed on a sharp point of time like a butterfly wriggling upon a pin—just as he held his victim within a telescopic sight, a solitary player upon a fatal stage, and his finger would squeeze, slowly, slowly. . . .

The glow reddened, flickered, became certain.

It came from a depression backed against the sheer wall. Fire painted scarlet figures and dancing shadows on gray granite.

Horn crawled around the depression, silently, just beyond the fire-tinged rim of dust. The voices stopped him. One was a man's voice, mumbling, indistinct. The other was high-pitched, shrill, and vaguely feminine. A woman? Here? Horn shook his head and listened.

"Come, now," she said. "A little food. A tiny morsel? A forgotten grain? Shake out that old tin box. Surely you'll find a bite for starving Lil."

The man mumbled something.

"Search, old man. Look hard! I'm not asking for diamonds, you know, even a little one no bigger than a seed. Please? For Lil? A bit of coal? A speck of dust? You're an ungrateful old man. Day and night, sleepless, Lil works to feed you, to keep you alive when you should have been dead long, long ago, and you won't give poor Lil the smallest crumb to keep her from starving. . . ." The words faded into soft sobs.

Horn stared at the shadows leaping against the rock face. One, darker and more distinct than the others, slowly became solid and real, a projection of fantasy against the gray solidity of fact. It looked like a squat, black demon with two heads, one round and featureless, the other hook-nosed and fiercely dominant.

Horn looked away and crawled on. Every few meters he stopped to listen. The desert sent no warning. When he completed the half-circle, against the mesa wall once more, he knew that there was no one near except an old man and a weeping woman.

The sobs broke into a scream. "All right, you old sot. If you won't give me anything to eat, at least don't keep all the liquor to yourself. Give me a slug, you depraved old man, you befuddled rum-pot, you. . . ." The description that followed was fantastically scurrilous and inventive.

Horn raised his head cautiously above the dusty rim. And froze, stunned.

Below, between the campfire and the mesa wall, an old man leaned against a rounded boulder. Below a tight, scarlet skullcap was a wrinkled, yellow face. Slanted eyes were half-closed. A dirty yellow handkerchief knotted around a short neck was the color of the skin that peeked through a torn shirt of bright, green synsilk. A single suspender held up a baggy pair of space breeches.

Behind him, perched on the boulder, was a gaudy, red-and-green bird; it balanced itself precariously on one leg as the other tilted a half-liter bottle into a preposterously big bill. She was bedraggled and disreputable. One tail-feather was broken and several were obviously missing. She had only one eye; it blinked in the firelight.

A small pot hung over the fire. From it drifted an odor that brought a jet of saliva into Horn's mouth. The only other thing in the hollow was a battered metal suitcase close beside the old man.

Horn took a deep breath and launched himself into the camp, his pistol in his hand. One foot kicked dust over the fire as he passed. It died, smoking. Horn stopped with his back against the rock wall.

The bird strangled. She dropped the bottle and fluttered into the air on battered wings. The old man sprang to his feet, black eyes wild and staring, fat quivering on his round face and short, stout body.

"Pirates!" the bird croaked. "Stand by to repel boarders!"

The color of the man's wrinkled, ageless face had faded to a pale yellow. "No killee!" he said in an archaic dialect. His voice quavered nasally. "Please no killee poor China boy." He hiccoughed. Horn caught a faint whiff of synthetic alcohol. "Poor li'l China laundly boy no makee bother noblody!"

It sounded phony to Horn. Phonier, even, than the ridiculous pair being here below the ruins of Sunport.

Horn glanced at the suitcase beside the man's feet. There was lettering on the side; it was scratched, faded, and archaic, like the old man's speech. It said: *Mr. Oliver Wu, Proprietor, New Canton Sanitary Laundry*. Horn took four quick strides to the right. On the other side, he read: *Lily. The Mathematical Parrot. Can Do Sums.*

"Poor China boy will get himself killed quick with a fire on the Forbidden Ground," Horn said deliberately. "A hunting party of the Golden Folk trailed me to within half a kilometer of this spot."

Wu's face got paler. His legs gave way under him. He sank down in front of the boulder. The parrot settled on his shoulder, staring at Horn with her one good eye.

"Poor li'l China boy," Wu said shakily. "No gottee nothing. One stupid bird." He cringed as the bird bit his ear. "One dirty clothes." His patched, outsize boot kicked the battered suitcase. "No makee tlouble noblody."

"The hunters will kill you just as quick," Horn said casually. "They're gone now, but they'll be back. If we're still here. . . ." He let it hang in the air, unfinished.

"No one talks well," the parrot said, "with gun in face."

Horn laughed, mirthlessly, and dropped the gun. The cord pulled it up tightly to his chest, ready to the slap of his hand. "Smart bird," he said. "Very smart. Smart enough to talk better than his master."

Slowly the color returned to Wu's face. "They aren't close then?" he panted. "The hunters?"

"You can speak the lingua! Maybe you can speak it well enough to tell me what you're doing here."

Wu sighed and breathed easier. "Even miserable creatures like us must live—or think we must," he said sorrowfully. "When the rich feast, crumbs fall under the table. Hunger is a fearful goad. It drove us a weary distance across the dreadful desert to reach the

Victory Dedication. Tormented by thirst, chased by the hunters."
Wu shuddered. "We saw three men die for their sport."

Lil waggled her head, her eyes gleaming in the darkness. "The
bloody, bloody hunters. And the dead men all had guns like yours,
stranger."

"Odd," Wu mused, "that they should have unitron pistols. Eron
guards them jealously." He glanced slantingly at Horn. Horn stared
back, his arms folded across his chest, his lips a straight, immobile
line. "Many died," Wu went on, "but we got through the desert and
the hunters, and tomorrow we will be at the ruins. And there we
will find means to continue life a little longer, eh, Lil?"

Horn's eyelids flickered.

"The weak are killed," Lil said flatly. "The fit survive."

She cocked her head and stared at the ground. The bottle had
long since spilled its contents into the dust. "Oh, the lovely, lovely
liquor. All gone, all gone." A large tear gathered in her eye and
dropped onto Wu's green shirt.

Suddenly Wu scrambled to his knees. Lil flapped into the air,
complaining raucously. Wu knelt beside the ashes of the fire and
peered into the pot. "Dust in the stew. Ah, me! But maybe something can be saved." He picked up a battered spoon, carefully
skimmed off the surface layer of liquid, and cast it on the ground.
The second dip he raised to his lips. He tasted it critically. "Marred
but edible. Insignificant as our lives are, stranger, you have dis-
rupted them considerably."

"Horn is the name." A flick of his hand sent a glistening crystal
disk spinning through the air; Wu caught it deftly. "I'm in nobody's
debt."

"A five-kellon piece," Wu said, raising the gold-banded disk to
his eye. The clouds had begun to scatter; a few stars peered through.
"Genuine, too. The beautiful new regent. Beauty and value. A rare
combination. It will more than repay us for our inconvenience, eh,
Lil?" The coin disappeared in Wu's voluminous clothing.

"What is beauty to an empty stomach?" the parrot grumbled.

"Proof Lil has the soul of an earthworm." Wu began ladling stew into two chipped plastic plates. He held one out to Horn. "Here. Since you have paid, you deserve a share."

Horn hesitated momentarily and then walked forward to accept the food. He retreated to the wall, squatted on his heels, and waited. Ignoring Horn's caution, Wu dived into the mixture with thick fingers. After a moment, Horn began to eat. In spite of an occasional bite that gritted between the teeth, the stew was surprisingly delicious. Small chunks of meat were identifiably rabbit; the other ingredients were obscure.

It vanished quickly. Horn tilted the plate to his mouth and let the last of the broth trickle down his throat. For the first time in many days, his stomach felt warm and full. He was sleepy and tired; taut muscles and strung nerves relaxed. The warmth swept out toward the fat old man and his bird like a wave of gratitude—

Horn straightened, scoured his plate in the sand at the base of the rock wall, and dropped it at Wu's feet. "Thanks," he said flatly. He went back to the wall, wiping greasy fingers on the rags of his pants. He squatted again and keyed his senses to their habitual, restless awareness.

Wu had pushed his plate away with a contented sigh. He turned to the suitcase beside him, his body blocking Horn's view. When he swung back, the suitcase was closed and another half-liter of alcohol was in his hand. He took several generous swallows and held it out, inquiringly, to Horn. Horn shook his head. Lil, who had eaten nothing, grabbed the neck of the bottle with eager claws. She turned it up; the clear liquid gurgled down her throat.

Wu rummaged in a deep pocket and finally pulled out a battered plug of lethe weed. Fastidiously cleaning one corner of lint, he gnawed it off and began to chew, his eyes half-closed.

Horn studied him. The last man he had seen mix the weed and alcohol had died quickly. At one time, Horn had smuggled the weed, but fumes from the hold had knocked out everyone for days and almost wrecked the ship. Wu seemed unaffected.

The old man spat. The dust turned a reddish-brown. "Here we are," he mused. "Three outcasts met on the Forbidden Ground. Did you know this was once the most fertile farmland on the continent?"

"I don't believe it," Horn said.

Wu shrugged. "It doesn't matter. I mention it only to illustrate the folly of men who think they shape their destinies. What strange eddy in the river of history swept us here? Where will it take us next?"

"It takes me nowhere," Horn said. "I go where I wish."

"So we think, so we think. In the middle of things, we see no pattern. But as we look back and view the picture whole, we realize how men are moved about by forces they do not suspect. The pieces fall into place. The pattern is clear."

Horn was silent.

"Lil and I, we think we go to the ruins of Sunport because we choose, but it is our hunger that drives us. And hunger is a force that has no equal. Why do you go there?"

The question was casual and unexpected; it took Horn by surprise. He blinked once before his eyes narrowed. "Who said I do?"

"Why else should you be here on the desert? Do you go to steal, like Lil and I, or to kill?"

"There is no other choice?"

"For a deserter with a gun? What else would he be doing at the Dedication? To steal or to kill, it makes no difference. The ruins will be better guarded than any spot in the Empire, and brute force must always bow to greater force. It is a pity for one to die so young."

Horn waited. He had schooled himself to wait until others had identified themselves and their purposes.

"We're three of a kind," Wu said. "We need have no secrets, one from the others. Lil and I, we have lived too long to be moralists. Men must live, and they must do what they must do."

"I won't die," Horn said.

"So we think, so we all think. And yet we do. But you may be right. You won't die now because you won't reach the ruins in time."

"You're wrong," Horn said calmly. "As you said, we are three of a kind. We need have no secrets. You are going to the Dedication; you will show me the way."

The cold certainty that the old man would be his guide had come a long time ago. Maybe he had known it as he watched from above the depression.

"No, no," Wu stammered. "I couldn't do that. I mean—that would be—"

Horn's eyes were icy on Wu's face.

Wu squirmed, shrugged, and sank back. "As you will. Outcasts must stick together. But you don't realize the chain of causation you are beginning."

"Men," Lil said darkly, "fashion their own nooses."

Horn stared at them silently, ridges slowly forming between his eyebrows. Wu yawned, shivered, and lay down by the cold ashes of the fire. He curled into a fetal position.

"No watch?" Horn asked sardonically.

"For what?" Wu's voice was muffled. "Death will come, just as dawn will come. If they come together, there is no help for it. I'm not going to stay awake to watch for either."

"How have you survived so long?"

A yawn reached Horn's ears. "By eating regularly, sleeping whenever possible, and not worrying about tomorrow. The wall is to our backs. Where would we run? Besides, Lil will watch."

Horn shrugged and climbed with habitual caution to the rim of the depression. After his senses had adjusted to the silence and the night, he let them roam out into the desert, but they brought him no warning. He settled down against the mesa wall to wait out the night.

The clouds had vanished. The stars were out, and the sky was brilliant. He could see a long way into the desert; it was lifeless. He pinched the heavy belt inside the waistband of his pants. A coin was ejected into his hand. The crystal disk had a silver rim. He held it up between his eye and the stars.

His hand trembled. He caught it quickly, stopped the tremor, held the coin steady. The strain had been great for a long time, but it would be fatal to let loose now.

Garth Kohlnar stared at him out of the coin. His massive, bronze face, his stiff, reddish hair, his yellow-gray eyes were startlingly lifelike. Powerful and dominant, the General Manager of the Eron Company fixed the holder of the coin with unwavering eyes, as if to say:

"Here is money. Here is the stuff of trade, the symbol of empire. Here is good money, hard money, crafted so carefully that counterfeit is impossible, backed by all the might and wealth of Eron. You have toiled for it, but your toil was not wasted. You hold your reward in your hands, a work of art, a token of value. Whatever you have done to get this coin was worthwhile. You own a share of Eron. Ask for it. It will be delivered without question."

The night wind was cold on Horn's half-naked body. He resisted the impulse to shiver. He laid the coin in the dust of the desert and drew out another and another until five of the crystal disks lay side by side, silver-rimmed, orange, green, blue, black. The General Manager and four of his five Directors: Matal for Power, Fenelon for Transport, Ronholm for Commerce, Duchane for Security.

Five faces: thin and round, long and short, bold and cunning. The differences were unimportant. They all had the golden skin of the pureblood, and an even deeper kinship spoke through the eyes. It was the kinship of power, an imperial hunger only half-satisfied and basically unappeasable.

The sixth coin was gold-banded like the one Horn had tossed to Wu. The symbol of the Directorship of Communications. Horn held the coin up to the stars.

The coin held a woman's face as a morning flower holds a drop of dew, mirroring in it the limitless possibilities of the world that begins again. Her skin was softly golden against red-gold hair confined by a fillet of immense white diamonds. Her red lips curved gently in the faint beginning of a smile; they promised an empire to the man who could win them. And her head, held proudly, told him that an empire would not be enough to lay at her feet. Her tawny eyes looked out at Horn, sank deep into his eyes, judging, weighing. . . .

Is this the man?

"The lovely Wendre," a voice wheezed. "Wendre Kohlnar, the new Director, daughter of the General Manager."

Startled, Horn turned at the first words. His hand darted toward his gun, dropping the coin. Wu knelt beside him. He was unarmed. Horn's hand fell back to his side.

"Beautiful," Wu went on casually, "and heir to all that." He waved a careless hand at the star-studded sky. "If she can find a man strong enough to hold it for her."

"All except that," Horn said. He pointed toward the seven sisters of the Pleiades Cluster, just rising on the horizon. "Eron has conquered the Quarnon League, but keeping it is another matter."

"The tides of empire rise," Wu said softly. "A few always flee in front of it, but the waves crash after them. Now they have crushed the Cluster. They have smashed it flat. It will never rise again. When the tide recedes at last, it will leave only sand-strewn ruins."

"The defeat isn't final. Not while the Liberator lives."

"You think Eron doesn't know that?" Wu asked. "Peter Sair was sent to Prison Terminal. Vantee. A few months ago, he died there. Or so it is said."

"Dead?" Horn said. He stared toward the horizon, toward the Pleiades, toward the cluster of stars that were close enough for civilization without the Tube, where freedom had died. He stared toward home and realized for the first time that he could never go back.

Three hundred light years separated him from the Cluster. Six hours by Tube; half-a-dozen lifetimes by the next quickest means.

And the Tubes led through Eron; he had barred himself from Eron by what he had done and what he was going to do.

Why am I here? Horn wondered, and pushed the thought away.

"Goodnight, idealist," Wu whispered, and was gone.

Horn shrugged and scooped up the coins in front of him.

Whatever you have done to earn these coins was worthwhile.

He reached for the pistol under his left arm and pulled it down easily. He held it between his knees, pointing toward the desert.

He hadn't earned them yet. He would earn them tomorrow.

THE HISTORY

Civilization. . . .

Like everything else, it has a price. The down payment is freedom. For the privilege of living together, men surrender the right to do as they please; they make laws and restrict themselves within them.

When civilization is conferred from outside, the price is even steeper: someone else makes the laws.

Only the Tube made possible an interstellar civilization. And only Eron knew the secret of the Tube.

Some people will not pay the price. They buy freedom instead and pay for it with toil and hardship.

So men fled before Eron. They fled down the starways in rusty ships ahead of the expanding sphere of civilization and empire.

In the star cluster once called the Pleiades, freedom stopped running. The stars were close enough for loose federation and trade but too far apart for conquest. Slow ships could link them together into the Quarnon League. Instead of a ship, its symbol was a man.

And there in the Cluster, freedom died, crushed by Eron in two great wars. For freedom is contagious, and bridges are profitable.

The news traveled fast: Peter Sair was dead.

But Sair was a symbol. And symbols, like freedom, cannot die as long as one man still believes in them. . . .

3

THE NARROW BRIDGE

Horn came awake instantly, his nerves tingling with alarm.

The pistol was in his hand as he glanced out over the desert. The eastern horizon was beginning to gray. The stars had faded there. But the danger wasn't in the desert. It was lifeless.

He looked to the left, but the depression was still dark. Dark and still. But something had changed.

A man in constant danger learns to depend on his intuition, that subtle analyzer of unconscious perceptions. He has to. Danger will not wait for judgment.

Stiffened muscles protesting, Horn crept silently down the slope. The hollow was deserted. Only the black ashes in the dust were evidence that someone had been there.

Wu and the parrot were gone. They had picked up their few belongings and left soundlessly in the night while he slept.

That was the disturbing factor. For longer than he could remember he hadn't allowed himself the luxury of real sleep. His sleep was only a step below consciousness, a drowsing broken by the slightest change of environment. How could they have gone without waking him?

He hadn't planned to sleep at all. The closer he got to the goal, the greater the pitch of danger. Had it been the rebellion of a body driven beyond endurance? That was ridiculous. And yet he had slept. He felt more rested, more alert than he had since leaving the cruiser.

If he had been drugged, in spite of his caution, Wu had been clever. Horn added another stroke to the implausibility of their presence here and the greater implausibility of their appearance.

Horn finished the automatic process of covering the ashes and shrugged. He felt no aftereffects.

It was unfortunate, nevertheless. The old man would have been useful; Horn was convinced that Wu had known a way to the mesa top. But anger was pointless. To Horn, Wu was a thing to be used. Wu had a right to avoid being used, if he could.

Horn considered the problem of climbing the mesa. By the growing daylight, he could see no break in the wall. It was likely that the search would take him all day. That was too long.

Horn ran up the slope beside the single set of boot tracks and studied the trail. It ran straight along the edge of the cliff until it grew indistinct in the distance.

Horn started after them at a steady trot. The tracks weren't too old, an hour or two at most, and the patches on the boots were plain. Horn read the trail skillfully. Here Wu had shifted the suitcase to his left hand; there he had stopped to catch his breath or take a drink. The undulations of a snake began and ended abruptly; farther on, a rabbit's tracks were beside the trail.

Horn passed a discarded half-liter bottle. The label said: *Ethyl Alcohol, synthetic, 180 proof. Bottled by Eron Export Authority.*

Thirst began to bother Horn. He took the last drink from the canteen, a tepid sip that was little better than nothing. He recapped the canteen and licked his lips.

Almost imperceptibly, the tracks grew fresher. Wu was only minutes ahead. Horn glanced up, as he had before, but there was only the sheer cliff face to his left and the red dust ahead.

Then he lost the tracks. They ended at a shelving of rock scoured clean by the wind and didn't return to the dust anywhere around the perimeter.

Horn stared up at the cliff. The bird could have flown over it but not Wu. Horn studied the bush that grew tight against the foot of the cliff. It was an unlikely green. Some of the leaves had been bruised recently.

Carefully, Horn pushed the bush aside. Behind it was blackness. A hole, a meter high, two-thirds of a meter wide. Horn didn't like holes or tunnels; there was too much uncertainty about them. But this one led toward Sunport.

The smooth rock was damp as he scrambled through the darkness on hands and knees. That trickle of moisture had been the reason for the bush. Water on the desert was a rarity. The clatter of the empty canteen against the side and floor of the tunnel reminded Horn how much of a rarity it was. It was torment to his dust-caked throat.

He grimaced and crawled faster. Slowly the darkness lessened, became a frame for brightness, and fell behind.

Horn stood up cautiously, the rocks at his back. After the drab desert, the colors were achingly brilliant, the all-pervading green broken here and there with red and blue and yellow. He breathed deeply, and his senses came alive to myriad odors. It was like coming back from death.

A thought intruded: he must pass from this to death again.

He pushed through the close-packed greenness, trampling the color and odor underfoot, until he came to a clearing. Over the surrounding trees and bushes he could see the bare, gray granite marching unbroken around the valley. He was no better off than he had been. And yet Wu had come this way.

The music of water was close. Horn made his way to it, ignoring the branches and thorns that tore at his arms and chest. He waited at the edge of the little brook. Birds in the trees had fallen silent, but as he stood motionless they began to sing again.

Horn stretched himself out beside the brook and plunged his face into the water. He let it trickle into his mouth, raised his dripping head, and the water washed down his throat, sluicing away the desert dust.

It was good water, incredibly sweet after the alkaline bitterness of the gypsum springs. He bent to drink again, deeply this time, when he saw the cottontail on the other side of the brook. Black eyes stared at him curiously.

Cautiously Horn reached for his pistol, set it at low velocity and took quick aim. He needed meat. But as the gun came down, the rabbit turned and disappeared into the brush in one giant leap.

A moment later, as Horn watched with narrowed eyes, a brown bird erupted from the brush and vanished toward the far wall. Horn followed its flight thoughtfully, drank again, and filled his canteen.

Horn trotted toward the distant wall, ducking under branches, circling clumps of bushes. As he drew near, he saw through the trees that here the cliff face had crumbled. Great sections of it had fallen, breaking into boulders and masses of rubble that piled against the wall in a steep ramp.

Coming out from under the last tree, Horn saw the small, dark figure toiling toward the top of the slide, loosening pebbles that rattled down the slope. Something smaller and darker circled in the air around the figure's head.

The pistol was in Horn's hand.

"Stop!" Horn shouted. The words echoed back and forth between the cliffs.

A white face turned back toward him. Horn raised the gun to his eye. Through the powerful telescopic sight, Wu seemed only a few meters away, caught upon the crosshairs. His eyes were wide and black as he stared down into the gun; his face was pale; indecision seemed to paralyze him.

Something brown and winged swept across the sight and disappeared into the blackness of the cliff.

"Stay where you are!" Horn yelled.

Wu moved then, swiftly for such a fat, old man, and swarmed up the rocks. The crosshairs swung to follow him. Annoyance flitted across Horn's face. The old man was a fool; he deserved to die. Horn's finger tightened on the trigger. At the last moment he twisted the crosshairs away.

The projectile whistled from the gun, fought its way through the air, and ricocheted from rocks a meter to Wu's left. And then the old man was gone, into the blackness in the cliff face, like the brown bird.

Disgustedly, Horn released the gun and dashed up the rocks, ignoring the way they slipped and turned under his feet and the dangers of starting a slide that would pull the natural ramp out from under him. Pebbles rattled down the slope. In a loose patch, he went to one knee, but in a few minutes he was staring into the black mouth of a cave.

Water trickled along a crooked channel carved into the smooth floor. It disappeared into the loose rock that fell away from the mouth. That and the long heating and cooling of the centuries had loosened the cliff face and pulled it down.

Horn stepped into the darkness. The mouth was unnaturally round; the walls were unnaturally smooth. This was a tunnel, not a cave.

It seemed straight. A light flickered far ahead in the darkness. Horn ran toward it, wondering if there might be wide, deep holes and pushing the thought away.

The light wavered, almost disappeared, and grew brighter. Finally Horn saw that it was a torch. Wu was holding it and walking wearily, his face turned back. The parrot was on his shoulder.

When Horn came into the flickering circle of light, breathing easily, Wu stopped, leaned against the tunnel wall, and sighed. Sweat trickled down his yellow face. His chest rose and fell raggedly.

"You are a determined man," he gasped. "In itself, that is an admirable trait."

"Character is judged by the ends it serves," Lil said harshly, her one eye gleaming in the torchlight.

Horn's face was calm. "I said last night that you would take me to Sunport. If this is the way, let's go on."

Wu put one hand to his chest as if to ease a pain. "I'm an old man. I've moved too fast. Besides, you shot at me. I might have been killed." There was horror in his voice.

Horn nodded. "You might have been. Lead the way."

The torch sagged in Wu's hand. Horn took it and motioned him away from the wall. Wu protested, but he moved ahead.

"How did you know of this place?" Horn asked.

Wu shrugged. "Men learn many odd things if they live long enough. Sometimes I think I've lived too long. When Sunport was young, this whole mountain was honeycombed with passages. The deeper ones are flooded. Most of the others are caved in. But this one should lead to the top."

Twice they had to crawl on hands and knees over piles of fallen rubble that almost choked the tunnel. When Wu began to complain again, Horn reached for the battered suitcase. Reluctantly, Wu gave it up. It was surprisingly heavy. Horn prodded Wu forward into the darkness that the torch forced into only a small retreat.

They walked silently into the darkness, slowly climbing, sloshing occasionally in the icy stream of water that ran along the floor or collected in pools where it had been dammed by refuse or rubble.

"A deserter," Wu panted. "A deserter from the Guard—with sympathies for the beaten Cluster—heading for the Victory Dedication at the ruins of old Sunport—with a gun. That paints an interesting picture."

"Glad you like it," Horn said.

"It presents some interesting possibilities, too. Where would a guard get money? Not from Eron. Not in those amounts. One might almost imagine that you came from the Cluster, that you were among those defeated soldiers who were permitted to enlist in the Eron Guard, that you came here with a purpose, determined to desert on Earth and make your way to the ruins of Sunport in time for the Dedication— But that is impossible. No one would have attempted it, and no one knew about the Dedication. It wasn't public knowledge until recently."

"You talk too much," Horn said curtly.

Wu stopped walking suddenly. Horn bumped into him. Lil flew into the air. Wu clutched at Horn and pressed himself back. Beyond Wu, Horn saw the pit.

Across the entire width of the tunnel, the floor had fallen away. They stood on the edge of a wide, black hole. Horn stepped forward past Wu and held the torch high. Across the pit stretched a rusty, metal girder to an uneasy resting place on the other side, more than five meters away. Someone long dead must have put it there. It was a narrow bridge across black infinity.

Horn knelt at the edge and held the torch out over the side. The light died away before it reached bottom. As he stood up, his foot dislodged a pebble. It rang and clattered against the sides for a long time before a distant splash told them it had hit water.

Wu stared at the pit and at the girder, half a meter wide, that spanned it. Sweat glistened in shiny beads on his round, yellow face.

Horn set one foot on the girder, testing its balance. It didn't move. He put his other foot on it. It didn't sag. Steadily then, without haste, he walked across the bridge, putting one foot down and swinging the other one around in front of it, until he stepped safely onto the other side.

He put down the suitcase and turned, holding the torch up so that it lighted the other side. "Come on," he said. "It's getting late."

Lil flapped across and settled down beside Horn. She looked back at Wu, who hesitated at the end of the girder.

"I'm an old man," he wailed. "I'm old and feeble. I can't do it. I've been running all day and creeping and crawling and climbing through a mountain's black heart. I can't do it. I can't stand the thought of heights. I feel dizzy already."

Horn grunted impatiently and put his foot on the end of the girder. Lil stared at Wu with her one good eye.

"Come back," Wu moaned. "Come back, my friend. I've been a sentimental fool long enough. After this you can eat coal."

"Life is more precious than diamonds," Lil said obscurely. She winked with malice. "Maybe this strong young man would like to find diamonds for me."

"You wouldn't leave me to die?" Wu gasped. "Wait. I'm coming." But his voice trembled.

He started out unsteadily, his breath coming fast and shallow. His fat arms were spread out for balance, and his eyes stared fixedly at a point in the darkness beyond Horn's shoulder. He sidled across, one foot inching forward, the other scraping behind.

When he was halfway across, the girder wobbled under Horn's foot. Wu stiffened, swayed, and stopped.

"Ah, no!" he said breathlessly. "Don't let it move. My poor, mistreated heart—it can't stand much more of this."

"I think," Horn said slowly, "that it's time we had a little talk."

"Of course," Wu said. "Talk, talk. Anything. I'll talk. I'm the best talker you ever heard. Only wait until I'm over there." Sweat was streaming down his face.

"I'll get better answers if you're there," Horn said calmly. "Don't move."

Wu had started to inch forward; the girder wobbled again. Wu gasped and stopped.

"What shall we talk about?" Horn asked casually. "About Sunport and why old men go there? About tunnels and valleys? About rabbits that turn into birds? About snake tracks and rabbit tracks that start suddenly and end just as abruptly? About—"

"Anything—" Wu gasped.

"What are you?" Horn asked. "And what is Lil? When I saw her the first time, her one eye was on the left. Now it's on the right."

"I'll tell you," Wu moaned. "Only let me cross. I can't talk here. I'll fall—"

"Don't move!" Horn looked down at the parrot. "Don't you try anything either, whatever you are, or your master will—"

But as Horn looked down, the girder twisted under his foot. Wu screamed and tottered, his arms contorting themselves grotesquely.

Before Horn could move, the old man had toppled into the black pit.

THE HISTORY

Port of the sun. Sunport. . . .

It rose from its own ashes, phoenixlike, and launched its gleaming, wingless children toward the stars. Outward they spread in a vast sphere, seeking the new worlds, the virgin worlds, carrying with them a spark of the immortal flame. Where they landed, the spark leaped and grew.

Sunport waited, but they did not come back.

They found all kinds of worlds: some so sweet they could not leave, some so bitter there was no time for anything but struggle. . . . They relaxed, or they fought. They shaped and were shaped.

Weary, like Earth, Sunport waited. Exhausted, like the soil and the mines, Sunport waited. Still waiting, Sunport returned to ashes.

And at last they came. They came as conquerors. But they were still the children of Earth. Changed a little, they were still men.

Something stirred in the ashes. . . .

4

PHOENIX

While Wu was still toppling, something whirred beside Horn and disappeared swiftly into the darkness. Horn glanced quickly around. They were both gone, Wu and Lil. Horn listened. The seconds passed, and there was no distant splash from the pit.

Horn put one foot on the girder and held up the torch. The fat old man was dangling under the girder, his mouth opening and shutting in mute terror, his arms and legs pushing downward as if they could shove the blackness away.

A wire gleamed. It circled the rusty beam. A bright metal hook went through the waistband of Wu's baggy breeches. Where the wire joined the hook was blue brilliance, burning in the torchlight with a cold, splendid luminescence. It was faceted, like diamonds, thousands of them sparkling. . . .

Kicking, gasping, Wu swung jerkily back and forth. Horn shook himself. He walked out on the beam, stooped, took hold of the unexplainable wire. It moved liquidly in his hand, and he almost dropped it and the living burden it supported. His hand tightened. Inside it was a comfortable handle.

He backed along the girder, his chest rigid with strain, shining with sweat. Wu swung heavily below, each swing threatening to send them both into the gulf. Finally one backward-reaching foot touched solid rock. Horn strained backward. Wu swung in, rising. His hands caught the edge of rock. He clawed his way desperately over the brink, crawled meters from the edge, and collapsed, panting and trembling.

The thing in Horn's hand flowed again. Horn looked down. The parrot was perched on his finger, her ragged wings drooping wearily.

"Disaster," she said breathlessly, "is the crucible of human hearts. We thank you, my master and I."

Wu sat up slowly. "Indeed, indeed. You are a noble young man, brave—"

"It won't go away if you shut your eyes," Horn said.

He stuck the torch into a crevice in the wall. It flared smokily over the scene as he sat down and pulled his gun forward between his knees so that it pointed toward the old man and the bird perched now on his shoulder.

"I toppled you off the girder," Horn said. "I'd just as soon toss you over the edge again."

"It was a stupid thing to do," Wu said. "You can't get answers from a dead man."

"Obviously. What is your life worth to you? It's immaterial to me whether you live or die."

Wu sighed and shook his head. "Ah, violence! You give us no choice. An old man and an old bird, what chance do we have against youth and callousness and a gun?"

"Answers," Horn said.

"How old do you think I am?" Wu asked.

Horn stared at Wu's ageless face. "Seventy? Eighty?" he said, and knew that he was wrong.

"More than fifteen hundred. Fifteen hundred weary years. Searching for peace and never finding it. Longing for rest and afraid of dying. Lil and I going on and on."

Horn's eyes narrowed, but the rest of his face was immobile.

"Like Lil, I am the last of my race," Wu went on. "When I was born on Stockton Street in San Francisco, my people were the most numerous on Earth. And the oldest. But they clung to Earth while others went out to the stars. With Earth, they died.

"I was different. I immigrated to Mars. At Syrtis City, with youthful folly, I established the New Canton Sanitary Laundry. But water was scarce and cleaning fluids were dear. It was cheaper to weave new plastic clothes than to clean them.

"I became a ship's cook on a small, prospecting vessel. Its owners struck the richest treasure in history. On one of the asteroids, we found the Diamond Cavern."

Wu crawled warily to the suitcase close to the edge of the pit, dug into it, and crawled back with a bottle. He lifted it to his lips; his throat moved convulsively twice before he lowered it and handed it to Lil. Wu sighed; his small, black eyes blinked.

"Living diamonds, sir. Carbon deposits in a mountain torn from an exploding world. The cavern was underlaid by uranium. For a long time, that energy fed Lil's race; when it began to fail, they learned how to fission individual atoms. When the uranium was used up entirely, they learned to gather thermal energy even from very cold molecules, in defiance of the Second Law of Thermodynamics. Improbable? True. But all life exists in a kind of defiance of the Second Law.

"Living diamonds. But the creatures were more wonderful than their crystalline skins. As you have noticed, Lil is no parrot. She is a pseudomorph of the Diamond Cavern."

A tear sparkled gemlike in Lil's one eye and dropped to the dusty tunnel floor.

"Lil's race had many things to offer men. They had a culture almost as old as Earth itself. Energy was low there; time moved slowly. They were almost immortal. But the ship's crew saw only one thing: the diamonds. One radiation bomb destroyed the cavern and all the creatures in it, discoloring and ruining most of the diamonds in the process. Only Lil was saved. I hid her in the galley. We have been together ever since."

Lil moaned thinly. "Poor old Lil," she sobbed. "She's all alone. Ah, ah, ah. Her people, all gone. Her world murdered and forgotten. No friend in all the universe but poor old Wu. Oh, the lost wonder, the beauty. . . ."

She wilted. Horn's gun lifted. Wu held up a warning finger. "Sh-h-h," he said softly. "You are going to see something that no one alive but me has ever seen."

Lil's gay, disheveled plumage flowed. The yellow legs collapsed into pliant pseudopods. A glittering surface of diamond was uncovered. Everything else ran shapelessly into an opening at the top, leaving a diamond the size of a man's two hands clasped together.

Torchlight struck it. The diamond threw it back, multiplied, in an incredible glory of prismatic colors. Horn caught his breath.

"Wait," Wu whispered. "Wait until she opens."

Seams appeared in the top of the burning, thousand-faceted spheroid. Six diamond petals bent slowly down. Above them rose six slender, living tendrils. Reaching pink fingers, they grew and divided into delicate and intricate membranes like a pure white web.

"With those and her amorphous body," Wu said, "she can assume any form she wishes. Those tracks you saw, the rabbit who looked at you across the stream, the bird that flew to me—all Lil."

The pistol slipped from Horn's relaxed hand; it slithered up under his shoulder. At the sound, the diamond thing leaped explosively into the air. Its splendor was concealed, in an instant, by the parrot's ragged feathers.

Lil swayed and moaned again. "Gone, all gone."

"Don't cry, Lil," Wu said softly. He rummaged deep in one pocket. "Here's a little trinket I've been saving for a bitter hour. It came out of the stickpin of a grafting Company inspector who tried to jail us for vagrancy."

Lil stopped moaning and flapped to Wu's shoulder. Her strong beak took the gleaming, pea-sized diamond delicately from his thick fingers. A muffled crunch and the stone was gone.

"One tomorrow," she said cheerfully, "is worth a million yester-days." She rubbed her beak affectionately against Wu's wrinkled cheek. "A most beautiful diamond."

"She can assimilate almost any form of carbon," Wu said. "But she prefers diamond. When we're prosperous, that's what she eats. Recently we've been reduced to anthracite."

"The secret," Horn said coldly. "How have you lived so long?"

"Lil," Wu said. "Her people learned many things in their long, almost eternal existence: life, probability, atomic structure. . . . That was only one of the things mankind lost through greed. She keeps me alive, and I help her find food.

"We wander. If we stay still very long, Duchane's Index will find us. That vast collection of memory would quickly fit our descrip-tions into a thousand-year-old record of jewel thefts. We would like to stay on the frontiers, beyond the reach of Eron, but there are few diamonds there.

"Wanderers, eternal vagabonds, we have seen a hundred worlds and known them all and have only our memories that go back too far to show for it. We must keep moving. Men would wonder why I don't die. My secret would rouse in them the same madness as Lil's diamond carapace. They would kill me for it.

"Yet there are consolations. There is always tomorrow—a new ship to catch, a virgin planet waiting. When memory grows too long, there's a way to blot it out. The weed for me, and diamonds for Lil, and rum for both of us."

Horn studied them for a moment. "That's all you've done with it?"

Wu shrugged. "What would you do?"

"It would give a man a different perspective," Horn said thought-fully. "You could do something for all humanity: in science, poli-tics, philosophy. You owe it—"

"For what?" Wu asked dryly. "Humanity had nothing to do with it. It tossed away its chance when its representatives wiped out Lil's race."

"Original sin?" A smile flickered across Horn's face. "If a man could think things out thoroughly, plan carefully, act slowly," he mused, "he could guide his people into better, wiser paths. If a tyrant arose, like Eron, he could—"

"One man against an empire?" Wu broke in. "Empires rise and fall, and that cycle is dictated by forces ignorant of things as insignificant as a man. They are as vast and mysterious in their workings as fate itself. Eron will fall—in its own time. But you will probably be long dead, and I myself may be dead. Even Lil can't push that finality away forever."

"Forces!" Horn shrugged. "They are only men in the mass. One man can lead them or push them. And one man, acting at the right time, at the right place, in the right way, can topple the greatest boulder."

"And get crushed himself when it falls," Wu said. "No, thank you. As long as I have lived, as weary as life sometimes grows, I cling to it—more desperately even than you. What have you to lose but a few unhappy years? It is easy for you to be foolhardy and contemptuous of danger. I must be timid and cowardly. This miserable carcass, which has lasted me so long, may last me as long again, with care."

Horn was on his feet. He pulled the torch out of the wall and motioned with his head for Wu and Lil to go in front. Wu picked up his suitcase and turned his head back to look at Horn.

"Don't you believe me, sir?"

"You aren't in the pit, are you?" Horn answered. The question Wu asked was something Horn couldn't answer directly. For the moment he was willing to accept it as a working hypothesis; it fitted the observed data. In addition, it was too fantastic not to have an element of truth. "Keep moving. We may be late as it is."

"We mustn't make you late for your appointment with destiny," Wu said. The words floated back mockingly.

The tunnel began to widen. It spilled them into a great chain of vast black areas: warehouses, Horn guessed, for the first interplanetary commerce. Sloping ramps led them up and up again. With the first distant suggestion of sunlight, Horn ground out the torch against the wall and, a little farther on, leaned it against the side of the last broad tunnel.

Storms had washed mud and debris into the crumbling entrance. The narrow exit that remained was well concealed by a gnarled juniper tree. Horn peered between the leaves. Beyond were ruins: mounds of weathered rubble pierced by an occasional rusted spear, a tottering wall. It was deserted. Horn climbed through the hole and slipped down under the lowest branch. Wu followed with a muffled sigh of relief.

Horn crept to the shaky wall and glanced quickly over it. He stifled an exclamation. "The Victory Monument!"

It towered against the noon sky, eight hundred meters away, where once the Mars Docks of Old Sunport had been. But even Sunport, at her proudest, couldn't have built this.

Its base was an immense black cube capped with a black hemisphere. It was at least nine hundred meters high. Towering endlessly above that rounded pedestal was a great, cylindrical column. It was faced with luxion and glowed with rising waves of living color. Blood-red just above the black hemisphere, it shimmered through orange, yellow, green, blue, indigo, and violet. The top faded to a shining white.

Crowning the pillar, four kilometers overhead, was a huge, steel-gray sphere, smooth and featureless except at the poles. There, thousands of slender golden spikes bristled in every direction.

"Eron!" Wu said at Horn's elbow.

"I've never seen it," Horn said.

"It's a good reproduction," Wu said. "That's it. Eron. Your boulder. Let's see you topple it."

Horn turned his eyes away from the monument and studied the area surrounding it. Only around the vast perimeter of the mesa were the ruins visible, and the other side was so distant it dwindled away grayly. Everywhere else the ruins had been sealed under a marble-smooth surface inlaid with murals.

"Sunport," Wu said softly. "They built it high and tall, on the ruins of a city called Denver, so that it would be nearer the stars. Like Eron, it ruled the known world. Legend says that a great barbarian leader sacked Sunport in its greatness. He led his nomad bands upon it, the legend says, and tore it down and gave it back to the sun, its might and its oppression."

"Eron, too, can be destroyed," Horn said.

"A straw man." Wu chuckled. "Legend is not to be trusted. Sunport was dead long before then. Created by a historic need, it died when its job was done. That tribal hero cremated a corpse."

Horn shrugged. There were immediate problems; he was intent upon the crowded surface of the sealed ruins.

Across giant doors in the black cube's face was a broad platform. Obviously temporary, it had the solidity of permanence. Like the broad steps that led up to it, the platform was gleaming, golden plastic. Emerging from under it and stretching far across the field were deep, metal-lined tracks. Facing the platform were concentric semicircles of bleachers, their tiers capable of seating many thousands.

Pavilions were a riot of color everywhere. Milling among them were the Golden Folk. Surely there were more of them here, Horn thought, than had ever been gathered together before. Below him was the aristocracy of Eron, the heirs of the universe, proud, powerful, arrogant—and effeminate. Not one of them could have done what he had done to get here.

The voices rose to Horn, their laughter, their gaiety, high-pitched, nervous. It sounded like the music for a last palsied dance before dissolution.

They were leeches, bloodsuckers. It would be pleasant to have the power to crush them all. The white, anemic worlds would bless him and grow strong again. But only one of them was to die. There would be time for only one.

The Golden Folk were no threat. Danger lay only in the strength they bought. Guards, sprinkled thickly, outnumbered their masters. They lined the perimeter of the paved mesa, alert and watchful. Units were posted in strategic spots. They clustered around the base of the black cube. They seemed unusually tall there, even at this distance. They were the Elite Guard, Horn realized, the three-meter Denebolan lancers.

It wasn't a question of being afraid of them. They were only a complication to be considered.

Monoliths ringed the edges of the mesa. They were the tall, black spires of battleships, their one-hundred-meter diameters and half-kilometer lengths dwarfed only by the monument. Two broad, golden bands, fore and aft, adapted them to passage through the Tube. Nothing projected beyond them; it was understood that they kept the ship from touching the Tube's deadly walls.

There were nine of the monoliths, each one a sleek, efficient, ruthless fighting machine. Each one carried twelve thirty-inch rifles. The thrust of their unitron helices could throw twelve-ton projectiles at velocities sufficient to vaporize them on impact. One shot would have split apart a mountain.

Only the rifles, normally retracted into flat turrets in the N-iron hulls, were busy, roaming restlessly in search of targets in the pale sky or on the mountains beyond that seemed close but were actually kilometers away. They found nothing to stop their searching.

Other ships were in the sky and on the ground: cruisers, scoutships. . . . Eron guarded its rulers thoroughly.

One small pistol against the massive power that had crushed a star cluster. It was not too uneven. Horn wasn't fighting with battleships, and brute power isn't efficient at swatting gnats. It takes only one small bullet to kill a man.

They thought eight hundred meters was an impossible range for a portable weapon. Horn smiled grimly. Eron didn't know its own devices.

Something whined above him. Instinctively, Horn threw himself down in the brush-covered hollow and turned his head to glance upward. The fantastic black mass of a battleship was poised above them, its hull rippling with iridescent color, betraying the infinitesimal power loss of the unitronic field that lifted and drove it.

Wu squalled and jumped to his feet. With one hand, Horn dumped him unceremoniously into the brush and held him there.

"Shut up and stay down!" he shouted above the whine.

Wu shivered helplessly, his face pressed into the dirt. "My ancestors, preserve me!"

Gently the giant stern lowered, passed them not a hundred meters away, and slowed to a stop on the field below. Colossal, tripod landing skids unfolded and bit into the mountain. The ground quivered under them. From behind them came the rumble of falling rock. Horn thought of the tunnel and hoped, briefly, that it hadn't been blocked.

He raised his head above the wall, shaken now so that it was only half as high. He could still see the monument and the platform in front of it. The ship served him instead of Eron; it gave him a shield from casual observation.

He glanced upward at the black tower, and Lil fluttered across his vision. For the first time he realized that she had been gone.

"Guards are as thick as lice on a beggar's bed," she reported. "But that monster is nothing to worry about. A man in armor pays no attention to ants underneath his foot."

Wu groaned, unappeased. "Can't a man pick up a wretched handful of diamonds? Must the Company send ships enough to blow the whole planet into atoms?"

Horn unclipped the pistol from the cord around his shoulder. There was little to go wrong with it, but even that little was a chance that need not be taken.

With the quick efficiency of the Guard, he stripped it down. Out of the butt he shook the small, flat dynode cell. Its molecule-thin films stored the energy of a ton of chemical explosives. The little magazine of fifty bullets was well oiled; the projectiles slid easily. The helix-wound barrel was clean and untarnished.

It was in perfect working order. When he pulled the trigger, a bullet, armored against atmospheric friction, would leave the gun with the velocity of an ancient cannon shell.

Wu looked at the dismantled gun and shuddered. "It seems as if all these precautions are for you," he said slowly. "I urge you: don't use that pistol! One man's death means nothing—except to himself. And the death that gun holds is yours."

Horn stared silently across the mesa toward the monument and thought again: *Why am I here? To kill a man*, he told himself, *to do a job no one else could do.*

"The man of violence," Lil said suddenly, "is a dangerous companion."

"You are right, Lil, as usual," Wu said.

Before Horn could stop him, the fat, old man had grabbed his suitcase and vaulted the little wall with surprising agility. As Horn listened to him slithering down the other side, his hands were busy snapping the pistol back together.

He pointed the pistol over the wall—and lowered it slowly. Wu and the parrot were already mingling with the throng below. A shot would accomplish nothing now but betrayal.

And yet— Horn indulged in a rare moment of self-reproach. This was the price of softness. It was obvious that the yellow man was going to sell him to save his own ancient skin.

Horn shrugged. There was nothing to do but wait.

THE HISTORY

Secrets don't keep. . . .

The facts of nature are written duplicate in atoms, which reveal them with the same phenomena everywhere, for intelligence to see. Intelligence can't be monopolized.

Yet one secret kept for a thousand years.

Men died to learn Eron's secret: scientists, spies, raiders. The theory, the mathematics, the technical details were all available in thick manuals and thicker textbooks. Captured technicians could build Terminals, but they couldn't link them together. One thing was missing: the imponderable, the unguessable. The secret.

Of the many ways to keep a secret, only one is perfect: tell nobody. But some secrets can't be allowed to die.

Someone had to know. Who? The Directors? The General Manager? At least one of them was always present when a new Tube was activated.

The secret. What was it? Who knew it? Eron guarded it well.

If all men could build bridges, who would pay toll? . . .

5

ASSASSIN

The seconds passed slowly, but they passed without alarm. Horn's pulse began to slow. He risked another glance over the wall, his pistol clenched in a sweaty palm. No one was looking toward him. There were no guards in the crowd clustered around Wu and Lil.

Wu stood on his battered suitcase haranguing the curious Golden Folk in a surprisingly loud voice of blustery confidence. Some of the phrases even drifted to Horn.

". . . Space-kings! Master-engineers of mighty Eron. . . . come to visit the mother-world. Pause a moment and see her latest wonder. . . ."

Lil stretched her ragged wings on Wu's shoulder, her eye fixed on something in the crowd. The conquerors were tall and blond and proud. Even the men were gorgeously dressed with padded bosoms and femininely symmetrical legs covered with heavy synsilk and furs. And jewels. A huge diamond flashed prismatically from the throat of a bulky matron.

". . . the bird with a human brain," Wu bellowed nasally. ". . . educated in the arts of calculation . . . will give the correct answer to any mathematical problem you wish to ask. . . ."

The purple-clad matron jabbed a jewel-studded cane at the parrot and said something Horn couldn't hear.

Lil flapped to Wu's outstretched finger and screamed, "Two and two are four. Four and four are eight. Eight and eight—"

Wu jerked his hand. Lil shut her beak.

A tall man pushed his way forward. On his tunic was the jeweled golden star of a retired space-officer. "Here's a problem for you," he shouted drunkenly. "State the elements of the curve of synergy for a unitron vessel entering a G-sub-four type binary system at forty-six degrees to the ecliptic plane and preparing to land on a mass-18 planet in an E-3 orbit. Deceleration constant at 80 G. Planet 8 degrees past relative conjunction."

Wu turned away hastily and said something to the crowd, but Lil launched herself from Wu's finger and flew to the officer's shoulder, croaking in hoarse imitation of his voice.

"You will find the synergic curve to be type y-18 times factor e/¢ plus G-field correction point oh oh nine four."

The man looked startled.

"Upon complete solution of your problem, however," Lil went on mockingly, "you will discover that such a landing would be unwise. An E-3 orbit for a mass-18 planet about a G-sub-four binary is radically unstable. In fact, within four hours after crossing the E-3 orbit, the planet in question will collide with the inferior sun."

The officer gasped. He pulled an astrogator's manual and a small calculator out of his pocket and started computing feverishly.

Lil flew back to Wu. Horn noticed that the white diamond was missing from the center of the spaceman's golden star.

Trumpets snarled across the field. The vast, amoebic beast that was the crowd stopped flowing aimlessly and froze, their eyes turned toward Horn. Horn dropped behind the wall, his heart beating fast.

But there was no sound of assault, no firing of guns. There was only the snarling trumpets. Horn waited until waiting became unendurable. Irresistibly his head came up.

Guard companies had cleared five paths from battleships at the perimeter to the monument from across the field. A company of marching, Denebolan lancers led it, their two-meter strides covering the distance effortlessly. The brilliant enamel on their N-iron link armor was blue. Blue, too, were the plumes on their upright, ceremonial lances. Holstered at their sides were gray, unitron pistols.

The shimmering blue car that followed floated a meter above the ground. Its torpedo-shape came to rest at the foot of the steps leading to the platform. Horn raised the pistol to his eye and stared through its telescopic sight at the man who stepped out of the car. It was a young man. He climbed the stairs briskly, tall, his back lean at the waist and swelling to well-muscled shoulders. As he turned, applause beat against the hills.

It was a young man's face, golden with the pure blood of Eron, hard with confidence and pride. It was smiling now. Horn recognized the man: Ronholm, Director for Commerce.

Along a second lane, another procession was approaching. Its color was green. Green for Transport, Horn translated. Thin, aristocratic Fenelon mounted the steps without haste and turned his hatchet face to the crowd. His eyes were deep-set and powerful. They blazed imperiously at the crowd, demanding its homage. They dragged it out of the formless beast.

They came more swiftly. Orange was next. Matal, Director for Power, panting as he hoisted his short, fat body up the steps, smiling broadly, his yellow jowls shaking as he acknowledged the applause. But the gun sight brought that face close to Horn. Horn saw the eyes, almost concealed in puffy flesh, peering out calculatingly over the crowd and shifting to eye the men on either side of him. *Greed*, Horn thought, *greed and gluttony*.

Then black. Black for Security. Black for Duchane. There was no sleek, unitronic car for him. He came on the back of a black hound. The massive beast, almost two meters tall at the shoulder, slavered on the steps as Duchane rode him up onto the platform.

Duchane swung down from the saddle and sent the monster to

sit, mouth gaping, like a red-eyed shadow at the back of the platform. The crowd was silent, but that seemed applause enough for Duchane. The square, powerful face on the heavy body looked out over the heads of the people standing beyond the bleachers with a pleased half-smile.

His face was sallow. With his darker eyes and hair, he seemed atypical. But he was, Horn knew, one of the most powerful men of Eron. Certainly, he enjoyed it the most. Ruthless, cruel, lustful, Duchane was the most hated man in the Empire. His agents were everywhere; his power was close to absolute.

Duchane had been staring almost directly at Horn. Horn dropped back. One finger stoppering the barrel, he dusted the gun carefully. When he returned to the wall, there was no chance of betrayal from a sudden reflection of sunlight.

Duchane's eyes had shifted a little. Horn saw what he had been staring at. A fifth procession had been making its way from the battleship beside him. It was halfway to the monument before it came into view. Its dominant color was gold. Gold for Communications.

Horn stared through the sight at the lone passenger of the car. The softly golden shoulders and red-gold hair shining down across them could only belong to Wendre Kohlnar. Was she as beautiful as her image in the five-kellon coin? It was impossible, Horn knew; no woman could be so beautiful.

As she climbed the steps, straight, slim, and proud, Horn's breath stuck in his throat. He waited for her to turn. She turned. Horn gasped as her face filled the gun sight. Here was a woman worth a galaxy, worthy of the name of Eron.

Her bare arm lifted to a thunder of applause; her head, crowned by the same fillet of white diamonds, bowed in recognition. When she looked up, her eyes seemed to look again into Horn's. Tawny eyes, wide and wise and clear.

Horn looked away.

The trumpets screamed a newer, more violent note. And then fell silent.

The silver of the General Manager was approaching the stand. The guards were silver; the car was silver. Silver, too, was Kohlnar's hair as he sat at the foot of the long steps, not stiff and red as it had been in the coin. He waited. Two giant lancers came forward and lifted him out of the car and helped him up the steps.

What was wrong with Kohlnar?

At the platform, he turned and grasped the railing and raised one hand to the thousands in front of him. It was a sign of victory. The Golden Folk exploded with shouts and cheers.

They couldn't see what Horn saw. He stared through the sight, unbelieving. The face was like an old woman's. The seamed, yellow skin hung in loose folds. The cheeks were heavily rouged. The lips were painted scarlet. The hairless eyebrows were penciled black. Flesh had shrunken from the nose; it left a thin, yellow beak.

It was a patient, cunning, ruthless face. It had all the powers of the other Directors, and it held them chained to an iron will. But the General Manager of the Company and through the Company, of Eron, and through Eron, of the Empire, was a dying man. He had spent his strength in a long drive for power and in the use of that power to conquer the Cluster.

Now, at the moment of his triumph here upon the ruins of the world from which the human race swept out into the stars, when Eron was truly the master of all the human-held galaxy, Kohlnar was dying.

While the Directors retired to seats at the back of the platform, Kohlnar clutched the railing with quivering yellow claws. Under the rouge, the lax folds of his skin were a sickly gray. Sweat stood out on his forehead. But when he began to speak, and amplifiers picked up his words and flung them to the far corners of the immense field, his voice was harsh and strong.

"Men of Eron," he grated. "Sons of Earth. We are here to celebrate not the victory of Eron but the victory of man. Nations, worlds, empires have won many battles. They have lost others. And in the end it did not matter whether they won or lost. The only victory that must be won is man's. And so we have come back to celebrate one more victory in the long, glorious sequence of man's conquest. We have come back to our origins, to Earth, to the mother-world. But let us go back even farther. Let us go back to beginnings."

He stopped. His breathing came in labored gasps as his fumbling finger found a button. Against the blackness of the monument base behind him, a vast mosaic sprang out, colorful, almost three-dimensional in its reality.

In the background was the primordial universe, vast chaos churning with unborn life. Closer was the misty glory of a spiral nebula, its arms far-flung as it slowly turned. Against it flamed a curling row of suns illustrating the sequence of stellar evolution. Red giants shrank. Planets condensed. At one corner of the scene was gentle Earth. At the other was harsh Eron.

"Out of chaos, order," Kohlnar said. "Out of order, life."

He pressed another button. The scene flowed around the corner of the cube and was replaced by another.

This was Earth and the evolution of life. At the left of the broad panorama, something shapeless but alive crept out of a primal sea. Monsters fought in steamy jungles. A caveman kindled a fire against the sharp-toothed cold. Men hunted and planted and reaped and wheeled their produce to market in small villages that grew into empires with marching soldiers. The empires rose and fell but man went on, building higher and better, destroying himself and rising again until he built the towers of Sunport, reaching out toward the stars. At the right Roy Kellon—legendary father of the Golden Folk—stood at the *Nova*'s valve ready to set out upon the first interstellar flight.

"For this, man built and suffered and labored, to claim his heritage—the stars."

Kohlnar pressed a button. The scene on the black face of the cube gave way to another.

Eron. It gleamed cold and steel-gray like the great sphere overhead. Like it, the golden spikes radiated from it toward the far corners of the Empire. Only here they did not end in points. They connected everything to Eron, the near stars and the distant ones. All kinds of stars: giants and super-giants, dense white dwarfs and faint red ones, and the blue-white, white, and yellow of those between. Everywhere there was life and profit, the Tubes reached and siphoned them away to Eron. And one massive Tube stabbed far across the galaxy into the heart of giant Canopus.

Eron. A fat gray spider, Horn thought, *sitting in the center of its golden web, waiting the tremor that announced the capture of another victim.*

Horn shrugged. The Golden Folk screamed their appreciation. "Eron! Eron! Eron!" they shouted, until it rang against the hills.

"Eron, yes!" Kohlnar said, and his amplified voice overwhelmed the shouting. "But more than that—man! Man's greatest achievement—the civilization of the stars. Eron! Man at his peak, one great culture reaching out from Eron in every direction almost five hundred light years, only possible because of Eron. And here—Eron's most recent victory!"

He stabbed a button.

The Cluster behind. In front the colossal ruins of the last demolished fortress on Quarnon Four. The surrender of Peter Sair. Small, stout, white-haired, old, the Liberator knelt in front of a tall, stern Kohlnar and signed the articles of capitulation. Behind Sair were the kneeling ranks of his defeated troops, receiving their yellow number disks. Behind them, symbolically, were numbered slaves toiling in the fields and mines and factories beneath hovering, black, gold-banded cruisers.

"Victory!" Kohlnar's voice was husky and low. "Not for Eron. For man. Those who challenge Eron challenge not the Empire but man's greatness. Let this be their answer. Eron will preserve man's goal, man's inheritance—the stars, strong and united. This is Eron's mission. She will not let it die, though we and others die to preserve it. Now, as a symbol of man's continuity of striving, we dedicate this Tube, uniting Eron with the place from which our ancestors launched the first ships toward the stars."

Behind him, the Directors stepped forward. Wendre stepped quickly to his side and placed her right arm around him. Duchane and Matal stood at his right, Fenelon and Ronholm at his left. Kohlnar rested his hand upon a golden switch on top of the railing; the others placed their hands on his. They pushed it closed.

The Tube. Suddenly it was there, golden and real, reaching out from the far side of the black cube toward the east, rising through the air, spearing out into space, crossing the thirty light years that separated Earth from Eron.

Horn's eyes followed it up and up until the distance narrowed it to a thread and then the thread was gone. He wondered if it was perspective alone that shrank the one-hundred-meter diameter into nothing. He remembered, vaguely, something about a real dwindling. . . .

Earth and Eron, linked now a second time, joined by a new umbilical cord. Not to feed the mother, worn and barren from the long agonies of childbirth, but to drain away the last, slow streams of life.

The Empire, held together by these golden cords, nourishing in the womb a great, greedy child. It had grown too large to live independently. It must protect these cords or starve.

Strange, Horn thought, that strength makes weakness. Through being strong, Eron had become the most dependent world in the Empire.

And yet, looking at the Tube, Horn couldn't deny its beauty.

His eyes slid back down the golden cord. A buzzard brushed incautiously against the Tube wall and burned brilliantly. Here and there along the Tube, it flared as insects leaped at it blindly.

That was the Tube: deadly beauty. Beauty to Eron, food for the greedy child. To all others, it was death.

The guards swirled near the reviewing stand. Horn looked down in time to see Denebolan giants drag a man from under it. Horn stared through the gun sight. It was Wu. The ragged old man was protesting vigorously and clinging desperately to his battered suitcase. There was no sign of Lil. Wu was hurried away. On the back of his neck was a large, red carbuncle Horn had never noticed before.

Horn's lips twisted. So it was the thief who was caught, not the assassin.

The gun sight drifted back up the steps to the group on the platform, separated a little now as it acknowledged the audience's enthusiasm.

Like the finger of fate, the sight moved across the faces of the rulers of Eron.

Young, proud Ronholm, flushed with triumph.

Thin, sardonic Fenelon, contemptuous of the herd.

Wendre Kohlnar, radiantly lovely, holding her father's arm with a slim, golden hand.

The dying man, Kohlnar, blinking in the sunlight, his face set with the effort of keeping himself erect.

Duchane, powerful and arrogant, his eyes searching the crowd for those who did not cheer or cheered without enthusiasm.

Short, fat Matal, eyes small and calculating as they estimated how much of the applause was for him.

Which one! The question was idle. Horn knew which one. That was why he was here. To kill a man. To shoot one man down from ambush. The sight wavered.

Why am I here? The answer this time was a little different. *Because someone wants this man killed.*

It had nothing to do with Horn. He was just an instrument. Suddenly he resented that, resented the necessity of doing something he had no interest in doing. The getting here was something different. This thing was easy and distasteful.

But the necessity was there. He had taken the money to do a job. The job was not yet done.

The crosshairs steadied. They centered themselves on the dying man.

Horn gave the thumbscrew another half-twist, estimated the air velocity, and peered through the sight once more. The gun, resting on the wall, didn't waver. The General Manager of Eron seemed only a few meters away. The symbol of Empire waited for the executioner.

Slowly Horn's finger squeezed the trigger. The pistol jumped, just a little. For a second Kohlnar looked surprised, and then his face sagged, blankly, and his body folded gently to the platform.

THE HISTORY

Star-wandering. . . .

That strange, wonderful period after the breakdown of the first interplanetary civilization. That irresistible bursting-forth which scattered man's seed hundreds of light years across the stars. That time of struggle and adventure, villainy and heroism.

There were heroes in those days, men larger than reality and magnified in the retelling. Men like Roy Kellon, they became the demi-gods of a new mythology.

Man didn't emerge from the star-wandering quite the same. The engines of the first interstellar ships were poorly shielded; that changed him. The worlds he settled changed him. Isolation changed him. And he traced his ancestry from heroes and demi-gods.

From such origins should come the superman. But the changes were insignificant. Men were still men, even the three-meter Denebolan giants who formed Eron's elite guard.

Even the Golden Folk of Eron, who lived, loved, and died like other men.

Still, it is unwise to underestimate the psychological importance of a slight variation in pigmentation.

How do you define the superman? The Golden Folk knew. . . .

6

FLIGHT

The scene was frozen under an afternoon sun. All eternity seemed concentrated into a moment, unchanging, unchangeable. And then—

Chaos. . . .

The Directors scattered. Only Wendre remained, kneeling beside the crumpled thing that had been her father, then rising, straight and unafraid, to search the edge of the field.

Horn held her face in the gun sight. It was a caress. His finger was far from the trigger.

The charging guards reached the platform. Their ranks became a living shield, three meters high. The last thing Horn saw was the black hulk of Duchane's hunter. It was dead against the monument. The bullet had passed through Kohlnar and struck down another killer.

The amplifier shouted orders in a sure, powerful voice. *Duchane*, Horn thought.

The voice was quick and accurate. No one would move except the guards. They would assemble under their officers at this side of the monument.

Scoutships climbed into the sky, were launched by battleships, circled with misleading laziness around the field. Companies of guards moved outward from the monument. They carved a pie-shaped sector. Its point was Kohlnar's body; its base enclosed, unerringly, Horn's hiding place in the hollow behind the wall.

"The General Manager is dead," Duchane said softly. It was a voice used to announce sacrilege and desecration.

For the first time, Horn realized what he had done. To Eron, it was sacrilege, it was desecration. Horn had shattered the symbol of empire, and Eron could not rest until he was caught and punished. All the resources of Eron would be thrown into the search.

Psychological factors are almost as important to empires as the fleets they can muster or the firepower they can assemble. Revolt would be futile, true; Eron could crush any world in a few hours. But let rebellion spring up here and there, continually, let the flow of trade falter, let the mercenaries themselves grow restless—and Eron would tremble.

Eron's rule rested upon a pedestal of omnipotence. No distance was too great for her fleet to go; no slight was too small for her dignity to overlook. Conquerors live by conquest; the first failure is a signal for the conquered to rise against them.

Omnipotence. How else could the Empire control a conquered population exceeding that of the Golden Folk by a million times? But let the slave worlds suspect that the pedestal is cracked—!

If not in outrage, then in calculated policy, Eron had to capture the assassin. Had to! No effort could be too great. And, once captured, his punishment must be salutary. Long, excruciating, and public.

Horn licked his lips. An empire against one man. It was like a death sentence. His chest heaved, sucked air deep into his lungs. The air smelled sweet to the dead man. The sun felt warm.

Horn shook himself. He was still alive. They must catch him first. He would give them a chase yet.

The guards had almost reached the base of the battleship towering close to Horn. The buzzards circling blackly overhead were wingless. It was time to leave.

Horn faded back through the branches of the juniper into the hidden mouth of the tunnel. As he turned his back to the light, he clipped the pistol to the cord around his shoulder and let the cord pull the gun tight to his chest. A few hundred paces into the darkness, a searching hand retrieved the torch. A moment later it was flaming.

The fugitive's walk was swift but unhurried. When legs are matched against ships, hurry is pointless. The pursuers would think of the desert long before the fugitive got there.

But how soon would they find the tunnel mouth? The hunted man broke into a trot. The trot became a headlong run. Panic ran with him.

Down the long ramps into vast blacknesses. Running through them wildly, the torch flame dancing and leaping into the darkness and swallowed up immediately. Running . . . running . . . lost. . . .

The tunnel went down too fast. It ended in a black pool. The hunted man stared at it with wide, dazed eyes. His gasping lungs began to ease. His mind cleared a little. Somewhere he had turned the wrong way.

He retraced his steps. In the echoing chambers, he tried to reconstruct the location of the right tunnel. Where it should have been was rubble. The hunted man fought his way through it, tossing the stones behind him with growing haste. The torch brushed out against a wall, and he worked in night, complete, impenetrable.

At last he felt a breath of air against his sweaty face. There was space in front of him. He scrambled upright and began to run again. One hand clung desperately to a useless stick of tar-soaked wood.

A subtle warning told him to slow down: a distant tinkling? A change in the echoes of his frantic footsteps? He stopped. He began to breathe again. Once more he started to think. He lit the torch again.

He raised the torch in front of him. A meter away was the pit, gaping blackly, hungrily. He walked toward it, his legs trembling wearily. He put one foot on the girder and stopped. He remembered Wu tottering, falling. . . .

He had crossed this bridge so easily a few hours ago. What stopped him now? The hunted man knew. This morning he hadn't known the shape of fear. He knew it now, and everything was tinged with it. His heart beat swiftly. His chest drew in greedy gasps of air. His hands trembled.

But behind him was certain death. Ahead was uncertainty. He edged out on the girder, carefully, thinking about the long way there was to fall, and the thinking made him weak and dizzy. He swayed, caught himself, and crossed the last meter in a clumsy run.

Panic caught him again, jumping the pit effortlessly, and shot adrenaline through his veins and spurred his feet, and he ran again and crawled where he couldn't run, and slithered where he couldn't crawl. And at last the light came, ghostly at first but growing, and it was like a promise of resurrection from the night of death. The hunted man threw down the torch and ran toward the light.

He stopped at the mouth of the tunnel, high above the little valley, and the sight calmed him. The panic was gone, suddenly, and he couldn't understand why it had ever driven him, and the long flight through the tunnel was like something that had happened to someone else. He was sane again.

More than half the valley was in shadows. Soon the cliffs would rise up in front of the sun, and the valley would be dark, and after that the sky would begin to deepen and the night would come. By that time he must be out on the desert. Night would be his chance. Once it had been an enemy; now it would be a friend.

Before dark he would have to be rested and sure of himself. His stomach complained. It must be fed. After getting away from the hunters, his body must take him far across the red-dust desert.

Horn picked his way carefully down the uncertain, rocky slope. He pressed through the bushes to the little stream. His hands worked quickly. They fashioned snares out of vines and branches and notched twigs. He glanced occasionally at the slowly darkening sky, but it was empty. So far, the hunters hadn't discovered this oasis.

With a bundle of leaves, he brushed away the human traces around the snares and backed away up the icy stream. He stopped when he reached a pool, dammed behind a fallen tree trunk, packed leaves, and pebbles. Horn knelt and drank deeply and refilled his half-empty canteen.

He stripped off his soaked boots and ragged clothes and plunged into the water. It bit into the cuts and bruises that scarred and mottled his chest and back, and it set his teeth to chattering in spite of a grim jaw. In a moment the shivers stopped, and his body began to glow as he splashed vigorously. Again and again he ducked his head under the water and came up shaking it from his hair in a flying spray.

When he finally pulled himself out and rubbed himself dry with his ragged shirt, he felt renewed. He passed his hand reflectively over his beard, got a long pocket knife out of a pants pocket, and honed it against a smooth pebble. He hacked at the beard, honed the knife again, and in a few minutes his face was reasonably smooth. His chin and cheeks were pale against the dark tan of his face, and the unveiled mouth was surprisingly sensitive.

Life surged powerfully through his body. With it came purpose and determination. He was clean again and young and strong and alive. He had done what he had set out to do, what he had been paid to do, what no one had thought possible. Maybe it hadn't been a proud thing, to shoot a man from ambush, but Kohlnar hadn't been innocent. There had been blood on his hands.

Let all Eron come against him; he would survive, because survival is more than an instinct—it is a desire, and in him the desire was strong.

These were the things he told himself as he strapped the heavy moneybelt around his waist, pulled on pants and boots, drew the still damp rags of the shirt around his shoulders, slipped on the cord of the pistol, lifted the canteen by its strap, and set out to inspect his snares.

They were empty, all of them. The sun was gone, twilight was fading, and he would have to go hungry into the desert.

He shrugged and followed the creek as it dwindled into a rivulet and almost disappeared close to the hole in the cliff wall. He crept through the small tunnel on hands and knees, annoyed by the way it seemed to whine, cautiously parted the bush at the far end, and peered into the lesser darkness. Here the whine was louder. It was not the tunnel; it was ships, many of them, in the sky above the desert.

The lesser darkness was broken by patches of light. They moved aimlessly across the desert. Horn crawled out onto the flat rock and stood up in the night, his back pressed against the warmth of the rock face behind.

The patches of light were almost square. They made a shifting, restless chessboard out of the desert: dark and light, light and dark, moving. . . .

Horn threw himself down at the base of the cliff, huddling close to the bush, just before the searchlight passed over him. A second later the whine came down to him, and he watched the light sweep into the desert.

Horn watched the crisscrossing lights, and there was a pattern. There was a consistency to the way the dark and light squares moved. The ships were using the sector principle. Hundreds of them swept the desert with eager, deadly fingers. Complicating the pattern were unassigned ships operating on a random-choice principle, lights on, lights off, darting here and there. There was no way of being certain exactly when a particular patch of desert would be safely dark or fatally brilliant.

Yet there was a pattern, and the fact that Horn could find it was a commentary upon empire. Mass government is government by rule and regulation. Obedience and conformity are overriding virtues; initiative is punished more often than rewarded. There are prescribed procedures for conducting a search, and no man can be punished for choosing rules over reality.

And yet, insofar as there is virtue in patterns, this was a good one. The sky whined with leashed desire, waiting to collapse on the hunted man. Horn crouched close to the protection of the bush, listening, studying the chessboard. He followed it on either side, far down the cliffs until it faded into distance and uncertainty. He could imagine what would happen if a sunbright beam chanced to pick him out.

He might dodge it for a moment, running this way and that in sudden twists and turns, but the ships would converge, pool their brilliance, and lay out a huge daylit square upon the night desert. In that square would be death.

He timed the passage of the ship in front of him, counting slowly to himself. When a random-flying ship crossed the pattern, he started to sprint, counting, choosing the safe, dark squares of the chessboard. Light and dark, light and dark. The patterns shifting, sweeping behind him. Veer this way, jump that way. Light and dark. Dark, dark. Jump!

He had almost miscalculated the ship's speed. It had come up behind him, and he had sailed into darkness just as the ship had turned upon another leg of its pattern. Horn picked himself up out of the dust and began studying the next pattern.

Only after three lines of ships lay behind him did Horn grow discouraged. The chessboard still marched across the desert in front of him. There was no end to it. The sky still whined above his head. It would go on forever; the whine had become a part of him, fraying his nerves, nagging at his mind until thought was an effort.

Then he heard the baying. A mounted party of hunters passed through a sweeping finger of light. The hunters circled there, back and forth, waiting for the man who was clever enough to pass the lights.

A line of hunting dogs, hell-hounds, completely encircling the patterns of light. That was how Horn would have planned it. They would have their sectors, too. They would patrol them, relieved by fresh hunters and mounts when they grew tired, and if he managed to slip between them, they would quickly pick up his scent and be after him. How long could he evade them on foot?

And beyond them, what? Another line of guards with ready guns? And beyond them another?

The desert night was cool, but Horn was sweating. His situation was hopeless. One man can never hope to escape an empire, if the empire is determined to find him. Not here on the desert, where there was no place to hide. The daylight would be more merciless than the searchlights. With the daylight he was dead. With the daylight, they would scout the hills and send parties of men ferreting out the smallest hiding places. They would leave no crevice unexplored. An empire had to find the assassin.

Horn realized then what he would have to do. A haystack is no place to hide a needle. The best place is among other needles. The best place to hide a grain of sand is on a beach. A man can only hide among other men. Horn knew where he would have to go.

He started to turn—and the searching finger found him.

It swept past. In that moment of passing, Horn sprinted. He sprinted away from the cliffs into the desert, tripped, and rolled in a choking cloud of dust down an arroyo wall. He landed, still running, but now the light was past and he was running in the opposite direction. He was running back toward the cliffs, back toward the mesa; he was running as if death pursued him.

The whine grew louder, became a chorus. The lights swept in. Horn ran, pressed close to the arroyo wall. In the distance the hounds began to bay. Horn ran a little faster, his breath coming into his lungs in great, burning gasps.

The lights swept past him and coalesced into a square behind. It was a restless square, moving this way and that as it picked out nothing but desert and then the bell-throated hounds and their armed riders. The square broke apart impatiently and began a new pattern. It was smaller now, and the dark squares were smaller as the arroyo dwindled away to nothing and Horn was running on the flat desert again.

He dodged and veered. Events were moving too swiftly now for thought and judgment. It was all instinct to pick out the square that would be dark next, instinct and luck as the squares shifted and merged and twisted. Instinct was right or luck held as the cliff face loomed up in front of Horn, and he threw himself in a heap at the base of it, and the lights roamed restlessly behind.

Left or right? Horn chose the right, only because he had to choose one of them, knowing that the wrong choice would be his last. He crawled along the base of the rocks, freezing when a light swept close, hoping that he looked like a fallen rock.

He crawled a long way, the baying of the hounds growing louder and urging him to speed he knew would be fatal, and the fear grew that he had turned in the wrong direction. But after an infinity he felt smooth stone under him, punishing his knees, and his left hand touched something that jabbed and rustled, and he slipped behind the bush and into the hole he had left—incredibly—only an hour ago.

He came back into the valley as if into peace, more blessed because it could not last. The hounds would find his trail. His doubling back might confuse them, but their masters would soon discover that they were making a giant loop into the desert and back to the cliff, and they would find the hole behind the bush because it was the only concealment anywhere on that loop.

He crawled beside the trickling stream for a moment, because there the bushes didn't grow as thick, and then, slowly, he collapsed and rolled over on his back with a weariness that was infinite. Chased, hunted, he had come close to the end. The long journey was almost over.

He had thought of that dark room on Quarnon Four as the beginning and the killing as the end, but the bullet that had shortened Kohlnar's life by only a few days had been an end only for the General Manager. Horn hadn't thought beyond it to the inevitable consequence—his own death. He wondered now if the dark room had been the real beginning. He knew that it hadn't.

All the little things that go to make up a life had shaped him for the decision that had started him on a three-hundred-light-year journey toward death. The Cluster had given him birth and molded him.

In the Cluster, individualism was sacred. There was too much to do to waste time on laws; they were obeyed or ignored as it suited the individual. Life was struggle; a man got out of it as much as he could take on his own. The frontiers were everywhere.

Horn had learned self-sufficiency early. The first Quarnon War had orphaned him; the casual government had ignored him. He bore no malice for either. That was life; the sooner a man learned it, the better off he was.

Everything he had ever had, Horn had struggled for. He grew strong and quick to learn. He became skillful in getting what he wanted and confident that he could get anything he wanted badly enough.

All causes were alike, good and bad. A man got what he could out of them. The only person a man must answer to is himself.

Above all, a man must not care. To care is to yield one's armor against the world; to care is to hand the world the power to hurt. Let the universe go its way; Horn went his and took, with his strength, what he wanted from the universe.

Horn looked up between the leaves at the stars. He had thought that people were like stars, separated by dark walls. But he saw them now connected by a network of nerves, bridged by sensitive filaments. No one exists in himself. No action is isolated. The black ships that had swooped down on the Cluster many years before had helped fire the shot that had entered Kohlnar's chest.

Is it like this everywhere? Horn wondered.

He rolled over and got back to his knees and crawled forward again. Perhaps he did not live just for himself. He hadn't been killed with his parents, and now a man was dead. If he lived now, would it have its effect somewhere else?

Something brushed against his face, something dangling and furry. He reached out. It was a rabbit, still warm, hanging in the noose of one of his snares.

Horn took a deep breath. It was a good omen. A rabbit died, and its death would give him strength. Perhaps that strength would give him life again.

Horn remembered what he had decided back on the chessboard desert. A hiding place. The only place he could hide. As he took the rabbit down and began to skin it, the plan unfolded in his mind.

THE HISTORY

Cultures aren't creatures. . . .

And yet they are much alike. A creature is a collection of cooperating cells; a culture is a collection of cooperating individuals. Like cells, the individuals specialize in their functions; they divide labor and sometimes inherit these divisions; they propagate themselves. Sometimes they grow wildly and, unless controlled, threaten the whole organism.

Like a creature, Eron needed blood, nerves, and food. Eron itself was the heart, the brain, and the stomach.

One thick, golden cylinder drove out from Eron into the greatest engine of all, into the flaming, yellow heart of giant Canopus. It was the master Tube. It was power. Power sustained the deadly walls of the other Tubes, and the walls transmitted it to power centers at each Terminal. Power. The blood of empire.

The Tubes were nerves. Along its walls raced variations—messages—bridging light years in hours.

And through the Tubes, just as swiftly, sped the giant ships: freighters, cruisers, liners. The cradles inched them into the locks; massive doors closed behind; air was sucked out. Doors parted in front of them, and they fell, fell into darkness, fell toward the narrowing center of the Tube until they passed it and began to slow. Only the golden bands that encircled them insured against a fatal contact with the invisible walls. The food of empire.

The analogy can be extended, but analogies don't bleed on the dissection table. Eron was more and less than a living thing. . . .

7

THE DARK ROAD

The lights roamed restlessly from artificial peaks, fleeing across the smooth pavement, illuminating for a second a dark form that turned its head away from unbearable brightness, jumping into the rocks, climbing the hills, crossing another beam like a giant sword, gleaming from the black flanks and golden bands of battleships with their own, roving cyclopean eyes.

The changing, prismatic colors of the monument and the radiance of the golden Tube stretching starward from it made the center of the field bright with wonder and imagination. But the perimeter of the field was dark, and guards stood in the darkness like patient shadows, unmoving, waiting for dawn to give them rest.

Among the shadow guards, a shadow moved; it was a little shorter than the others. A cloak and hood gave it a humped shapelessness. It passed from guard to guard, stopping for a moment and moving on.

The great sealed ruins of Sunport were quiet. Elsewhere there was noise and life; here was only silence and shadows and the sweep of searchlight. The day's thousands were gone, inspected, passed, shipped elsewhere, through the Tube at the domed base of the monument or through the older Terminal on Callisto. Only half the battleships remained around the edges of the field and the guards that were their complements. The only other ship was a small scout, insignificant beside the towering bulk of a battleship.

The desert was stirred into a sea of climbing dust by ships and hunters; they soared over the mountains and toiled over the hills and probed the hollows. But here there was quiet. The assassin had escaped for the moment, but he would not get far. Certainly he would not return.

"Guard!"

The shadow stiffened as the shapeless shadow stopped beside him. It was a woman's voice, low and soft.

"Yes?"

"What have you seen?"

"Other guards."

She was passing, but she stopped and peered up at his shadow face. It was too dark to make out features. The guard saw nothing but a pale blur under the shadow of the hood. A faint fragrance drifted to him; his nose wrinkled. His pulse quickened. He had never been so close to one of the golden women. He could reach out now and touch her, if he dared.

He stood straight and still, staring ahead.

"You don't think the assassin will come back?" the woman asked.

"Guards aren't paid to think."

"I'm asking you to think, now." Her voice became reflective. "They laughed when I said he would be back. They said they would catch him on the desert." She spoke to the guard again. "What do you think? Will he come back?"

"If I were he, I would come back."

She peered at his face again, curiously, futilely. "Your accent is odd. Where were you born?"

"In the Cluster."

"You enlisted after the War?"

"Yes."

"Then you don't know this area."

"A little."

"Then where did the assassin come from?"

"The desert."

"But the hunting parties were out. There's no food and almost no water."

"A strong man could do it. A clever man could get through."

"But how would he get here? And how did he get away?"

"Beyond the ship, there, is a tree. Behind the tree is a tunnel that cuts down through the mountain, down close to the desert. He never had to get closer than that."

"You knew this? Why didn't you say something?"

"To whom? I gave the reason before."

"Guards aren't paid to think?" The woman was silent for a moment. "Maybe you're right. But then you don't love Eron, do you?"

"Should I?"

"Why did you enlist in the Guard if you didn't want to serve Eron?"

"There was another choice?"

"And yet Eron pays you, feeds you, shelters you. What do you give Eron in return?"

"What Eron asks of me and everyone: obedience."

"You think we are hard masters then, the Golden Folk?"

"Masters are good and bad. Eron remains the same. It didn't grow strong by kindness. Eron is fat; the rest of the Empire starves."

"Then why doesn't it revolt?"

"With what? Fists against battleships? No, Eron is safe as long as it has the Tube."

The woman was silent for a long time. The guard stood straight, but his breath came quickly.

"Why will the assassin come back?" she asked finally.

"Where else can he go? The desert is suicide. The hills will soon be as deadly. His only chance is to come back here and steal a ship. Once among other men, you will never find him."

"I think you sympathize with him."

"He is a man like other men. Deluded, perhaps, but he did no more than any guard is paid to do."

"At least you're honest," the woman said. "I won't ask your number. I'd have to report you for treason, and you've helped me tonight. I'm grateful."

She turned away. As she turned, they heard a faint groan. The woman started to swing back and found herself inside the arc of the guard's powerful arm, a sweaty palm clamped over her mouth. She took a quick, sharp breath and started to struggle.

Horn cursed softly to himself as he fought against the woman's unsuspected strength. Her body was surprisingly firm and youthful, and her muscles twisted wirily inside his arms.

A few minutes more and he could have dashed for the scoutship, but the woman had blundered along before he was more than dressed. It wouldn't have mattered if he hadn't been weak and talkative. Those had trapped him.

He should have killed the careless guard, the fool who turned his back to shadows, but at the last moment he had slowed his hand. Here was a man, like himself perhaps, trapped into serving Eron; why should he die? He was no enemy. And Horn had let him live, to groan. And then he had kept the woman here with foolish chatter when she wanted to leave.

Why? Horn decided to trust his intuition.

The woman struggled fiercely, silently; she twisted and kicked, and her breath came hot and quick against Horn's hand. Suddenly she stopped fighting. Her body stiffened.

"Yes," Horn whispered. "The assassin."

A wandering light swept close. Horn drew the woman back with him into the shadows. The diffused edge of the beam touched them. The woman's hood had fallen back from her shoulders, revealing a long, tumbling mass of red-gold hair and the gentle sweep of a golden cheek. For an instant Horn's arms relaxed; she almost got away from him then.

In his arms was Wendre Kohlnar, the lovely face in the coin, Director for Communications, daughter of the man he had killed.

Horn's arms tightened just in time. "I don't want to kill you," he whispered. "But I will if you make me. It's up to you. I'm going to let you go in a moment. Don't move until I tell you. Don't shout or scream. The moment you take a deep breath I'll shoot you through the back. The pistol is turned to low velocity; it won't make any noise. Understand?"

She nodded. Horn's arms dropped away. She drew in a quick breath. The pistol barrel jabbed into her back.

"Careful!" Horn whispered.

"I couldn't breathe," she said quickly. "You bloody killer!" she added bitterly.

"I killed one man," Horn said. "How many billions did your father kill? Not just men, either. Women and children, too."

"You know, then?" she said, starting to turn.

"Keep your eyes ahead," Horn snapped. "Yes, I know who you are."

"That was different," Wendre said.

"It always is."

"But why?" Wendre asked. Her voice was puzzled. "He was dying."

Horn didn't answer. He didn't know the answer, and he had asked himself the same question. Why? Who had wanted Kohlnar killed? Who had paid Horn to kill him? And why was it important that Kohlnar didn't die a natural death?

It was important. Someone had gone to a great deal of trouble and expense and risked his own life to set the plan underway. It had to be important. But it wasn't as important right now as getting away and staying alive.

"We're going to walk across the field," Horn said slowly. "You'll walk in front; I'll follow. Head for the scout. Climb the steps. Order the crew out. If you try anything, you'll die."

"All right," she said.

"Let's go," Horn said.

She walked in front of him across the field. It wasn't far to the little ship, maybe two hundred meters, but the reflected glory of the monument was brighter as they went toward it.

Wendre's walk was a little hesitant and stiff, but Horn decided it would pass unnoticed. Who would question one of Eron's Directors? Horn marched behind her at a respectful two-pace distance and a little to the left. It would take keen eyes to see, in the darkness, the pistol held low against his right thigh.

Half of the distance was behind them. Still no challenge. No suspicion. The field lay in night and silence, stirred only by the sweep of roving beams and the brisk click-click of their footsteps on the pavement.

The steep stairway leading up to the dark port of the scout was only a few steps away.

"Slowly," Horn whispered.

Obediently, Wendre slowed her pace.

Suddenly the odor of danger was stifling. Horn felt like screaming or running madly for the steps that led up toward freedom, up toward safety. He clamped his teeth firmly on his lower lip and stilled the eager trembling of his muscles. Of course there was danger. The farther he went, the more dangerous the situation became. It would build higher and higher until the scout blasted away from the mesa and got beyond the range of battleships, beyond pursuit.

In front of him, Wendre's shoulders straightened.

"I don't want to kill you," Horn whispered.

The shoulders slumped. She started up the steps.

Danger. Stirring close. Crouching in the darkness. Horn's eyes were busy in the masklike calm of his face. But he saw nothing.

Calm! Calm!

Horn climbed behind Wendre, watching her back, quickening his pace a little to close the gap between them. When they entered the ship, he must be only half a step behind.

Two more steps. One.

Danger! It exploded! Something moved in the shadow of the little ship. At the first flicker, Horn shoved Wendre forward, instinctively.

The bullet whined between them and screamed off the rounded hull of the ship.

"Guards!" Wendre was shouting. "The assassin. Guar—"

The clanging of the port cut off her words. That way was closed. Wendre had tricked him. But it hadn't been a trick. There had been a shot.

And Horn was spinning, waiting for the second shot, braced against it. Before it came, his own gun spat. A muffled thud came from the shadows beside the ship. A groan. A whisper of cloth.

A sound of men running. Shouts. The searchlights hesitated and began to converge.

Horn was leaping down the steps. Two long strides brought him to the ground. He didn't hesitate. He ran toward the center of the field, toward the glowing monument.

Feet drew close behind him, many of them.

"There!" Horn shouted. "There he is!"

He ran hard, holding his gun in front of him. Behind, the running feet came on. But there were no shots.

They were running into a fantasy of leaping, shifting, many-colored shadows, painting them with paint-dipped fingers. . . .

"There he goes!" someone shouted.

Behind, distantly, came the creaking of an opening port. A woman's shouts were indistinguishable.

You're quick, Wendre, Horn thought. *But not quite quick enough.*

A hunter has to know what he is hunting. The guards didn't. No one knew what he looked like, not even Wendre. She knew that he was dressed like a guard, but she was the only one. As long as the chase continued, as long as the guards weren't mustered, inspected, questioned, searched, they couldn't find him. Before then, he would have to fade back into the hills. The far hills, this time.

Someone pulled abreast of him. The long desert trip, the thirst, the hunger, the lack of sleep had weakened him. But the guard beside him was looking ahead, looking for an assassin.

Assassin, assassin. The word hammered in Horn's brain. What is an assassin? What does he look like? How can you tell him from other men?

The Victory Monument drew close. Guards streamed by on both sides as Horn's stride faltered. His breath came raggedly.

He had time to wonder about the bullet that had passed so close to him. Close but too far. A foot in front. Fantastic inaccuracy for a guard. It had passed through the space where Wendre had been a moment before, where she would have been if Horn hadn't pushed her through the lock. Wendre? Had the bullet been meant for her?

Were there other assassins?

And then Horn was beside the towering cube, glowing with the giant picture of the Cluster's surrender. The platform was gone, and he wondered why he was here instead of running with the guards toward the distant hills, and then he understood. He could never make it. He could never survive another chase; he didn't have the strength to escape again. Again his instinct had been quicker than his judgment.

Here was escape. The only possible escape. Dangerous. Possibly fatal. But escape, if he lived through it. There was no other chance.

He tried to remember the Terminal he had inspected on Quarnon Four, the Terminal that stood outside the capital like a monument to futility. Somewhere in the Cluster there had been another, just like it, identical with Eron's Terminals to the minutest detail. They had never come to life. They had been dusty mausoleums for years.

Horn felt along the smooth black wall. Close to one corner was a crack. He traced it as high as he could reach; it went on up. Down, it turned a corner a few centimeters from the pavement, paralleled it for a meter and turned up again. A rectangle. The door.

Horn leaned against it. It swung in. Horn slipped into a dimly lit room and let the three-meter-tall door swing shut behind him. There was no one in the long room.

Horn turned back to the door. Beside it was a circular disk, slightly recessed into the wall. Horn put his hand over it and tugged at the door handle. It was immovable.

Horn turned back into the room, feeling a moment of security. Where were the technicians? Gone to aid in the search? Or hadn't they moved in yet? Perhaps the Tube wasn't ready for operation. Horn felt a flash of panic.

It subsided as he inspected the room. He remembered. This was a dining hall. Plastic plates stacked at the far end of the room for disposal were soiled.

Horn passed through an archway into a room lined with bunks and lockers. Four doors opened off it. The first would be the control room, the second a communications room, the third—

Horn palmed the disk beside the door. The door slid aside. Horn stepped into a huge, domed chamber, nine hundred meters high and almost as wide. Offset a little from the center was a massive, N-iron mounting for a giant, gun-shaped tube. It slanted upward. At a hole even larger than itself, the tube joined the dazzling brilliance of the real Tube. The floor trembled a little, as if the whole thing were in steady movement.

It was, Horn realized. It would have to follow the apparent movement of Eron.

At this end of the metal tube was a hinged cradle. The ships were brought into the cube on the many-wheeled dollies that rolled along the grooved tracks. The cradle lowered to receive them, raised them up, and shoved them forward into the main lock.

Horn ran toward the mounting and scrambled up the ladder welded to one of the beams. The first joint was two hundred meters from the pavement. Railed steps led upward toward the main lock at a thirty-degree angle. At the top was a door. Beside it was a disk. Horn hesitated and palmed it.

Beyond was a small room. The walls were lined with spacesuits, supported at the armpit by pegs. *Personnel lock,* Horn thought. He closed the door behind him.

He picked out a suit that seemed about the size of the one the Guard had issued him. He got into it with the ease of long practice.

He lowered the plastic helmet over his head and clamped it down. He shoved his hands into the gauntlets and felt them click against the metal cuffs. Gauges reflected their information against the front of the helmet. Air supply: 12 hours. Water: one liter. Food: two emergency rations. Closures: airtight.

He brushed his hand against the breastplate. The dials vanished. He walked heavily toward a door in the far wall. It slid aside to reveal a narrow cubicle lit by a single glowing plate in the ceiling.

Opposite Horn was another door. He palmed the disk beside it, but it didn't open. Instead, the door behind him closed. For a moment he stood there helplessly, feeling the sweat begin to trickle down his sides, and then the door slid open. Horn walked into a great tube, half a kilometer long, one hundred meters in diameter.

He began to run toward the far end of the tube, closed by giant doors. When he reached them he was winded again. At eye level, just to the right of the crack between the doors, was another disk. It was red. Above it was printed: DANGER—EMERGENCY.

Horn took a deep breath. Beyond the doors lay the Tube, and the Tube led to Eron, away from Earth and danger.

Was Eron better than Earth? For him, it was. Earth was death. Eron, at least, was uncertainty. Once there, if he could blend into that teeming hive of humanity, he could disappear. They would never find him.

He stood at the mouth of a second, darker tunnel and thought the thoughts he had thought before. Only this tunnel was deadlier. He remembered the buzzard that had flared so brilliantly against the Tube wall. The touch of the Tube was death.

Could he make it in a spacesuit?

Slowly he raised his hand toward the red disk. The metal gauntlet closed over—

He fell, fell into endless night, fell toward Eron, thirty light years away. . . .

THE HISTORY

Eron. . . .

Bitter child of a negligent mother. Spawned and forgotten.

Eron. Man's greatest challenge. Man's greatest triumph.

You had nothing but hate; that you gave freely. You froze man while he compressed your thin air to make it breathable. You scourged him while he searched futilely for useful minerals and fertile soil. You changed him; you made him as hard and bitter as yourself.

It's not surprising that he turned from you to the endless seas of space. Trade; raid. There was little difference between them.

Legend says that Roy Kellon found you, but legend is mistress to any man. Why should he have chosen you? Almost any world would have been fairer, sweeter, kinder. And you are nearly thirty light years from Earth, the journey of a weary lifetime.

Eron. Where are you now? Man changed you more than you changed him. He hid you beneath an expanding skin of metal and put you at the center of a star-flung empire. You sit there, tamed, obedient, holding it together with golden strings.

Eron. You are the Hub. All roads lead to you. . . .

8

OUT OF CHAOS...

Nothing. Nowhere. Lightless, soundless, weightless. . . . Nothing. Nothing to see or hear or feel. Formless, unreal. . . . Nothing.

The universe was dark, was dead, was gone. The world had ended. No stars, no warmth, no life. The night had won, and the light was forever gone. Death had conquered. The great clock of creation had run down. The great energy gradient had been flattened. Hot, cold—there were no words for those. No motion. Nothing.

Infinity was a dark sameness. Here, there—the terms were meaningless. Nowhere was everywhere; everywhere was nowhere.

One consciousness in the eternal night, stunned, reeling, afraid. One life living in the endless death. One thing aware when awareness was futile. One mind thinking when the time for thought was done.

Horn screamed. Soundlessly. Without movement. It was a shocking, mental thing without physical extensions, imprisoned with the narrow, impervious shell of the mind. It was lightning captured in a hollow ball.

No breath dilated his nostrils or stirred his lungs. No pump throbbed rhythmically in his chest. No muscles tensed or relaxed. He was a consciousness, hopelessly alone.

One mind, spinning in infinity.

Think! Think!

Infinity split. Creation!

Consciousness in the womb, weightless, eternally falling, endless distances below, above, around. *That's wrong. Think!* No up, no down. All directions were outward.

Consciousness. A mind to think. Existence. Circular proof. Outside of this, nothing.

Birth!

Upon one fact a man can construct a universe. Always one fact, always the same. I think—I am. Reality begins with me. I am the universe! I am the creator.

Create, then. Everything is destroyed but you. There is nothing alive but you. There is no thought, no memory, but yours. Create!

The universe was falling through the void. Falling or weightless? Distinction meaningless: identity. Falling. Hold fast to that. A thing must fall from somewhere, fall to somewhere, fall through something.

Cling to it. Cling to sanity. Create.

Falling from somewhere. From a place of weight and solidity. Earth. Horn created Earth, complete, with green plains and gray mountains, rivers, lakes, and seas, blue sky, white clouds, and sunlight. He peopled it with animals and men. Earth. His creation filled him with longing. But Earth was behind him. He was falling from there.

Falling to somewhere. To a place of weight and solidity. Eron. Horn created Eron, complete, steel-jacketed, cold, the hub of a giant wheel, spokes reaching across the stars. Beneath the icy metal skin, he tunneled it out and peopled it with mole-men, scampering blindly through the tunnels. Eron. It was in front of him. He was falling to there.

Falling through something. Falling through one of the golden spokes. The Tube. Horn created the Tube, complete, a golden shimmering of energy outside; within, a black nothingness, an empty, timeless void, foreshortening space or expanding time so that a distance of light years could be spanned in hours. He peopled it with a man, himself. He was falling through it.

Reality. Horn created it. . . .

Memory returned. With it came sanity. Sensation was still missing, but he had these two, and he must hug them tightly or go mad. He had fallen up into the Tube, up into nothingness and insanity. He was still there, but now he had a mind that worked.

He willed his mind to feel. At the end of eternity, he gave up. Either his mind was isolated or there was nothing to feel.

Eternity. The Tube was timeless, too. Every instant was eternity.

This could be death. Horn considered the possibility calmly. He tossed it away. It was an unprofitable assumption. If true, his condition was unchangeable; if not, his acceptance of it might make it actual.

He was in the Tube. These sensations—or these lacks of sensation—were a result of that; probably they were the effect of it.

He had been in a Tube twice before: going from Quarnon Four to Eron and from Eron to Callisto. Both times he had been unconscious. *Gas*, he had thought the first time. The second time he had held his breath, lying strapped in the guard-quarters bunk, but it hadn't delayed the blackness. They could have other means.

He had suspected then that it was a precaution against revealing a clue to the nature of the Tube. Now he was not so sure. It was obviously—if not entirely—a precaution against insanity. He knew himself to be tough-minded, and he had come dangerously close to irreversible madness.

He returned to the problem. He was in the Tube, falling from Earth to Eron. The effects were these: no light, no sound. . . . Better: no movement. Still better: no energy. Or the effect was this: no sensation.

Was there a way to tell which was the actual state of affairs? The effect on his consciousness would be identical, whether there was no stimulus or no reaction. Or, perhaps, if there is no reaction, the stimulus does not exist. Is there a sound where there are no ears to hear it?

Horn cut the thought off. That was a metaphysical blind alley. He had to assume the reality of things outside himself; this existence was self-centered enough, and he had no desire to return to the universe-creator illusion.

There should be tests to determine which of the alternatives was true. But how can a mind test anything? The mind has three functions: memory, analysis, and synthesis. Memory. . . .

A man, dressed in a gray uniform, looking at his watch: "I thought these trips took three hours; not even a minute has passed."

Analysis. . . .

1) Eron lied; the trip is instantaneous.

2) The man was mistaken; his watch had stopped.

Synthesis. . . .

If 1) is true, then these thoughts I am thinking are instantaneous. Can this trip which seems infinitely long be infinitely short? Time is man's invention, true, and it may not exist in a way we can understand it inside the Tube, but I am conscious of duration, however long. Moreover, instantaneous transmission implies the existence of a thing in two places at the same time. Judgment: implausible.

If 2) is true, then motion ceases inside the Tube. This would include: light, sound, all manifestations of energy, breathing, heartbeats, all internal activity including neural. . . . Then how do I think? Is intelligence incorporeal? Judgment: more likely.

The hypothesis was self-consistent and fitted the observable phenomena. If it were correct, then both alternatives could be true: there was no stimulus and the senses could not receive impressions and transmit them to the brain. If he could test it—

Horn recognized the familiar wall. At least he had a hypothesis, and that was better than nothing.

The walls—he remembered them suddenly, and he remembered that they were dangerous. He must not touch them. That was the function of the gold bands around the ships, to keep them from touching the walls. But he had no gold bands, and he had no way of keeping away from the walls and no way of knowing when he was close to them. Even now he might be edging close, imperceptibly—

He caught himself and drew back from the edge of panic. It was pointless to worry about the walls. If he touched them, it was all over, and there was nothing he could do about it.

He remembered how the Tube had seemed to taper. He had seen a sketch of a Tube once. He tried to visualize it. It had tapered. Like a tube of glass heated in the middle and pulled at both ends, the Tube had been drawn out to a slender filament. Was it wide enough to let him through?

The ships were much bigger. They got through. But the gold bands could be responsible for that. When he got to the narrowed section—

It was necessary to do something. Fatalism and inactivity might be natural under the circumstances, but they could be disastrous psychologically.

He decided to concentrate on just one sense. He tried to see. And failed, after an eternity of mind-wracking effort. He was troubled, however, by a vague feeling of something impenetrable equidistant on all sides of him. Could that be the Tube? If the mind were something distinct from the brain, could it sense directly, especially in circumstances like these? He accepted the possibility, and saw no way to prove it or put it to use.

The endlessness of the trip oppressed him. Time might be man's invention and his tool, but it could also be an enemy to destroy him. With nothing to measure its passing, he could grow senile waiting for an instant to elapse. The objective duration of the trip might be three hours; subjectively it was eternity multiplied.

He had escaped one trapdoor to madness only to find himself standing on another. He must keep his mind busy; he must fill eternity with thoughts.

He planned what he would do when he reached Eron. The Tube would take him to one of the Terminal caps at the poles, a cap bristling with Tubes. The caps didn't rotate with Eron. If they did, the Tubes would soon be twisted together like spaghetti. The broad, spiked caps floated in a shallow pool of mercury. They turned in the opposite direction of Eron's rotation, or, rather, motors kept them motionless while Eron turned underneath.

The ships pushed through airlocks into the space around Eron. They located their assigned elevator. The massive elevator lowered each ship past level after level until it reached the appropriate one. The freighters went deep, close to the ancient, sterile rock of Eron itself. The fighting ships stopped at the barracks-level. The liners, reserved almost exclusively for the Golden Folk, dropped only a little.

But ships were useless to him. Even if he could steal one and get it into space, he would have no place to go. Not into Eron. The elevators were operated from inside the skin of the world. The nearest planet was years away by conventional drive; he would be recaptured quickly.

There had to be some way to get from the caps to Eron itself, other than by ship. Could he walk out on the surface in his spacesuit and find a way in? No, that wasn't the way. Even if he could jump from the stationary cap to the spinning world without disaster, he would be dangerously exposed while he was searching for an entrance, if any.

There should be a direct connection. Not at the perimeter, although the relative motion would not be so great after all. If the caps were fifty kilometers in diameter and Eron rotated as rapidly as Earth, the relative motion would be less than seven kilometers an hour. But it would be awkward, waiting for doorways to align themselves; Eron would never plan it like that.

The nearer a man approached the pole, on the other hand, the less the linear velocity would be until it dropped away to zero directly over the pole. There, if anywhere, should be an entrance to Eron. Horn planned, in as much detail as his knowledge of Eron permitted, how he would get to Eron from the cap and what he would do when he got there.

But he could never quite forget the mouse of insanity nibbling at the edges of his mind. *How swift is thought? How slow is time? How long is three hours?*

The insensate mind that called itself Horn floated blind and helpless within a formless area, carried along by an unfelt force toward a shrinking goal. Only faith could sustain it, and the only faith it had was in itself.

It was irony, Horn thought, that when he was most alone, most independent of outside influences, he was unable to react with his environment; a completely isolated individual, he could not move a muscle, he could not alter his circumstances in any way. Perhaps there is a lesson in that, he thought.

Maybe it would have been better to have believed in something, he reflected, even though belief is a form of surrender to the universe. It might have sustained him now, if he could believe, as the Entropy Cult preached, that there was a great, beneficent force behind the apparent aimlessness of the wheel of creation.

He did believe in something: he believed in Eron, in its skill and its power. When Eron built something, it worked; the Tube worked, and it would take him to Eron. But believing in Eron was only a form of believing in himself; it was believing in his senses, his judgment, the validity of the external environment.

How swift is thought? How long to Eron?

It was not such a bad thing to believe in: himself. Would he have got so far if he hadn't, if he had believed in something else instead? He knew that he would not. It had saved him from self-pity, from easy satisfaction, and from soft acceptance, this belief that a man's fate is in his own two hands. Few things are impossible; fewer are inevitable.

It had taken him to wealth three times; twice he had tossed it away riotously. The third time he had wasted it fighting a futile war with Eron. It had taken him into countless adventures on a dozen worlds in the Cluster, found profit in them, and brought him out again. It had taken him three hundred light years across the Empire to Earth and a rendezvous with assassination.

The only way to get to Earth had been through Eron. Horn had taken advantage of the general amnesty to enlist in the Guard. After brief training on Quarnon Four and a taste of the fierce discipline enforced by barbarian mercenaries, Horn had been shipped to Eron. There he was handed over to the molding hands of Eron's drillmasters.

None of the recruits died; the officers called them the lucky regiment. But Horn couldn't count on the lightning stroke that assignment to a ship with orders to Earth would be. He got himself attached to the headquarters staff; when the duplicated stacks of orders arrived, he leafed through them, found one for Earth, forged with practiced skill the name of his own company, and less than a day later was on Callisto, satellite of a giant world in the solar system that included Earth.

The trip to Earth was far slower. Once there, he spent days searching for a way to escape from the ship. One night he was stationed as a guard at Port Three, whose massive rifle had been dismounted for rewinding. He had gone through it as soon as his fellow guard was stunned and tied.

It had taken him a week to avoid recapture and reach the tall, electrified N-iron fence that separated the food-plantations from the great American desert. It was patrolled, and the fence went too deep to dig under in the time available. Eventually, he had to fight his way through a gate, leaving two out of the four dead because one man was too alert.

Through the desert, believing in himself, taking what he needed. The nomad's pony, the stick man's life. The pony had been forfeit, like the nomad's life, when he had crept up on his camp, on foot; if Horn could catch him, he would never have escaped the swarming hunters. The stick man had been dead anyway; why should two men die when one is sufficient?

Horn remembered the terrified Chinese, the incredibly ancient Wu, teetering on the twisting girder above the black abyss, gasping with fear, toppling, screaming. . . . Horn supposed he hadn't meant to twist the girder, but without the threat of it he would never have learned the truth about Wu and Lil. As it turned out, it hadn't mattered, but he couldn't know that.

Horn wondered if death had caught up with them at last. That or imprisonment and, of the two, death was more likely.

With a twinge of shame, Horn remembered the screaming panic of his flight after Kohlnar's death. He remembered the valley and the chessboard desert and the man who moved only on the black squares, the despair, the return to the valley, and the rabbit. The strength of that had brought him here, up through the dark tunnel for a third time to this darker tunnel.

He remembered holding Wendre Kohlnar in his arms, and it was a good memory because there was no feeling left in his body. He remembered the slim firmness of her body struggling against his arm and her breath hot against his hand. It could almost make his heart beat again, thinking of her beauty and her courage and the way she had talked. . . .

How swift is thought? How far to Eron?

It was folly, thinking of Wendre, heir to the Empire, but it was better than madness. It was better than the eternal death that madness would be, because he had a hunch that he would need a mind that worked before he was out of the Tube.

Death. The bullet had whistled through the spot where Wendre had been. It had been meant for her; Horn knew that now. Who had wanted to kill her?

Who had hired him to kill Kohlnar?

That was behind him. Ahead was Eron. Surely he would be there soon!

He tried, once more, to see. Again he had a vague impression of impenetrability equidistant from him. Except in one direction. His mind strained. Was it light? Was it imagination? Was it delusion?

Distantly, an impression shaped itself inside the insensate mind. Brightness, coin-sized, growing. Along, barrel-shape beyond. Getting nearer, clearer. The image of the main lock grew more vivid in Horn's mind. Was this some kind of extrasensory perception, or was it illusion, the first step toward madness? There was no way to be certain, no tests to make. The brightness appeared to grow closer. *Think!*

If he were sensing this directly with his mind, why should there be a limit on it? Why couldn't he have seen this long ago? Answers: maybe he could, maybe there is a natural limit, maybe. . . . *Too many answers, too many questions.*

The brightness was growing larger more slowly. Too slowly. If he were seeing it, he would estimate the distance as twenty meters. Fifteen. Thirteen. Twelve. Eleven.

Too fast. Too fast!

Was it possible that he wasn't going to reach the lock? Was this real, what he was sensing, and was he going to fall short for some reason? Because he didn't enter the Tube with any velocity of his own, perhaps? Would he fall short by ten meters?

Ten. Ten. Ten. Eleven.

He had to act as if this were real, not a projection upon a hysterical mind of its own fears. But he couldn't act. There was nothing he could do—do— He couldn't move. . . .

Twelve. Thirteen.

Think! What are the chances, say of something falling thirty light years through a straight tube and never touching a wall? No chance. Meaningless. No—no! Something must have kept him equidistant, if this is real. The mind? Some force it exerts in this strange universe? Try it! What can you lose?

Only your sanity.

Horn *pushed.* There was no other word for it. Gravity caught him, yanked him crashing to the lock floor. Light blinded him, sensory impressions of every kind overwhelmed his mind.

Horn let out a gasping breath that started as a sigh and ended sounding much like a sob.

He had made it. He had reached Eron, and it seemed like an old friend.

But that was only a mask. It was suicide to think otherwise.

THE HISTORY

Dreamer, builder. . . .

Like the ant, man builds cities. Unlike the ant, he builds them consciously. Because they are convenient and economical, not because he needs the city life or likes it. He hates it. Always. And yet the city-building was something which, once started, could not be stopped.

All things tend toward ultimates, but it is the nature of ultimates that they can never be achieved. If Eron, then, was not an ultimate, it is because of the definition. Eron was the dream of Man, the City-Builder.

Trace the steps, the dreams. Ancient Paris and London; old New York and Denver; mighty Sunport. But they were rubble before Eron began.

Eron the City. A world encased in a metal skin, gleaming coldly in the light of its distant sun. One world, one city. As Eron grew powerful through the Tube, the Golden Folk built up and dug down: space, more space, still more. Warehouses and trading centers, schools and barracks, tenements and residences and palaces, amusement centers and factories, restaurants and communal kitchens, control rooms and power rooms. . . .

Eron was the center of a star-flung empire: politically, economically, socially. Every extraplanetary shipment, every message, and most of the Empire's power went through Eron. Eron grew, automatically. As long as the golden Tubes led only to Eron, that growth would never stop.

Eron. Megalopolis. . . .

9

SPIDERWEB

Horn pulled himself together. It was an effort, as if part of himself were still on Earth and he had to wind it in through all the weary distance, the danger, the darkness, and the fear.

If that's independence, he thought wryly, *I've had enough to last me for quite a while.*

His senses had eased their angry battering at his mind, and his mind started working again in its usual way, collecting information, weighing it, acting on it. He pushed himself to his feet. The giant doors were closed behind him, sealing the mouth of the Tube. Horn looked at the red emergency disk and turned away, shuddering. He walked quickly down the long, gleaming barrel.

The door to the personnel lock was in the same position. It swung open readily, closed behind Horn, and in a moment the door opposite opened. The walls of the small room were lined with spacesuits, supported at the armpit by pegs. They were all identical, these Terminals, constructed to rigid specifications. This one was exactly like the one he had left on Earth. He had no way of knowing, really, that he hadn't returned there.

Faith sustained him. Faith in Eron and faith in the Tubes that were Eron's greatness. Eron built well, and the things that Eron built worked.

Still, Horn thought, it would be ironic if he had returned to Earth. He should have made some mark— He had. He had taken away a suit. There was no vacant space now. He must be on Eron.

He pushed one of the suits to the floor and stood in its place. Before he removed anything, he stopped and thoughtfully brushed the breastplate with his gauntleted hand. The gauges sprang to life against the helmet face. Air supply: 12 hours. Water: one liter. Food: two. . . .

No change. He had used no air while in the Tube which seemed like proof that the bodily activities were suspended. Now, though, it would be a good idea to eat and drink. He might not have another chance for some time.

He worked the tube into his mouth and drew in half a liter of tepid water. He let the tube go and clamped his teeth on the food ejector. A pellet dropped into his mouth. He let it dissolve slowly, savoring the meaty flavor. When it was gone, he finished the water. He began stripping off the suit—

The room trembled.

Horn paused, half out of the suit, and listened to the reverberations. They could only be one thing: a ship entering the main lock a few meters away. A ship from Earth close upon his heels could only be pursuit.

He stepped free and made himself hesitate, studying the long line of suits against the wall like decapitated monsters, all gray, ungainly, limp. He stuck his hand inside the neck of one and squeezed the ejector. A pellet squirted into his hand. When he reached the door, he had five of them. He dropped them into a tunic pocket.

Horn opened the door and stepped onto the railed steps slanting down. They shook as he ran down them, hundreds of meters from the pavement. He grabbed the rail and looked back. A ship was coming out of the lock into the cradle, stern first. it was a small ship, a scout.

Horn raced to the joint, where the ladder began. The whole mounting shuddered as the cradle swung down toward the pavement below. When it stopped, Horn started down the ladder, swinging down swiftly, scarcely touching the rungs with his feet. A glance at the ship told him that he couldn't beat it down. The shaped dolly had reached up to receive the ship and was lowering it to a horizontal position. A faint shimmering revealed the tiny power loss of a unitronic field.

Horn swung his body around the ladder quickly. A body of guards had marched into the room from the side doorway. Now the mounting was between him and them. There were a dozen of them, dressed in gray uniforms like the one he wore. They didn't look up. They headed purposefully across the floor toward the ship.

Horn moved down cautiously, silently. A dark opening grew oval and round in the scout's hull, became bright, and flickered as gold-uniformed guards emerged and came down the dolly's built-in steps to the pavement. There were six of them. They glanced at the waiting gray guards, shrugged, and looked back up the steps toward the ship. They waited. The gray guards waited. Horn, who had dropped within meters of the floor, waited.

Wendre Kohlnar came through the port and ran down the steps. As she reached the pavement, the gray guards, with perfect timing, clubbed down Wendre's guards. While they were still falling, two more sprang at Wendre. She struggled in their arms, indignant, confused.

The noise covered Horn's final descent. Sheltered behind one of the giant beams, he stared speculatively at the scuffle. He fingered the butt of his pistol indecisively, fighting an unreasonable urge to help the girl.

He had no idea what was going on, what sides were represented here. There were too many of the gray guards. This wasn't his battle. Why should he trouble himself over a woman who would only turn him over to Eron justice? Let them fight their fights. His business was survival.

They had vanished into the ship again, taking Wendre with

them, leaving the guards like molten gold on the pavement. The port closed.

Horn walked briskly across the broad floor toward the door in the side wall. He breathed deeply trying to shake a dark mood of depression and worthlessness. The hell with them. The hell with all of them! It didn't help much.

"Get her?"

Horn looked up quickly. A technician was standing in his way. His golden features were almost pure. "Who?"

"The assassin."

"Sure," Horn said and tried to brush past.

The technician held him back. "Something funny came through from Earth. Said the assassin was in the Tube. But the pronoun was 'he.' And it didn't mention a ship. It said 'suit.'"

"Garbled," Horn said. This time he succeeded in getting past. The giant room he had left was rumbling.

He swung around at the archway that led into the dining hall. "Didn't you know who we picked up?" he called back. "That was Wendre Kohlnar."

The technician looked blankly incredulous for a moment and then spun toward the control room. Horn walked quickly through the dining hall and out into a corridor over two hundred meters wide. Deep, metal-lined tracks were recessed into the floor. Horn turned to the right and walked briskly away.

The corridor was empty. The rumbling sound he had heard had been the ship being raised back into the cradle. The main lock would rotate it into position to launch itself into space. It would circle Eron until it came to rest on the elevator that would lower it—to whoever wanted Wendre. They should be out in space now if they were going to get out at all.

The capture had been carefully planned and skillfully executed. Horn decided they would get out before the technician could convince the control room to stop the ship. But the confusion should cover his escape.

Horn came to a broad cross-corridor. It seemed to curve inward. That meant he was moving away from the center of the cap. Good. If the cap were constructed logically—and Eron was predominantly logical—it would be a spiderweb with a set of straight, radial corridors intersected by circular, concentric ones. At the center would be the spider, a sensitive and dangerous area of some kind. It was where he had to go, true, but not at this level. He needed to approach it from another direction.

The corridor he was on was definitely radial. It ran straight in both directions until, although it was well lighted, it faded into indistinctness. The concentric corridor's curve was gentle, but Horn found it impossible to judge the degree of curvature by eye. It could be anywhere from several to twenty kilometers from the center of the cap.

Horn trotted on along the way he had been going when the intersecting corridor stopped him. Before he came to another, he found a relatively narrow ramp leading downward. He turned into it without hesitation. Within a descent of a few meters, the ramp crossed a level corridor, darker and narrower than the ones above.

The ships didn't get down here. Horn crossed the corridor and continued down the ramp. The second level was even narrower and almost dark. The floor was dusty; the only footprints Horn could see were his own. It smelled musty and unused. Horn turned to the left, toward the center of the web.

The corridor thrummed gently with a constant vibration. He was close to the shallow pool of mercury in which the cap floated. Somewhere there would be massive motors, compensating for Eron's rotation. The vibration would be due to one or the other, or both. Horn trotted toward the center of the cap.

The corridor seemed unending, unchanging. Horn coughed a little in the dust raised by his feet. He slipped a food pellet into his mouth and sucked on it and found himself wrapped in the unreality of a childish memory.

Someone had told him about Eron—could it have been his

mother?—and the description had created as vivid a picture as a child's imagination can contain. It had been all false, of course, but it had all the truth of a fairy world. The golden Tubes, the metal world, the broad, rotating caps floating in seas of quicksilver. . . .

The quicksilver sea—that had been the most wonderful part. The boy had dreamed about it, surging and splashing metallically, gleaming like molten silver. He had cherished the illusion for a long time, and when he had learned that the mercury was only a few centimeters thick, it had been like the breaking of something infinitely precious. It was his last dream.

And here the corridors were dark and dusty, without beauty or illusion. He was actually in the cap that floated on the quicksilver sea, and he couldn't dredge up the smallest relic of wonder or delight. He was on the threshold of Eron, searching for a doorway into long-lost dreams; he wouldn't find it. Eron wasn't a dream world to him, only a refuge, and he was only tired with the eternal necessity of awareness.

The radial corridor he was on stopped abruptly as it was intersected by a concentric corridor. Ahead of him the perceptibly curving wall was unbroken. Horn turned to the right, trotting. After a few hundred meters, he was able to turn left along another radial corridor continuing toward the center.

Horn nodded. Obviously, all the radial corridors couldn't meet at the center. For an extensive area, there would be no walls—only corridor.

And this corridor ended in a blind alley. Horn stood in the box-like end, pressed against one wall to let the distant light filter past his shoulder. The walls, the floor, the ceiling met flush against a fifth plane set at right angles to all of them.

It should be a door, Horn told himself. It had to be a door. There would be no logic in a pocket like this.

There was nothing to brush or press along the walls. Horn pushed against the partition. It was solid and unyielding. He let his hand brush the edge. Something clicked. Horn threw his weight against the barrier. It gave a little, squealing, and stuck. A bright line of light appeared at the right.

Horn took a deep breath and tried once more. Complaining, groaning, the door swung open. Cautiously, Horn stepped into a large room shaped like a fat cylinder. In the center, reaching from floor to ceiling, was a smaller cylinder, about four meters in diameter. The room was empty.

Horn closed the door behind him and circled the room looking for an exit. Exit? Entry. Entry into Eron.

The surface of the small, central cylinder was smooth and unbroken. Opposite the door he had entered was another door in the curving wall of the room. When he had pulled it open, there was only another long, dark corridor behind it. He slammed it shut and leaned against it.

His shoulder slumped wearily. His legs trembled a little. It had been a long time since he had rested.

He leaned his head back against the cool metal and closed his eyes. He forced them open quickly. If he let them stay closed, he would fall asleep, and he couldn't afford to sleep. The silent desertion of the lower levels of the cap was deluding. There could be no peace for him, just as there could be no sleep. The hunt went on, somewhere, and if he stayed too long in one spot, the hunters would catch up with him.

He saw the wheel against the ceiling.

It was below the ceiling a few centimeters, connected to it by a thick, threaded bar. Beside it, against the wall, was a ladder. It started three meters from the floor.

Horn jumped, caught the bottom rung, and pulled himself up hand over hand. When his head was close to the ceiling, he wrapped one leg around a rung and leaned back to grab the wheel. Above the wheel was an opening in the ceiling about a meter in diameter; it was covered from above by a metal plate.

From his position, Horn couldn't exert much leverage, and the wheel was stubborn. Horn gripped it firmly and pushed with his legs and back. It began to turn. He sweated with it, his back muscles starting to cramp, until it was almost flat against the plate in the ceiling.

He rested for a moment and wiped his face on his sleeve, braced himself again, and shoved upward. The wheel lifted, taking the plate with it, and toppled to one side. Horn grabbed the edges of the circular hole and lifted himself into the room above, realizing that caution was useless after the noise he had made.

The room was almost identical with the one below. The differences: it was cleaner, better lighted, and the central cylinder was cut off a few feet from the ceiling. This room was empty, too.

Horn was interested in the central tube. It led down. From here. It ended here.

He circled it. The first thing he noticed was the disk just below eye level. Then he saw the hairline crack beside it. He palmed the disk and waited. Nothing happened for a moment.

He felt a slight jar under his hand. The crack widened. A door swung open toward him. Behind it was a little, circular room, just big enough for one person.

Horn waited until his heartbeat slowed and stepped into the room. It had to be a way into Eron, an elevator or a tube car. He sank gratefully into the single, room-filling pneumatic chair. He stared at the curved, softly golden wall. It was a pleasing color, but featureless.

No controls. No way of knowing where the car went or how to stop when it got there. It had to be automatic, then. With no choice, there was only one possible destination. That, logically, would be the other Terminal cap. If he went straight through Eron and out at the other pole, he would be no better off than if he stayed here.

Horn frowned. That meant there was no way directly from the caps to Eron. It didn't seem reasonable.

He reached out for the handle of the cylinder door and brought it gently toward him. Before he closed it completely, he hesitated and then, defiantly, slammed it shut. The lights went out. In the darkness, something nudged Horn's arm into the car and slid shut. Horn wondered why he felt no movement, no sense of falling.

Eight glowing disks floated in the darkness in front of him. Six of them were in the middle. To the left of these, separated a little, and a trifle more than half a diameter beneath the straight line that passed through the center of the others was a white disk. The six in the middle were colored: silver, gold, orange, green, blue, black. The last one was barely discernible against the deeper darkness. And, separated by a space to the right, there was a red disk.

Controls! They had to be. He could pick a destination inside Eron. All he had to do was figure out the meaning of the disks and pick one—the right one.

The white one at the left was easy. It should be for the south Terminal cap. If he had been at the south cap, that disk would be out and there would be one lit above it. At one of the other destinations, both of them would be lit, and a passenger could choose between them.

The colored disks—he could only think of one meaning. They could stand for the directorships. If he covered one of those, the car should take him to the residence of one of the Directors. It was a sobering discovery.

He had blundered into the Directors' private transportation system. It seemed to be the only route direct from Eron to the caps. It would take him into Eron, sure, but right into the hands of those most anxious to find him. Like the Tube that had brought him from Earth to Eron, this only postponed the imminence of capture in favor of greater inevitability.

But there wasn't any choice. A quarry has only one function: to run. When he stops, he is finished; the game is over. Horn sat in the near darkness staring at eight floating choices and reflected how inevitability had channeled his actions since he had left the Cluster. Since he had accepted the money from the voice in the darkness, there had been only one step to take, and he had taken it;

one path to follow, and he had followed it. Beyond, it had seemed, there would be choice; never now.

So it had led him on, step by step, comforted by the self-nurtured illusion of free will, guided subtly, unyieldingly, by the iron tube of determinism. Once started, he never had a chance to turn back. There was only one thing that could have prevented his appointed meeting with Kohlnar—death. And death is almost always the greater of evils.

"I go where I wish," Horn had said, there at the base of the cliff.

And the ancient Mr. Wu had replied, "So we think, so we think. In the middle of things we see no pattern. But as we look back and view the picture whole, we realize how men are moved about by forces they do not suspect. The pieces fall into place. The pattern is clear."

In other words, when somebody moves, something has pushed.

Choice. Where had there been choice? Having deserted, he would have been insane to stay in the occupied lands. In the desert, the hunting parties had forced him toward the mesa. Backed against the cliff, he had only one way to go: through them.

Wait. Twice there had been choice: at the beginning and at the end. He could have turned down the job. Could he? Given his condition, his experience, his background, his environment, had he chosen freely? Or had the choice been determined for him?

With the crosshairs on Kohlnar, he could have refused to pull the trigger. Couldn't he? Perhaps he couldn't. Perhaps that, too, had been determined by the built-in set of a lifetime.

And then, after the assassination, even the illusion of choice had vanished. Driven, guided, pushed. Down the dark tunnel to find the desert closed. Back to the mesa to find only one way open: the Tube. And through the Terminal cap to this spot.

Was it true that a man's only real choice was to live or die? Even then the dice are loaded. Roll them as often as he likes, the dice will come up: live! It is better to suffer than to feel nothing. The conscious mind may rebel; it may even, in a brief moment of sanity, win a surprising and final victory. But it is infrequent, and who can say whether that, too, is not determined.

"I won't die," Horn had said.

"So we think, so we all think," the fat, yellow man had answered. "And yet we do."

And now another choice, a choice of colors: silver, gold, orange, green, blue, black. You pays your money and you takes your choice. Not free. Not now or ever. Because the coin is life.

The other Directors might well be back by now. Only two would not be home: Kohlnar, who was dead, and his daughter, who was captured. Silver or gold? In any case, there would be guards, and they would be watchful and on edge. What choice? A choice of staying here, where he would certainly be caught, or postponing his capture for the duration of the trip through this private tubeway.

Horn's lips curled wryly. The quarry has no choice. He must run until he can run no more.

Silver was probably the better choice; the General Manager's household would be confused, disordered, headless. But Horn had a curious reluctance to go there.

His hand stretched out toward the disks, hesitated, and dropped over gold. He had chosen Wendre. Or had something pushed?

The thought was cut off as the chair dropped out from under him. The glowing disks vanished. Blackness was a blow, and he remembered nothing.

He opened his eyes to darkness and the unpleasant disorientation of free fall. For a moment he thought he was back in the Tube, but sensation was still with him. Behind him was smoothness. He gave himself a gentle push and floated through the darkness, his hands groping ahead. In a moment he had pulled himself into the chair and strapped around his legs the belt he hadn't noticed before.

He rubbed the back of his head gingerly. The colored disks

were dark; it hadn't been all unconsciousness. Only the red disk on the far right was still glowing. As he watched, it blinked.

He knew then what it was. He slapped his hand over it, hoping he was not too late.

Then the panel was completely dark. The car began to slow.

THE HISTORY

Hope. . . .

It springs from the hopeless. It is all they have.

True religion comes from the slaves. It is a survival factor; for them, the major one.

The Entropy Cult, with its visionary hope, was born among the endless, numbered slaves of Eron. Its symbol was the bisected circle; its promise was a rebirth of matter and spirit when the eternal circle swung back to rest upon its other foot.

The day of regeneration. The poor, the hopeless, the oppressed waited for the promised reversal, when those that were low would rise high and those that were high, fall low.

Out of the darkness it was born. In the darkness of the deepest warrens and catacombs, it grew. Poor bastard-child of science and despair.

Officially, the Cult was banned. Unofficially, the Golden Folk considered it something which, if it had not existed, they would have invented. It kept the slaves docile.

But oppression and despair can breed other things. And a symbol can cover a multitude of meanings. . . .

10

THE HOLLOW WORLD

Horn was pressed hard into the yielding chair for a moment, and then his body was straining against the belt around his legs. The car or an inner shell had flipped over. Suddenly the pull ceased; normal gravity took over. The car was at rest.

At rest where?

Horn looked at the disks which were floating once more in the darkness. All of them were on, even the two white ones, one above the other at the left, even the red one. He was nowhere. For Horn, it was better than somewhere.

Horn unfastened the belt and fumbled with the panel of the car before he found the button that pulled it back. Beyond it, a door swung aside. Light flooded into the car. It was blue.

The red disk had been an emergency stop. This was an unlisted exit into the hollow world. There might be dozens of them. There had to be more than one; otherwise the red disk would have gone out.

Horn stepped out of the car into the blue room. It was empty. He turned and studied the tube door. He suspected that when it was closed the thin line of its juncture with the wall would be completely concealed by the living mural on the luxion facing.

The blue world. Around the walls and across the ceiling the

mural flowed, constantly changing. The sky was the blue of midnight; the foliage was blue-veined white fernery tossing gently in a breeze he couldn't feel. Horn had an uneasy feeling that blue-furred animals moved silently behind them, peering out with strange, cautious eyes.

The floor was carpeted with blue grass. In one corner the floor rose to a wide, mossy mound. Horn suspected that one would sink down deep into it. He shivered. Beyond the bed a brook sprang musically from the wall and streamed across the floor in a narrow channel.

The tube door was similar to the other walls except that there was a small, blue sun toward one edge. It was a little too blue to be realistic; it should have been blue-white and hot. Instead it chilled the room. Horn shivered again. He didn't like this room. The night sky was brilliant in the Cluster, rivaling the day. Nights on Earth had been bad enough. This gave him a shuddering, choking feeling.

He put his hand over the blue sun and felt something click. That was the lock and the signal for the tube car. He hesitated and then slowly shut the door. This was better than he could reasonably expect to find at another tube car destination. But the click-click had an ugly sound of finality. He thought about the car falling through the metal tube to wherever its depot was, for it wouldn't stay outside the blue room, blocking the tube.

Half an hour in the blue world was twenty-five minutes too long. Horn fought a desperate despondency as he searched for a way out of the room. But half an hour was the length of time it took him to find it. He had knelt on the blue grass, reluctantly, and sipped the blue water. It had been cold and sweet and vaguely effervescent. He had opened a closet filled with diaphanous blue and white clothing; there were also some stained things that could have been nothing but whips. At last Horn found the door.

He stepped into the yellow hall with a heavy sigh. The change in his attitude was remarkable. He felt invigorated, potent, powerful. He fought that, too, and moved cautiously down the hall. The doors he passed were marked with colored disks. When he passed too close to some of them, he heard high-pitched laughter and screams and low moans and animal-like grunts. If he had had any doubts about the nature of this place before, they were dispelled. After that he stayed in the middle of the hall. He wasn't squeamish; it was merely that some pastimes were not to his taste.

He met no one along the straight corridor that stopped, eventually, against an immovable door. Horn stared at it blankly. There was no disk to palm, nothing to press, nothing to turn; the only clue was a slot a few centimeters long and about a quarter of that wide.

Horn frowned. It was a simple door, at the end of the hall, obviously meant to be used. It would be irony to be turned back now. The slot was obviously meant for something.

Horn pinched coins from the money belt and fed one into the slot. It clucked contentedly, but it didn't open. Horn kept count. When the total reached five hundred kellons, the door swung out.

Horn grimaced. It had been an expensive exit; it had eaten a sizable hole in the price of Kohlnar's death. Escape and the exotic came high on Eron. He shrugged as the door closed behind him and another opened in front. He had never kept accounts.

He stepped warily into what seemed to be a roofed alley. It was dimly lit, a perfect spot for thugs and thieves. But perhaps the area was patrolled. The alley was deserted.

The alley opened into a broad, colorful roadway. Horn had seen slideways before but never so many and so swift. The ceiling overhead was a neutral color, reflecting without glare the light that streamed against it from hidden sources. The slideways were crowded; the golden-skinned people on them were dressed fantastically. The women wore very little, and Horn realized that the air was warm, a little too warm. Brief skirts or shorts revealed long, shapely legs often ornamented with brilliants. Blouses were even more revealing; they were transparent, low-cut, only a half, or slashed strategically to give tantalizing glimpses of golden flesh.

What clothing the women had removed, the men had put on. They were overdressed in synsilks, furs, and jewels. Their bosoms were padded into grotesque imitation of their mates, and their legs, elevated on stilt-heel shoes, had a feminine symmetry. These were the Golden Folk, at home, and Horn wondered how he could pass among them without being stopped.

He squared his shoulders and stepped purposefully onto the first strip, his eyes watchful. Brilliant light drew his eyes to the left. Above a glowing, multicolored door, were wriggling letters. They spelled out: *THE PLEASURE WORLDS.* As Horn stepped to a faster strip, they were gone behind him.

As if he were carrying out a grim mission, Horn moved from strip to strip, his face set and determined. Men and women glanced at him and looked away, and in that flicker Horn read distaste and uneasiness and a touch of fear.

What is it you sense? Horn thought. *An assassin? Or is it only the vague knowledge that I could kill you so easily, I the barbarian, unsophisticated, savage, and powerful? Or is it your own society you fear and the security measures necessary to sustain it?*

The slideways moved through the eternal tunnels of plastic and metal, past the near-hypnotic displays of shopping centers, the tantalizing odors of restaurants, the garish beckonings of amusement districts. Urging, luring, demanding. The slideway was a living snake weaving to the changing tunes of a skillful charmer. People got off and people got on, but it was always the same snake. Helplessly, Horn moved with it, watching the strips that split off into other corridors or turned downward, thinking dazedly how a man could stand in one spot and go entirely around this world, how he could keep traveling all his life and never pass the same spot twice, how this went on endlessly, this headless snake swallowing its tail. . . .

Horn shook his head vigorously. Danger could be anywhere and was probably everywhere, but he had to decide where to go. He couldn't just stand and wait for the decision to come to him.

But it was hard to think while the snake twisted mindlessly to the compulsive rhythms of music and the pleas and commands to buy this! buy that! do this! do that! use this! use that! . . . Horn tried to close his mind to it, but words forced their way into his consciousness:

"*All guards not now in their assigned barracks will report there immediately. All guards—repeat—all guards will report to their assigned barracks. No excuses. No exceptions. Guards on post will wait until relieved. All unreported guards will be shot on sight. . . .*"

The snake turned to look at Horn. He walked quickly to the right-hand strip and stepped onto the first strip heading down. As it carried him away from the brilliance, he heard the voice saying:

"*A meeting of Directors has been called for some unspecified time within the next twenty-four hours. Presumably the most urgent business will be the election of a new General Manager to replace. . . .*"

Down. That was the right way. Down toward the barracks. Down in obedience to the general command, which could only mean that Duchane knew he was inside Eron dressed as a guard. The Guard would be inspected, a monumental task but one guaranteed to unmask an assassin hiding behind a gray uniform and a yellow identity disk his description did not match.

And if he didn't report, the manhunt would begin in Eron. Any solitary guard would be captured or shot.

Idly, Horn noticed the level number glowing on the wall as he stepped around a corner to take the next strip down: *111.* He had been on the top level then; there were one hundred and twelve numbered levels to Eron. It was an odd fact that occurred to him suddenly, and he felt an odd satisfaction in the reflection that he had been where few barbarians had ever been.

The hunt was about to begin again. Horn felt a familiar flutter of something between panic and excitement. His hands got cold; he suppressed a shiver. He breathed deep for calmness, turned a corner, stepped onto another moving ramp. Down. Down, seeking his level, seeking the level of rats and vermin and other hunted things.

Down past flickering lights and darkness, intermixed: residence levels, schools, middle-class shopping centers, restaurants, amusement areas, music, babble, people. . . . They blurred together; they became a kaleidoscope, bright, colorful, flickering, fantastic, meaningless.

As he was carried lower, men in uniform began to join him, guards answering the order to report. They became a stream fed by countless tributaries as it dropped lower down the smooth, sloping channel; inevitably the stream became a river.

The lights brightened. The slideway leveled out into a wide, low-roofed area where guards waited with drawn pistols. Between them the river flowed, Horn carried with it. Horn glanced at the faces bobbing in the river around him; they were blank and careless. But the men with the guns were watchful.

Ahead of them would be the long, narrow barracks with the stacked bunks against the walls and the eating benches between. Horn remembered them well. Once there his last chance would be gone. His eyes searched the walls ahead, searching for an opening; he kept his gun hidden beneath his arm. There were slideways leading down from here. Most calls for the guards came from below.

When the break in the walls appeared, Horn was ready. He saw the slideway when he was fifty meters away. He sneaked his pistol into his hand and edged toward the right side of the gray river. When the slideway was ten meters away, his gun was on his hip, slanting upward toward the low metal ceiling.

He pulled the trigger. The bullet screamed against the ceiling and ricocheted off a wall.

"There he is!" Horn shouted.

Guards turned to look. The river began flowing more swiftly. Men broke into a run. Horn lowered his shoulder and broke through the line of armed guards at the wall, dodged through the opening onto the slideway, and he ran down the moving strip in long strides, weaving from side to side.

The bullets that followed him were late. The feet that ran behind him were slow. In a few minutes, he lost them. He went down.

After innumerable turns and innumerable descents, the strips stopped moving. They looked as if they hadn't moved for a long time. The long inclines were darker, narrower, dirtier. Horn moved out into a roadway, his nostrils flaring to a general odor of decay.

Here the people were pasty-faced instead of golden; their clothes were drab and ragged; they had the blind look of moles. They trudged along the unmoving strips, their eyes down with their feet in the half-darkness, to no music except the shuffle of shoes on plastic.

The shops were dirty and poor. The plastic facings were cracked; large pieces had broken free. The goods on display matched the appearance of the stores they were sold in.

Horn walked with the ragged men and women, feeling a certain kinship with them. Like them, he was hungry; like them he had known that life was sorrow, and sorrow was eternal.

They walked among the factories where the sound of machinery shook the air, beat it with hammer blows, shattered it with explosions, and the air retaliated against the people who moved through it, swaying. They passed the open doors and the long, dirty benches of communal kitchens, where the odor of rancid, rotten food drifted out to them, and many turned aside and entered.

Horn hesitated, feeling his hunger like a living thing inside, but it was folly. He fished a final pellet out of his pocket and let the crowd carry him along. As they entered another stretch of miserable shops, Horn noticed that the people shuffling near him had begun to inspect him warily out of the corners of their eyes. Even here, he had no place.

It was the uniform. If he wanted to hide, he had to get rid of it. He swung into a half-lit doorway. It was a clothing store. Cheap overalls and sleazy wrappers were stacked in the window. The door had a handle. He twisted it and pushed it open and went in.

A bell tinkled somewhere in the back; it had a cracked, hollow sound. As Horn's eyes adjusted to the darkness, something white moved, came close. It was a claylike face above a crooked body.

"Yeah?" It was a throaty whisper.

"Clothes," Horn said harshly, annoyed by a feeling of revulsion.

The face shook from side to side, laughing with a cracked, hollow sound like the bell. "Nah! The butcher'll nah get me. No clothes for gray guns. It is the law."

"Clothes," Horn repeated savagely. "I'll pay for them."

The doughy face shook. It had lines of dirt in the wrinkles. After a moment Horn realized that the gnome was laughing again. "Nah! Gray guns nah make so much."

"Ten kellon," Horn said.

The gnome stopped laughing and hesitated before he shook his head. "Nah, nah."

"Fifteen."

They settled on twenty-five. The gnome handed Horn a thin pair of coveralls, reputedly white, and motioned for him to change in the back room. Someone might see.

Horn shrugged, opened the grimy door, and walked into a room stale with old odors of food and sweat. It was even darker than the shop. Quickly he opened his tunic and started to pull it off.

Strong hands yanked the tunic down over his arms, pinning them back. Something whispered through the air. Horn threw himself forward, going down on his knees, rolling. Something grazed his head as he went, but the man who had been holding his tunic sailed over his shoulder and hit against a wall with a thud and an explosion of air.

The tunic had ripped. Horn's arms were free. He was on his feet, turning to meet the expected charge. Something black flickered toward him. Horn threw up his arm and lunged with the other. The blow was numbing; his right arm was useless. But his left fist connected. As the second man staggered, Horn hit him again with a chopping blow that dropped him to the floor, moaning.

The first thug was rising dazedly. Horn turned, bringing up his knee sharply. The dark shape slammed against the wall again and slithered down it limply. The second one, on his hands and knees, was shaking his head like a sleepy bear. Horn chopped the edge of his hand against the back of the man's neck. He pitched forward.

Horn stood still, breathing deeply, listening. The room was silent now. He stooped and found the pistol that had been torn off in the struggle. He turned slowly, making a complete revolution. Nothing. Quickly, then, he stripped off the gray trousers and the remnants of the tunic and slipped into the loose coveralls. He pushed the pistol into one of the deep pockets and shook his right arm. The numbness had left it; there was a sore spot on the forearm, but it worked out as Horn clenched and unclenched his fist.

His eyes had adjusted themselves to the darkness. He paused at the door to glance back at the men on the floor. They were big, heavy brutes, but their features were puffy, doughy. They looked soft and degenerate. Horn shook his head and went back into the shop. His hand was holding the pistol in the deep pocket, but the look of shock and helpless fear on the face of the crooked man brought his hand away.

He had been lurking near the door. Horn turned to him, his mouth twisting. "A cap," he said.

The second one he tried on fit well enough. He pulled the misshapen bill down low over his forehead. He stepped close to the shivering, silent shopkeeper, his hand held out. The man drew back fearfully.

"Here," Horn said. He dropped the coins into the man's grimy hand. "I'm paying for the clothes. You'd find a way to betray me if I didn't. I'd advise you not to try. The Guard or Duchane's agents would find the money. They'd take it away and you, too. They'll never believe you didn't help me. Forget you ever saw me."

The man nodded, his eyes rolling.

"Give me an identity disk for a warehouse laborer," Horn said.

Clutching the coins, the gnome bent beneath a table piled high with cheap cloth. In a moment he came up with a yellow disk hyphenated with numbers.

"Get rid of that uniform," Horn said, as he pinned the disk on his cap. "Fast. And you'd better take care of your boys. They're going to be unhappy with you."

Horn walked quickly to the front door. He stood there for a moment, studying the twilight street. Even the slaves were ready to rob him, kill him. He hadn't found his level yet. He would have to go lower still, down to the lowest levels, the warehouse levels.

Or perhaps, he thought, *an assassin has no natural allies.*

He saw a guard burst through the shuffling mass of slaves and speed past and disappear again. Horn's eyes narrowed. The workers milled. A rising murmur reached Horn's ears, became shouts and curses. A squad of guards fought its way through the barriers of obstructing flesh, clubbing their pistols right and left to clear a path. Sullenly, the slaves parted.

When the tumult and shouting had passed on into the distance, Horn slipped through the door and joined the roiled stream. He let it carry him along for minutes, trying to see whether any faces followed him for long. There were so many of them, and they seemed so alike that he gave up. He turned aside at the first wide ramp leading down. The air, which had been fresh, although warm, at the top levels, was stale and hot here. It became worse as he passed through huge, dark caverns cluttered with stacked crates, boxes, barrels, bales. There were occasional working parties, but Horn kept well clear of them. Twice he saw thick, squat freighters in their wells, being loaded or unloaded. They were distant and well-lighted. Horn kept to the deepest shadows as he made his way deeper into Eron.

Downward, fleeing, where the rats scurried away from his footsteps and flying things brushed, flapping, past his face. The passages grew narrower, dustier, hotter. Sometimes there were holes in the ramps. The dark caverns, dotted frequently with thick, N-iron beams, were deserted. They had been given up to rot and decay centuries ago. The air was stifling.

Horn tried not to think about the overpowering weight piled above him, supported by these long-forgotten beams. The mass of human flesh alone was a shuddering thought.

Horn stopped. He was in a dark, narrow corridor. The floor was rough underfoot, and the walls were chiseled rock, warm to the touch. Dust was thick in the air; cobwebs clung to his face. He swept them away with a coarse sleeve.

He was below the lowest level. He was down into the ancient catacombs in the heart of Eron's rocky crust. He tried to take a deep breath and walked forward wearily.

The corridor eventually turned right and widened. The light took Horn by surprise. Hours in the hewn passageway had covered him with cobwebs and dirt. Horn blinked. After a moment he saw that the light was only a dim reflection. He went on, turned left, and stopped at the edge of a vaulted chamber cut out of the rock.

Crude wooden benches were arranged neatly on the rough floor. The rows faced toward the far end of the room. That end was bright. Blackly, massively silhouetted against the light was a symbol carved out of the living rock; it was a circle bisected by a thick line extending above and below it and ending in horizontal arms and feet.

Horn recognized it. It was the scientific symbol for entropy, and this was an Entropy Cult chapel. There were a few people scattered singly on the benches, their heads covered and bent in thought or weariness. Their clothing was ragged. Horn sank gratefully onto a bench and bent his head into his arms.

He had run until he could run no more; this was the end. He had run from the naked desert of Earth deep into the rocky heart of Eron; he could run no farther. But what could a quarry do except run?

Eron wanted him, needed him as badly as it ever needed anything. It would never forget. It would never rest until he was in its hands, Horn the Assassin, smasher of images, threat to empire. There was no hope for him.

And he realized what he would have to do. Even the most timid animal will fight when it is cornered. While there is a chance for escape, it will run, but when it can run no farther, it will fight. And so Horn would fight. The only way to survive was to destroy Eron. Horn clenched his jaw: he would destroy Eron.

Only long afterwards did the decision seem funny: one man declaring war against man's greatest empire. At that moment Horn only knew that it was logical and just. Eron could be destroyed; he would destroy it.

It went no farther than that. In his weariness, he didn't think of odds or means or plans. There was only the decision, implacable, unshakeable, and—

His arms were seized, twisted behind him while he came up off the bench. Helplessly, Horn braced his shoulders against the pain.

THE HISTORY

Atoms and men. . . .

They are moved by certain general forces in accordance with certain general laws, and their movements can be predicted in certain broad generalizations.

Physical forces, historical forces—if a man knew the laws of one as well as he knew the laws of the other, he could predict the reactions of a culture as accurately as the reactions of a rocket ship.

One historical force was obvious—Eron. It couldn't be overlooked. Its influence was universal.

Challenge and response. That was a force. Eron challenged; man responded with the Tube. Out of the Tube sprang the Empire.

But now the greatest challenge was the Empire itself; it shaped its own responses. By its own grim pressures, it created the forces that threatened it. It created its enemies and cut them down and found new enemies rising behind, beneath, within.

It created the Cluster and destroyed it, as it had destroyed other growing cultures and would go on, creating and destroying, until it grew too weak to respond with renewed vigor and was itself destroyed.

And there were other forces working, unseen, inexorable, sweeping before them men and worlds and empires.

What of a man? Is he at the mercy of these forces? Is he helpless to determine his own destiny?

The laws of classical physics are statistical; the unpredictable, individual atom enjoys free will. . . .

11

THE TURNING TIDE

Horn woke to darkness.

He woke with the dream still vivid, remembering the sensation of being tossed and driven in the fury of the flood that rammed irresistibly through the tube, remembering the choking, gasping helplessness and the long, wild tumbling into nothing. He remembered, too, the sudden surge of decision and energy with which he had caught a handhold in the tube, blocked it with his body, withstood the furious battering of the raging water, and slowly, surely, forced it back upon itself. . . .

Under Horn was rock, warm, worn smooth. The air was dusty and stale, but it was breathable. Horn sat up, recalling the narrow dimensions of the cell, and felt rested, restored, and alert. He sat in the darkness, hugging his knees to his chest, and remembered how he had been brought to this place.

On either side of him, there in the Entropy Cult chapel, had been a dark-cloaked man, his face shadowed and anonymous under a hood. Horn's arms had been twisted up tightly behind him; the hands holding him had been strong and sure, and he could get no leverage. They had moved him easily, silently, across the rough floor. None of the bent people on the benches had even looked up.

As they went through a break in the rock wall into a dark

corridor, Horn glanced back over his shoulder. Uniformed guards poured into the room through an entrance near the carved entropy symbol, like a gray wave. Horn and his escort moved quietly through a maze of black tunnels before they stopped.

They tied his hands behind his back, took his gun away, and fitted two nooses around his neck. One cord led to the man in front who led the way; the other trailed to the hooded figure behind. If he tried to escape, he would be strangled.

Horn trotted anxiously between them, trying to keep the cords slack. It was a nerve-wracking, exhausting effort that kept him at a constant half-run with no time for thought of anything except the tightening cords around his neck. They seemed to walk forever, through eternally branching, eternally dark corridors cut out of the rock. Horn started to stumble; it threatened to leave the silent figures with a corpse to carry.

Before Horn collapsed, they entered a room partially lighted by a hand torch blazing up from a metal bracket fastened to the wall. The ceiling was dark, bare rock not far overhead, but the light didn't reach the other walls of the room. From the echoes, Horn formed the impression that it was deep and wide.

Someone had been waiting for them. It was a man, shorter than his guards but dressed like them in a concealing, hooded robe. His face was hidden in shadows. On the breast of the robe was embroidered the bisected entropy circle.

Horn stood between them, struggling to stand straight. One of his captors spoke. It was the first sound Horn had heard him make.

"He fits the description. Found in chapel fifty-three."

The voice sounded hollow. It bounced back and forth between the rock walls. Horn looked straight ahead, his face immobile.

"Pull back his cap." The voice was firm and decisive.

As the cap was pulled back from his face, Horn caught a glimpse of the face under the hood. The light slanted across it as the man studied him. It was a hard, dedicated face. Horn had never seen it before. The voice, the face, both strange; Horn wondered why his intuition was making such an issue of it.

"It's the man."

They put him in the cell, cut his hands free, and gave him food and water. The food was coarse, but it was filling. Horn needed it after the bulkless nourishment of the food pellets. The barred, metal door had slammed behind them. It had been a solid, final sound.

Alone in the darkness and the complete silence, Horn had eaten and then investigated the cell. It was completely bare but clean. There was no exit except through the door, which admitted what air came into the room. Horn fingered the lock. It was newer than the door and escape-proof. Its small square of minute holes needed the insertion of tiny, magnetized filaments.

Before he had time to worry about it, he had fallen asleep.

Now, awake, he wondered what had awakened him. He heard again the odd, clinking sound that seemed loud in the total silence.

"Hurry!" someone whispered.

Horn felt his skin creep. He tensed his muscles. A final clinking sound and the door creaked. Before Horn could spring, a light was in his eyes. He blinked blindly.

"Ah, boy, boy," someone breathed softly. The light went out. "I've been a long, weary time finding you."

"Wu!" Horn said incredulously.

"The old man himself." Something metallic clanked against the stone floor of the cell.

Something rustled. "And Lil. Don't forget poor Lil."

Horn moved quickly to the door. It was shut, locked tightly. He whirled in the darkness, his back pressed to the bars. "Why did you lock it again? We've got to get out."

"Easy, my boy. We got in. We can get out as quickly. But first we must talk."

"Talk then. How did you get here? The last time I saw you, the lancers were leading you away from the Victory Monument."

"So they did. It is another mystery for Duchane's Index. Cells aren't made for Lil and me; locks cannot keep us in or out. The jail hasn't yet been built that will hold us."

"Not even Vantee?"

"Prison Terminal?" Wu said softly. "Perhaps. Vantee perhaps. But they would have to take us there, and how would they hold us on the way?"

There was no answer except a scurrying and rustling near the floor. In the brief flare of Wu's light, Horn saw that the old Chinese was dressed as he had been before. His battered metal suitcase was beside his feet. And on the floor was a glowing-eyed cat with matted fur and a scarred face. It trotted toward them triumphantly, a limp rat dangling from its mouth.

"What of you?" Wu asked. "I know, of course, that you were bold enough and foolish enough to carry out the assassination of Garth Kohlnar."

Briefly Horn described what had happened to him since Wu and Lil had leaped over the ruined wall. After Horn finished, Wu was silent for a few minutes.

"I could help you escape from here," Wu said finally, "but where would you go? Where in Eron is there a hiding place for the assassin of the General Manager?"

"There isn't any," Horn said quietly. "Eron must be destroyed before I'll be safe."

"Then you've given up?"

"That isn't what I said."

"Oh." Wu chuckled. "One man against Eron. A delightfully daring thought—but hopeless. Empires fall when they are ready and not before."

"When a tree is rotten," Lil interjected suddenly, "the lightest breeze will topple it."

"You, too?" Wu sighed. He was thoughtful. "Undaunted youth," he said. "I would like to feel those emotions again, those convictions that there are no mountains unscalable, no seas unswimmable, no odds too great. How do you plan to start?"

"I don't know," Horn said slowly. "Maybe with the man who hired me to kill Kohlnar."

"Who was that?"

Horn shrugged and then realized the gesture was meaningless in the darkness. "It was in a room as dark as this."

"You would recognize his voice?"

"I don't know."

"Then how do you expect to find him?"

"By something you said once. When we were in the tunnel. I was hired in the Cluster, you see, right after the surrender of Quarnon Four. You said nobody knew about the Dedication then."

"That's right," Wu agreed.

"Somebody knew about it. Kohlnar must have known. Whom did he confide in? Who did he trust? Who betrayed him?"

"I see," Wu said softly. "That eliminates his enemies, in the Cluster and elsewhere, and leaves his friends. His close friends. To which of them did he tell his dreams?"

"Exactly," Horn said. "It seems to me that it would be one of the Directors. Which one stood to gain most from Kohlnar's sudden death?"

"The hunter," Lil said hollowly, "the bloody, bloody hunter."

"Duchane?" Wu said. "Perhaps. He or one of the others might hope to retrieve from chaos what he couldn't get by an orderly transfer of authority. So far Duchane has seemed to gain the most. He has moved swiftly and surely; at the moment he is the most powerful man alive. His position is pretty; it would be even prettier if he had caught the assassin. Or if the lower levels were not on the edge of rebellion. He could have counted on the first; perhaps he could not have expected the second. Duchane. Or perhaps one of the others."

Horn heard light metallic sounds. He identified it with the opening of Wu's suitcase. A bar of something was pressed into his hand. He heard a gurgling sound bringing the pungent odor of synthetic alcohol. He bit into the bar gingerly. It was sweet and rich with oils. He ate it hungrily.

"Don't forget poor Lil!" the parrot said quickly.

The light clicked on briefly. Horn glimpsed a pouch in Wu's hand and the glitter of huge diamonds sliding from it.

"How did you find me?" Horn asked suddenly.

"Lil and I are used to finding hidden things," Wu said. "We found the lovely Wendre's diamond tiara, eh, Lil?"

For answer there was only a muffled crunch and a sigh of satisfaction. "Lovely, lovely," Lil said. Horn couldn't decide whether she was referring to Wendre, the tiara, or the diamond.

"It must have been through the Cult," Horn said.

"You're a clever man," Wu said softly. "Yes, the Cult owes me a favor or two, and I called on it to locate you."

"It must be an interesting organization; even more efficient than Duchane's. That's surprising in a religious cult."

"Isn't it," Wu agreed. "And it is—efficient, I mean—in its way and at its level. It followed you for some time, sent out some red herrings to draw the pursuit away, and brought you here."

"That was the guard who ran past the shop," Horn exclaimed.

"No doubt," Wu said.

"Why did you want to find me?" Horn asked.

"You have a right to be curious. And I have a right to refuse to satisfy it. You may credit it to your own charm or an old man's whim, if you like. You are interesting, you know. Hired killers always are. Not admirable, but interesting."

"I've never asked for admiration," Horn said mildly. "This isn't the epoch for admirable characters. They die young. My only interest is survival. But then I don't suppose anyone would apply the adjective to you, either."

"True," said the old voice in the darkness. "But our survival characteristics are slightly different. Yours are skill, strength, courage, and amorality. Mine are craft, weakness, cowardice, and immorality. I recognize the great social forces and work through them; my infirmities keep me alive."

"It is a strong man," Lil said in a deep voice, "who recognizes his own weakness."

"You, on the other hand," Wu continued, "ignore the social forces and outrage them, and your strength has pitted you against an empire. And yet I like you, Mr. Horn. You are right; this is no time for admirable characters; and I am glad you recognize the historical necessities that mold and move us, willy-nilly."

"I've been used and moved," Horn said firmly. "No more. From this time on, I'm a free agent, moving but unmoved." He chuckled; it was an odd sound in the darkness. "Let Eron and history beware."

"It is a weak man," Lil said in the same tone as before, "who knows only his own strength."

"How do you know," Wu said, "that in these decisions and these acts you are not an instrument still?"

"We're wasting time," Horn said quickly. "What we need is not questions but answers. Someone must have the answers. The person who hired me, for one."

"And if you find him," Wu said, "and if you find out 'why?'— how much better off will you be?"

"I'll know which way to move," Horn said. "One thing that could be done, for instance: cut off the Tubes!"

Wu gasped and then chuckled appreciatively. "A master stroke! It would take a man like you to think of it."

Horn thought he caught a note of mockery in Wu's voice. "Eron is dependent on the Tubes, totally dependent. She can't live more than a few days without fresh supplies from the Empire. And if fighting should start, the only chance for a successful rebellion would be if Eron were isolated. Without fresh troops—"

"You needn't list the advantages," Wu broke in. "I appreciate them even more than you do. The Empire would be crippled, a wheel without a hub. But how do you propose to cut the Tubes? It isn't even known how they are activated."

"The Directors should know," Horn said.

"It comes back to them, doesn't it?" Wu mused. "I'm tempted to help you. Suppose we join forces temporarily. I say 'temporarily' because I can't guarantee how long this quixotic spirit will last. I am an old, old man and easily tired. But we have no love for Eron, eh, Lil? We wouldn't be sorry to do the Empire an ill turn."

"Good," Horn said softly. He didn't underestimate the help that Wu and Lil offered; they hadn't lived so long without unusual talents and great cleverness. "We've wasted enough time," he said. "Let's go."

"Where? Like this? Blindly? Ah, youth, youth!"

"Well, where do you want to go?"

"Why, to the center of things, of course. But suitably attired and adequately prepared. Put these things on."

Horn felt heavy cloth pressed into his hands. He sorted it into pants, a tunic, and a uniform cap. He hesitated a moment and then stripped off his coveralls.

"A little light," Lil said impatiently.

In the brief flash Horn saw Lil clinging to the lock of the door. One claw ended in minute feelers which disappeared into the lock's tiny holes. Tumblers fell, clinking metallically. No wonder locks were no barrier!

Horn slipped into the clothing. It was a uniform, by the feel of it, and it fit surprisingly well. While he listened to Wu's sighs and rustlings, he had time to wonder where the clothing had come from. It could only have been that fabulous, inexhaustible container, Wu's battered suitcase, which was obviously much bigger on the inside than it was on the outside.

Wu sighed deeply and clicked the suitcase shut. "Here," he said. He laid a heavy object in Horn's hand. Horn had no difficulty identifying it. It was a unitron pistol, complete with cord. "You need this for at least two reasons."

"Disguise and defense," Horn supplied. He slipped the cord around his left shoulder and followed Wu's footsteps through the open doorway. They walked along dark corridors for minutes. Wu stopped once to slip his suitcase, regretfully, into a hidden niche. The second time he flicked a light onto a smooth rock wall. His hand moved into the light. Horn noticed that it looked different, somehow, but he had no time to think about that.

The rock wall opened outward. Beyond was the dimly lighted interior of a tube car. Wu was outlined against it. He was dressed magnificently in rich orange synsilk and furs. A padded bosom stuck out above his rounded belly. Lil seemed to be gone. Horn looked down at his own uniform. It was orange, too.

Orange, Horn thought. *Orange for the Directorship of Power.*

Wu turned his face back toward Horn. Horn drew back, startled. It wasn't Wu's face; it was the fat, golden, jowly face of an Eron noble. Tawny eyes peered out at him over puffy folds of flesh. The hair was stiff, reddish.

The pistol was in Horn's hand. He knew that face. He had seen it, close, not long ago. It was the face of Matal, Director for Power.

"Ah," Wu's voice said. "Then the disguise is effective?"

Horn was startled again. His hand relaxed. The gun flew back against his chest. "But—" he began.

"Another of Lil's many talents," Wu said.

"The clothes, the disguise," Horn said. "It's obvious that you had this planned."

"Planned?" Wu echoed judiciously. "I am always prepared, let us say, for opportunity."

"It seems to me that I am being used," Horn said gloomily. "What are you after?"

"We all are used. If I am using you, you, in turn, are using me. The question is: are we going where you want to go?"

"Where are we going?"

"To a meeting of Eron's Directors," Wu said softly. "They must elect a new General Manager. It is the most crucial meeting since the foundation of the Company. We will be there. We will take part in the decision, I as the Director for Power and you as my personal guard."

"Yes," Horn said. It was the right place to go; he could feel it intuitively. "But the real Matal will be there."

"Matal is dead."

"Dead?" Horn echoed.

"He was always a careless man. Greed and death caught up with him. Duchane's assassin found him alone. He was hurrying to a meeting with his head engineers. Power was shining in front of him, the power over men that is real power, and it blinded his eyes. He died at the south Terminal cap, clutching his belly. It was a poor substitute for an empire."

"Does Duchane know it?"

"Even Duchane wouldn't dare receive such a message. No, the assassin must make his way to the Director for Security as best he can, evading capture. He must come a long way, but if we delay much longer he may be there before us."

"How did you know about this car?" Horn asked.

"There are few things about Eron I don't know," Wu said placidly. "It is difficult to keep secrets from a man who has outlived civilizations. I was here when the Directors' private tubeway was built. Another thing I know, for instance, is that the car is meant for one person but two can squeeze in. I will let you have the chair."

Horn hesitated and stepped into the car. He sat down and strapped the belt across his legs. Wu painfully maneuvered his bulky, padded figure past Horn's knees. He squeezed and panted and complained, but finally he was wedged into the space at Horn's feet, his back against the wall under the control panel, his feet planted solidly under the chair.

"Close the door," Wu sighed. "This is extremely uncomfortable for an old man of my size and shape. Already I can feel my enthusiasm waning."

Horn looked down. There was something naggingly familiar about the way his face was shadowed. It eluded him; Horn shook his head and slowly closed the door. The click was followed by darkness and the nudge of the sliding inner door. Once more the many-colored disks floated in front of Horn.

"Which one?" he asked.

"Black."

Horn felt a shiver start up his spine. He frowned. "Duchane?"

"That's where the meeting is," Wu said. The colored disks cast an eerie, motley pattern over his reddish hair, but his face was dark. "To the center of things. Quickly."

Horn reached out and palmed the black disk. He felt again that uneasy sensation of free fall; there is no direction but outward. Perhaps it was half due to that, the suspicion that swept over him.

It was obvious, however, that Wu knew too much and he knew too little. All he knew about Wu was what the old man had told him; that could easily be lies and evasions. Wu could be anyone; he could be working for Duchane himself. He could be leading Horn into a trap. He had to have some organization behind him; he couldn't have all the information he displayed without it, not even with the help of Lil.

"You know a great many things," Horn said in the darkness. "Things that Duchane doesn't know: me and my location, Matal and his fate. And things that no one but Directors know: the secret tubeway and the meeting and its location. It is a wonder how you have learned so much."

"I am—"

"I know," Horn said impatiently. "You are an old man, and you have learned many things."

He started. Shadows over Wu's face. Put a hood over it. The resemblance clicked into place.

"You!" Horn said hoarsely. "You were the priest with the embroidered symbol on your robe."

"The Prophet," Wu corrected gently.

THE HISTORY

The pecking order. . . .

Among men, as among chickens, it is a necessity.

Hen A can peck hen B; hen B can peck hen C; hen C can peck hen D. Until the pecking order is established, there can be no peace in the henyard.

What chickens know instinctively, men must learn for themselves: power is indivisible.

Garth Kohlnar learned that rule well as he fought his way up the dangerous ladder of power politics from an impoverished nobility. Power is indivisible, and there are no means alien to it: intrigue, corruption, exposure of corruption, deals, betrayals. . . .

The management of the Company had been set up as a check-and-balance. The five Directors were chosen by competitive examination from all qualified engineers among the Golden Folk. Their duties: to establish policy, elect the General Manager, and preserve the secret of the Tube.

The General Manager was merely an executive. It had never worked that way. Kohlnar had ruled the Company with an iron hand.

His death shattered the peace of the henyard. The pecking order had to be rediscovered. . . .

12

STALEMATE

"Do you think," Wu asked, "that a man could live as long as I have with just the aid of his own senses?"

"Then the Cult exists only for your protection," Horn said sardonically.

"For my protection," Wu agreed, "and the consolation of the miserable. And possibly for other reasons which we can't go into at the moment. For we are there."

The car came to a stop. The door swung open. Outside it was a large, bare room with glistening, black marble walls. Wu motioned him out of the car. Horn unsnapped the belt and cautiously stepped out, his pistol in his hand. The room was empty.

Wu led the way to one black wall. A section of it slid aside as they approached. Behind it was a small, square room; its walls were black mirrors. It was lighted by hidden sources near the ceiling. Dark, disquieting faces peered out of the walls at them. As they turned around, the door slid shut and the floor pressed heavily against their feet.

"I have more eyes and ears than you think," Wu said, "but it is better to say no more. So does Duchane, and this car is probably tapped."

"It is." The heavy, powerful voice came from a side wall. Duchane was staring blackly out of it at them. "Welcome, Matal." His voice was impassive and unsurprised. "We've been waiting for you."

The car stopped. The door opened. Wu preceded Horn down a long hall. Like the other room below, it was walled in black marble. Even the heavy carpet underneath their feet was black.

"Your tastes run to the macabre," Wu said. His voice had changed; there was a bubbling breathlessness to it.

"Thank you," Duchane said. His voice came from near the ceiling. It was an unnerving experience, as if the building itself were alive, a part of Duchane. "It is, after all, my job."

They approached a door. Two impassive, black-uniformed guards stood on either side of it. It slid open in front of them. Beyond it was another short hall, two more guards, a second sliding door. And then a large, hexagonal room. It was black, as usual, but it was better lighted than any of the others. Horn watched the door close behind them. There was no visible seam. He tried to mark the spot.

The table was a polished, black hexagon to match the room. Three sides were occupied. Duchane had the door to his right; Fenelon was facing it; Ronholm had his back to it. A single guard stood behind Ronholm and Fenelon; each was dressed in the blue or green of the Directorship.

Duchane didn't have a human guard. Crouching beside his chair was a gigantic black hound. It was twin to the one Horn had seen dead upon the platform in front of the Victory Monument. Duchane's hand rested affectionately on the monster's head.

"You're late," Duchane said casually. "But now we can begin."

"I was—detained," Wu said breathlessly. "Where is the Director for Communications, the lovely Wendre?"

"She, too, is—detained. I expect her later—"

"I object to this entire air of intimidation," Ronholm broke in with quick, youthful anger. "I move that we hold our meeting, as usual, in the Directors' Room at the residence of the General Manager."

Duchane looked at Ronholm mildly. "There are obvious reasons why that is impractical. First, the General Manager is dead; we must respect this period of official mourning. Second, and more important, these are troubled times. Kohlnar has been assassinated. One of us may be next. The lower levels are muttering, and the word they use is 'revolt.' This is the only place whose absolute safety I can guarantee."

"I can guarantee the safety of my residence," Ronholm snapped, his handsome face flushed.

Duchane smiled broadly. "Can you?" He chuckled. "Can you really? The Director has made a motion. All in favor?" Only Ronholm's voice was heard. Duchane shrugged. "You seem to be in a minority."

Wu sank gratefully into a deep chair directly opposite Duchane. Horn stood behind the pseudo-Matal and watched Duchane.

Fenelon asked a pointed question in his high-pitched, aristocratic voice. "What can Security report about the assassin? Has he been found?"

Duchane's face, sprinkled with a golden powder, darkened. "Not yet. It is only a matter of hours. We know that he is on Eron. We are closing in."

"Are you?" Wu asked. "Are you really?"

Duchane shot him a swift, dark glance. "I'll get him. And when I'm finished with him, I'll give the remains to Panic." He caressed the huge, black head. "It will be justice for the death of Terror."

"You've mourned more over that hell-hound than you have about Kohlnar," Ronholm said bitterly.

Duchane's eyes were heavy lidded. "Terror was my servant and my friend. No, we haven't laid our hands on the assassin. Not yet. But we've found the person who is even more guilty—the one who paid for the bullet."

"Who?" Ronholm blurted out.

Duchane let his eyes slide from Ronholm to Wu, from Wu to Fenelon. "In due time, fellow Directors." His lips twisted into the mockery of a smile. "First let us consider a more pressing matter: the election of a new General Manager."

"Kohlnar's body is scarcely cold!" Ronholm objected.

"Events do not wait on sentiment," Duchane said softly. "The immediate stabilization of Eron's leadership is vital. Discipline proceeds downward. We must present the Empire with a strong, new government, united behind one man, unshaken. If the Empire sees us faltering, fighting among ourselves, the hints of violence will become reality. We must decide now, and close ranks behind our choice."

"Sensible," Wu said.

Fenelon nodded. Ronholm looked sullen.

"I ask for nominations," Duchane said, his eyes flickering over them.

"Wendre Kohlnar." Surprisingly, it was Fenelon.

"Wendre!" Duchane exploded. "I ask for strength, and you give me a woman. Everything is against it: tradition, policy, strategy."

"Everything except common sense," Fenelon said slowly, his lean, chiseled face intent. "A woman, yes. But a woman qualified by birth and training. You ask for strength. I say that strength is not enough. Only Wendre has the confidence of the people. Only Wendre has the popularity to make rebellion hesitate before attacking—"

"Coddle them?" Duchane exclaimed incredulously. "Pamper these conquered slaves with a General Manager they'll like? Appease their hunger with golden blood? No, by Kellon! The only fit food for slaves is the whip; the only answer to rebellion is death!"

Horn was surprised to hear Wu's bubbling voice say, "Hear! Hear! I nominate our vigorous, bloodthirsty Director for Security for the office to which he aspires."

Duchane's eyes gleamed with cold satisfaction, but he only gave a slight nod of recognition.

"Wendre!" Ronholm said violently.

"Wendre," Fenelon echoed.

Duchane studied them silently.

"But where is the lovely Wendre?" Wu asked again.

"Here," Duchane said.

A door to his left, opposite the one through which Horn and Wu entered, slid open. Wendre stood behind it, dressed as Horn had seen her last. Her red-gold hair was disheveled; her dark-blue cloak hung from her shoulders revealing glimpses of torn gold beneath. Her hands were together in front of her. They were fastened with a thin snake of gleaming wire.

"Here she is," Duchane said sardonically. "The lovely Wendre. Patricide."

The room gasped. Horn couldn't separate the reactions. Wu was the first to regain his voice. "Ah, no!" he said.

"Fantastic!" Ronholm exploded. He half rose from his chair.

"Clever!" Fenelon said quietly.

A hand shoved Wendre. She staggered into the room. The door slid shut behind her. She stopped, straightened, and stood proudly in front of them. For a moment her smoldering, tawny eyes rested on Duchane, and then they turned to the other three Directors.

"Ask him for proof!" she said. Her voice was clear and unafraid.

Ronholm sank back into his chair. "Release her!" he said with cold intensity.

"Yes," Wu seconded. "Release her, and then we will listen to your proof."

"Of course," Duchane said blandly. "If she will come close—"

Wendre hesitated and then took two quick steps toward him. She held out her hands above the huge, black head of Duchane's hunter. The dog sniffed once, curiously, and then looked away. Duchane reached toward Wendre, touched the metal snake. It slithered off her wrists into his hand. He toyed with the half-alive thing as Wendre turned and walked away. It coiled and twisted in his hand.

"Proof," he mused. "A delicate thing. Without the assassin, we cannot prove that he was contacted by Wendre or her agent, given his instructions and his payment, and that he carried them out. I can build you a substantial edifice, however. Consider these questions: who was responsible for the planning of the Victory Dedication? Who opposed the use of my men as guards? And who, except for the quick action of one of my men, would have led the assassin aboard her scoutship and from there to safety?"

Horn's eyes narrowed. The pattern became clearer. That bullet hadn't been meant for him. Duchane had acted quickly after Kohlnar's death. He had commissioned an agent to assassinate Wendre.

It could have been planned earlier than that. Duchane could have hired him to assassinate Kohlnar.

Duchane had recovered quickly from the failure of the attempt on Wendre. He had arrested her and assassinated Matal. But Wu was speaking.

"Is this true?" he asked Wendre.

"Half-truth, twisted cleverly like that chain he has in his hand. Duchane's agent is a curious contradiction. He was so close that he could identify an unknown assassin. And yet his eyesight was so poor that he couldn't see the pistol the assassin had at my back. And his aim was so bad that the bullet came closer to me than to the assassin. Duchane's story is absurd. I was arrested at the Terminal cap before he knew that the assassin had come back to the monument and escaped—before he could have known. What was my motive in hiring someone to kill my own father?"

Duchane seemed amused. "Practical or psychological? Need I point out that your father was dying, that you had no hope of succeeding him in a peaceful transfer of authority? Only just now we heard your candidacy for your late father's office argued on the basis of your popularity with the people."

Wendre's chin came up. "I have no désire to be General Manager. I won't accept the nomination."

Duchane's lips twisted. "A little late, my dear. Shall I go into your psychological motives? Shall I recite from the Index? Shall I prove that you hated your father for making a loveless marriage with your mother, for using her money and the name of Kallion as rungs in the ladder of his ambition, and then for casting her aside to make room for a succession of mistresses? Shall I—"

"Shut up!" Wendre shouted. And then, quietly, "I'm glad I didn't even consider your suggestion of marriage." She turned to face the other Directors. "That was his price for dropping this absurd accusation. Does he really believe I'm guilty, or is he willing to shield a murderer to further his own ambition? He can't have it both ways."

"I won't even deny it," Duchane said calmly. "I suggest a third interpretation. Guilt and justice are irrelevant abstractions compared with the future of Eron."

"A fascinating suggestion," Wu mused. "The marriage of strength and popularity. It might make all the—"

"Never!" Ronholm exclaimed.

Wendre glanced at him gratefully. "Never," she echoed calmly.

"Not even to save the Empire?" Wu asked.

"I don't believe the Empire needs such measures to save it," she said coldly. "But if it is that rotten, it deserves to perish. I'd rather marry a barbarian."

Horn's eyelids flickered.

"Duchane has accused me of hiring the assassin," she went on, "but his edifice of truth turned out to be a house of cards. As good a case can be built against Duchane. Who has gained the most from my father's death? Who tried to get the Dedication security arrangements under his control? Who was in the best position to hire or assign a man daring enough and desperate enough to attempt the assassination? Who tried to have me assassinated and, failing that, tried to pin on me his own guilt? Who—"

"Enough!" Duchane roared. Responsively, a menacing growl rumbled deep in the throat of the hell-hound named Panic. "I have additional proofs—"

"I suggest," Wu said quietly, "that these accusations are not only pointless but dangerous. If we fight among ourselves, how can we expect to suppress rebellion from below? Guilt has no meaning among us. If Wendre is publicly accused, Eron would suffer. She must be freed. In turn, she must forget your actions against her. It is a question of survival—our own and the Empire. We must not divide our forces now."

Duchane's dark eyes inspected the faces around the table. "A vote, then. A vote for the next General Manager of Eron."

"Wendre!" Ronholm said.

"Wendre," Fenelon repeated.

"Duchane," Wu said.

They all turned to look at Wendre. She hesitated and looked puzzledly at Wu. Horn couldn't see the pseudo-Matal's face. Wendre's lips tightened.

"Duchane," she whispered.

Duchane relaxed. "I should return the pretty compliment, but you all realize that I am not sentimental. Of course I vote for myself. The vote is three to two, the necessary majority—"

His voice broke off. His head swung to the right. The door slid open. A dark, little man in dirty, orange working clothes trotted into the room, sidled to Duchane's chair, and bent to whisper in his ear. Before he had time for more than one word, his restless eyes had darted around the room and stopped at Wu and widened.

The man stepped back. His hand darted toward the pocket of his ragged tunic. It came out with a pistol. Before the muzzle came up, the man was dead.

The bullet that killed him buried itself in the soft wall behind the falling body. It made a muffled *thunk*. Before then, Horn's pistol was centered on Duchane's black chest.

Beside Duchane, the giant dog was on its feet, poised, its massive head leaning forward, turning, jaws agape and drooling.

Without looking away from Duchane, Horn was conscious that the guards behind Ronholm and Fenelon had guns in their hands. Duchane faced the three muzzles without alarm.

"Assassination?" Wu said incredulously. "Here?"

Duchane's eyes were narrow with speculation. "He said your name."

"Obviously," Wu said.

The tension stretched thin. At any moment, Horn knew, it might snap and men would die. Anything could start it. The dog straining forward from Duchane's hand—

"Look at the walls," Duchane said quietly.

Horn didn't look away from Duchane. He didn't have to. Behind Duchane, three slits had opened in the wall. Through each one poked the muzzle of a unitron pistol. One of them was pointing at him. There would be other slits in the other walls. The exception might be the wall behind him. The path of the bullets would be toward Duchane.

"No sudden moves," Duchane said. "They might be misinterpreted."

"A wise thing for you to remember, as well," Wu said. "You can kill us, it is true. But remember that you will be the first to die. Keep your hands away from the table and the arms of your chair. Even the swiftest bullet can't stop a finger from squeezing."

Silence. In that moment the tension that Horn had thought could stretch no tighter stretched beyond endurance.

"You had this planned from the start," Fenelon said coldly. "But you underestimate us. Your residence has been surrounded ever since I entered."

Duchane smiled. "Your guards were disposed of long ago," he said easily. But he kept his hands in sight.

Only Ronholm said nothing. And his silence was difficult to understand.

Quickly, out of the corner of his mouth, Wu snapped, "Easy, there. Easy. There is no profit in that."

Ronholm sagged back.

"We seem to have a stalemate," Wu said quietly. "You can't assassinate us without being killed yourself. We are in the same predicament. I suggest that we find a solution quickly. There is a certain strain implicit in the situation. Fingers have been known to twitch involuntarily. It would be sad if the government of Eron were to destroy itself."

No one spoke. No solution was possible. Neither side could trust the other; the first one that lowered its guns would die.

Beads of sweat broke out on Duchane's broad forehead. Horn watched them trickle through the gold powder on his face. The gun in Horn's hand began to shake just a little.

THE HISTORY

Decay. . . .

The odor is distinctive. Any historian can identify it when the scent is strong and trace it to the first rotten spot. But it takes a wise man to spot the symptoms early.

Eron had the symptoms. Keen nostrils began to wrinkle.

The Tube was a splendid achievement, but it was also power. The saying was old before Sunport; power corrupts, and absolute power corrupts absolutely. For a thousand years, the Company stood as a magnificent and stubborn barrier to the further progress of all mankind. But the waters of life piled up behind it, and the barrier wore thin.

The space kings of Eron no longer fought their own battles. Mercenaries could be hired for that. The technicians, the spacemen, the engineers—they were barbarians. The Golden Folk clung only to shadows: hereditary wealth and titles, and a secret. The secret was the Tube.

The question: could a new challenge revive the lost vigor of the race?

A thousand years. For that long the Company, drawing upon the unlimited energy of a star, was able to dam the river of life. But it strained to break through and overwhelm those who sheltered themselves from it, and flow again. . . .

13

THE IRON STEPPES

"None of us wants to die." Wu's voice was shockingly loud in the silence. "There is only one way to keep the situation static until it can be altered without disadvantage to either side. Let us choose exits, all but Duchane. He, we hope, is in no danger from the gunmen behind the wall. At a signal, let us go to our chosen exits, keeping our worthy Security Director in aim, and leave simultaneously."

"There are only two exits," Ronholm objected. "And anyone leaving after the others would be at a disadvantage."

"Is that right?" Wu asked Duchane. "Are there only two?"

Duchane nodded, as if he didn't trust himself to speak.

Wu turned to Ronholm. "Then you may choose first. After you, Fenelon."

Horn took a deep breath.

"Well?" Wu asked, turning back to Duchane. "Is it agreed?"

Duchane's eyes shifted from face to face, not speculatively this time, but as if searching for an answer he couldn't find.

"The alternative," Wu reminded gently, "is death."

"All right," Duchane said hoarsely.

Wu turned to Ronholm. "Choose."

"That one," Ronholm said quickly. He pointed at the door by

which Wu and Horn had entered. Horn's jaw muscles tightened and relaxed.

"The right," Fenelon said, shrugging.

Wendre had come through that door. Horn didn't envy the aristocrat; it was little better than staying in the room. Objectively, there wasn't much chance for any of them. Even Ronholm would have to fight his way to the elevator which might or might not work when he reached it.

Perhaps it was better to stay here and take Duchane with him when the shooting started—

"We," Wu said carelessly, "will take the third exit. I am taking Wendre with me."

"No!" The word was torn from Duchane's lips. The hound beside him leaned forward, snarling.

"Careful!" Wu cautioned. "Remember the alternative!"

"Take her!" Duchane groaned. "Down, boy!" he whispered. The hound relaxed a little.

"Come, Wendre," Wu said, slowly lifting himself out of his chair. "And, companions in peril, back to your chosen exits. The doors should be open and the halls empty."

Ronholm stood up and began backing. He licked his lips nervously. Fenelon turned and walked briskly toward the door he had chosen. The guns of their guards were steady as they backed away.

Wendre was beside Wu. Wu backed toward the wall behind them. Horn kept his pistol steadily in the middle of Duchane's chest. He backed a little.

Wu scuffled his feet, as if he were turning toward the wall. In a moment Horn heard a whisper of movement; a breath of air cooled the back of his neck. There had been a third exit. Somehow Wu had known it and got it open.

Duchane's eyes were hot with fury. Horn's finger itched against the trigger.

"Ready, gentlemen," Wu said. "Slowly, now."

Step by step, Horn backed, feeling walls swing in on either side of him. Into his peripheral vision came the two other doorways. They were empty. The door whispered as it began to slide shut; the rectangle in front of him narrowed swiftly. Simultaneously, Horn heard the whine and screaming ricochet of bullets in the distance.

Horn snapped a shot through the narrow opening. Blackness threw itself toward him, over the table, jaws gaping to swallow the bullet meant for Duchane. Horn threw himself toward the sheltered wall with outspread arms. He crushed Wu and Wendre behind him. Three bullets whined through the narrow slit before the door slid shut.

"What's this?" Horn asked, turning quickly.

Wu trotted up the dimly lit corridor in front of Horn. Between them was Wendre, who glanced curiously over her shoulder at Horn as she ran.

"Duchane's mind is devious," Wu puffed. "It runs to traps and secret passages. This is one of the latter."

"I haven't had time to thank you, Matal," Wendre began.

"No time now, either," Wu said.

A long flight of narrow stairs led down into darkness. Wu didn't hesitate. He felt quickly over the wall beside the stairs. Another hidden door slid aside. Behind it, stairs led up. Wu pushed them ahead, up the stairs, and stopped to close the door behind them.

The stairs were interminable. They raced up them until Wu called a halt. He leaned against the wall, one hand pressed to his padded bosom, gasping for breath. Slowly color returned to his pale face.

"Go on," he panted.

Horn hesitated and then grabbed Wu's right arm. He draped it around his shoulders. With his left arm around Wu's thick waist, he half-lifted him, half-dragged him up the stairs.

"I'm all right," Wu protested, but Horn didn't release him until they had climbed into a small dusty room at the top of the stairs. Half a dozen spacesuits hung from their supports against one wall, transparent helmets racked above.

"What do we do now?" Wendre asked.

"Get out of here fast," Wu said.

"Where to?." Horn asked. "Duchane's got the power. No place is safe as long as he's General Manager—"

"Why did you want me to vote for him?" Wendre asked.

"How long do you think we'd have lived if you had been elected?" Wu asked softly. "But Horn is right; we must strike back at Duchane. The only way to do that is to cut off the Tubes."

"We can't!" Wendre protested, horrified.

"Can't?" Wu raised one eyebrow.

"Oh, it can be done, of course, but it would cripple the Empire!"

"Better that it be crippled temporarily than fall into the hands of a man like Duchane," Wu said gravely.

"Maybe that's true," Wendre agreed, "but think what it will mean in terms of lives! Power will go off all over the Empire. Everything will stop on thousands of worlds: factories, cars, planes, elevators, slideways. Homes will have no heat; food can't be cooked. Panic and accident will take millions of lives; children will starve, Eron itself will start dying; a few days without food—"

Wu shrugged. "All over the Empire men are dying, children are starving. If they can't survive a few days without the power that Eron pipes from Canopus, they don't deserve to live. Consider how many will die if Duchane consolidates his power."

"No!" Wendre said decisively, shaking her head. "That's not the way to save the Empire. We'll go to my residence. We'll be safe there while we build up a force to strike back."

"As you will." Wu turned away. "But we must hurry. Get into the suits." The old man turned toward the other wall. Set into it was a miniature visiplate. There were ten numbered buttons beneath it. Wu's fat fingers blurred as they pushed a series of eight. Wu turned to see Horn watching him. "Quick!" he said.

Wendre was fumbling her way into a suit. It gave him a curious, light-headed sensation when he accidentally touched her as he helped. He steadied himself.

"At the time of the capitulation on Quarnon Four," he said slowly, "who knew about your father's plans for the celebration?"

Her tawny eyes searched his face curiously. "I did. He mentioned it, idly, shortly after we arrived."

"Did any of the other Directors know?"

"Not unless he mentioned it before we left," Wendre said. "I was the only one to go with him to the Cluster. Why?"

Horn shrugged. "I don't know." He started to lower the helmet over her head.

She smiled at him. "Thank you," she whispered.

Horn felt an unreasonable warmth flood through his body. "A pleasure," he said, and clamped down the helmet. He pointed to the gauges. She nodded and brushed them away.

Horn turned back to Wu. The visiplate showed a small, empty room with dark gray walls. The few pieces of furniture in the room were overturned or smashed. Wu pressed another button. The screen went blank. He turned.

"Cult headquarters," he said, shrugging. "Raided."

"Where do we go now?" Horn asked.

"To the cap, of course, to turn off the Tubes," Wu said with wide eyes.

Horn glanced at Wendre and remembered that she couldn't hear them. Her eyes were curious; she stepped away from the wall clumsily, but in a few strides she had learned the short, quick steps that kept the heavy suit balanced. Wu hustled to the shortest suit on the wall. It was still too big, and he had a little difficulty in getting into it.

"What about her?" Horn asked.

"You're getting sentimental," Wu said gently. "Helping me up the steps, worrying about a woman. We'll bring her around."

"It isn't going to be easy getting to the cap," Horn said.

"True," Wu said. "But it will be no more difficult getting there than it will be getting anywhere."

"What was the real reason you swung the vote to Duchane?"

"Duchane was a fool. He had the substance, but he had to have the trappings, too. Wendre might have saved the Empire. The slaves fear Duchane worse than death; his term will be bloody but brief. Hurry! We've wasted too much time now."

Horn slipped into a suit. He had it locked tight within seconds. By the time he moved away from the wall, Wu had opened another door. Behind it was a second, narrower stairway leading up to a metal ceiling. Wendre was standing in it, half-bent. Wu motioned Horn past him.

Horn turned on the stairs and saw Wu slipping an extra gauntlet carefully between the jamb and the closing door. When the plate above them slipped aside, Horn felt an explosive push and then a diminishing tug as the air escaped past them into the blackness beyond. Freezing water vapor turned the air white; ice crystals formed around the edge of the horizontal doorway.

The air began to slow; the glittering crystals disappeared. They climbed out carefully—Wendre, Horn, and Wu—onto the gray, metal skin of Eron.

On the gray horizon, at the end of a dim, red, narrowing path, the feeble K_o-type sun hung against the blackness like a fading spark about to be extinguished in a frozen sea. There was no moon, and the unwinking stars gave almost as much light as the sun.

Horn turned slowly, staring out across the unbroken, monotonous grayness, seeing it curve away from him. It was like standing on a giant ball. Horn had the uneasy feeling that it would be easy to start slipping and slide across the smooth, curving metal plain and never stop. There was nothing to see, nothing to stop the slow sweep of the eye.

Horn blinked and shivered. He looked up. That was worse. He felt that he was hanging head downward toward the stars, glued insecurely to a thin, metal disk above.

Beyond one horizon, gold streamers fanned out, diminishing into the blackness of night. The metal skin reflected them dully. They reminded Horn of the familiar aurora polaris phenomenon, but that was atmospheric and there wasn't any air here. Horn realized, then, that the streamers were the Tubes.

One of the Terminal caps was not too far away, Horn judged, although it was difficult to estimate distance on this featureless plain.

Something was tapping on the arm of Horn's suit. He swung around. It was Wu's hand. Horn reached toward the breastplate of his suit to switch on the intercom, but Wu slapped the gauntlet away. Horn leaned forward, noticing that Wendre's helmet was pressed against Wu's. When Horn's helmet touched theirs, he heard Wu's voice, thin and distorted.

"No phones," Wu said. "Too dangerous. The airless room and stairways below will slow them down. They'll have to find suits, but we can't count on too much time. Duchane's clever. He'll have ships out within an hour, and there's no place to hide. The sanctuary I was counting on is gone, even if we could reach it."

"My residence," Wendre suggested again. Even filtered and hollow, her voice was low and lovely.

"Duchane will have guards surrounding it," Wu pointed out, "even if he hasn't taken it over by now."

"My guards are faithful," Wendre said firmly.

"Possibly," Wu conceded. "Even so, we need a safe way to get there. Even more immediate, we need a way out of this pitiless exposure and back into Eron. Once there, the best route is the private tubeway, which is basically safe. Duchane can't sabotage it within hours. But where we can reach it—or where we are now, for that matter—I haven't the slightest idea."

Horn pointed toward the golden streamers. "That's north or south."

"North!" Wendre said. "Duchane's residence is close to the north cap."

Wu raised his head and studied the display for a moment. "About sixty kilometers, I'd estimate, from the apparent size of the Tubes. Too far to walk. Wendre? Do you have a suggestion?"

She shook her head bewilderedly.

"The only tube entrance I know," Horn contributed, "is a place called the Pleasure Worlds."

"The Pleasure Worlds," Wu mused. "That sounds familiar. Let's see: Eron is divided three different ways. The longitude has letter designations; the latitude and level, numbers. The first two describe a truncated, inverted pyramid."

"It's on the top level," Horn interrupted.

"That's right," Wu said, frowning. "Let me remember! The location is—BRU-6713-112. Top level. South of here. If I'm right on my estimate of our present distance, about seven kilometers south. We'll head in that direction and try to think of a way to determine our longitude. Stick together. If one gets separated, we might never be able to find him."

They headed away from the golden streamers. They walked toward an unchanging, unmoving horizon curving gently away from them. There was no impression of getting anywhere. To the southwest, hanging unmoving above the horizon, was Eron's feeble red sun.

They tramped over the endless gray distances, Wu with a skill that soon matched Horn's. But then, Horn thought, Wu had enjoyed the experience of several hundred lifetimes. Occasionally Horn helped Wendre. He found even that metal contact oddly stimulating.

Time was meaningless; the sun was still. Horn wondered if their heavy footsteps were disturbing Eron's nobility below. They weren't, of course. The buffer zone for meteors and the insulation were impervious to sound.

Horn stopped suddenly. Wu, feeling the vibration through his feet, looked back. Horn motioned him to another helmet-to-helmet conference. His lips twisted as he thought how strange it was, their little group huddled together upon this gray world while beneath them humanity teemed like ants in a hill, living, loving, suffering, dying.

"The ships must have some way of identifying sectors," Horn said, "where to land and so on. Sight would be much too slow. It would have to be radio, and these suits incorporate planet-to-ship frequencies."

Wu nodded. "Everybody quiet."

Horn brushed the switch and tuned to the *pts* frequency. The inside of the helmet whined; it was an excruciatingly painful sound. Horn turned it off hastily and sighed. "Automatic. It would have to be, of course."

"Has anyone been looking down?" Wu asked. They stared at each other blankly; the unchanging horizon had a way of seducing the eye upward in the futile hope of seeing something different. "I thought not," Wu said. "Just before you stopped, I noticed something to the left."

In a few moments they were looking down at three letters painted beside a broad, golden stripe running north and south: BRT.

"Repairmen and working crews would need guides like these," Wu said exultantly. "And we're off less than one seventeen-thousandth of the circumference. At this latitude, that's about twenty-two meters. Which way do they letter? Oh, my poor, abused head!"

"West," Wendre said.

They headed west. In a few minutes they were standing over another golden line. This one was lettered: BRU. They had been marching south between the two lines.

They followed the stripe south until another stripe crossed it at right angles. It was numbered: 67.

"Sixty-seven kilometers from the pole," Wu sighed. "If my memory hasn't played tricks on me, the Pleasure Worlds is only one hundred and thirty meters south."

It was only when they began to look closely that they noticed the small figures painted regularly beside the stripe they followed. Gradually the figures climbed from "1" to "12" and then "13."

"Here!" Wu said. "Let it be here! We can't have much more time before the ships are out in force."

They scattered to search for a trap door. Wendre came running back toward them, almost falling, and led them toward a plate recessed into the gray metal. Painted across it clearly was the designation: BRU-6713-112.

"You try the door itself," Wu told Horn, "while Wendre and I stamp around the outer edge. There must be some way to open this from the outside."

They never learned the exact location of the latch. While they were doing their strange dance, the door suddenly started sliding under Horn's thundering feet. He leaped to safety beside Wendre. Starlight revealed an upper step. Horn started down.

The stairway seemed identical with the one at Duchane's. An outstretched hand touched metal. Wendre pressed close behind him. Back of her was Wu, bending painfully below the door level.

Wendre's helmet pressed against Horn's. It had the intimacy of a caress. "Matal says there will be a latch disk beside the door. Cover it with your hand."

Horn's hands were already working their way around both sides of the door. Unexpectedly, the darkness deepened and became impenetrable night. The trap door had closed overhead. Why didn't the door open in front?

It was the air, of course. The room was an air lock, and air had to be released into the little stairwell before the door in front could open. It opened, and Horn still couldn't see. Water vapor had condensed and frozen on their helmets. Horn brushed away some of the frost with his gauntlet and stepped into the lighted room. As the frost gathered again, the light sparkled and blurred and then the frost began to melt and trickle down the plastic.

Horn backed into an empty wall rack and braced himself against it as he stripped off his gauntlets and gingerly touched the helmet clamps. They were cold but not dangerous. In a moment he was out of his suit and helping the others.

They found their way down long stairs and finally into the yellow hall that Horn remembered. This time it was silent. They met no one. The whole place seemed deserted.

"The Pleasure Worlds," Wendre said. "What is it?"

"Here, for a price," Wu said, "men can indulge their passions, some strange and some not so strange."

"Oh," she said. Her golden face darkened.

"This is it," Horn said. The door had a pale blue disk.

Wu brushed it. The door didn't open. Wu knelt in front of the door and pressed his forehead against it. Horn glanced down curiously. Wu's eyebrows were moving like tiny snakes. They worked into the crack beside the door. The infinitely useful Lil.

The door swung in. Wu stood up and looked back. His eyebrows were back in place; his face was the face of Matal. They walked into the blue world.

Wendre glanced around the room and drew her cloak tight around her. "I don't like it."

Horn palmed the blue sun. A few seconds later, the wall swung outward. The lighted interior of the tube car was in front of them. They had reached—if not safety—at least the way to safety.

Wendre started to step into the car, but Wu held her back. He pressed his hand against the door jamb. The colored disks appeared palely against the front panel. Wu leaned into the car and covered the gold disk. Suddenly there were voices.

". . . hold her there. Matal, too, if he is with her. Or, if there is a chance you might lose them, shoot. . . ."

"Duchane!" Horn said softly.

"I understand, sir. You can depend on me."

The voices went on, but Wendre obviously didn't hear them. Her eyes were wide; her face was incredulous. "But that—" she began. "But that's—"

"Yes?" Wu said.

"That's my steward. He's been with me since I was little. I'd trust him with my life."

"That, it seems, would be unwise," Wu said gently. "All things can be bought if the price is right. Safety doesn't lie there. The question is: where can we go?"

Horn studied the pulse that was beating at the base of Wendre's throat and wondered if they had reached the end of the long flight.

THE HISTORY

Golden blood. . . .

They called it the Great Mutation. Roy Kellon was the father, legend said, and his son was the first of the Golden Folk.

Supermen. Fit to conquer and rule the universe. In everything, the golden blood was superior: intelligence, courage, stamina. And only the pure golden blood could make and control the Tubes.

Was that the secret? If so, it was not well kept. Eron let the rumor spread unchecked. Conquered hearts sank lower.

Hail the superman!

It was a most remarkable mutation. Almost unbelievable when one considers the millions of successive steps needed to create something as complicated as the human eye—and the millions of blunders that were automatically destroyed. The Golden Folk. Cut them, if you dare. They bleed red.

It was also said that only the Directors knew the secret of the Tubes. Take your choice. It could not be both ways.

Perhaps there was another secret—a secret even the Directors did not know. . . .

14

THE MASTER SWITCH

"What's wrong with him, Matal?" Wendre said dazedly. "He wants to kill us all."

"Power," Wu said somberly, stepping back from the car, "is a vision that drives men mad."

"We've got to stop him," Wendre said, drawing a deep breath. "We must kill him first. He'll shatter the Empire."

"We can't get near him now," Horn said.

"The slaves would take care of him for us," Wu pointed out, "if we could keep him from bringing in reinforcements."

Wendre stared at Wu. "Cut off the Tubes? All right. Let's go to the main control room in the north cap."

A frown slipped across Horn's face and was gone. Wu was using Wendre. He had maneuvered her, very cleverly, into suggesting that the Tubes be cut off. It wouldn't have surprised Horn to learn that Wu had arranged for that apparent conversation between Duchane and Wendre's steward.

They all wanted Duchane destroyed but for different reasons. To Wendre it seemed to be the only way to preserve the Empire. Horn wanted the Empire shattered; he knew that this would do it. Once let Duchane fall, and no new ruler could ever put the pieces together again. The myth of empire would be broken.

Horn wondered what Wu wanted. Amusement, relief from boredom? Or did he have deeper, more valid reasons?

"You two—get in that car," Wu said. "I'll follow in another as soon as you've gone."

"Both of us?" Wendre exclaimed.

"You two are young and slim," Wu sighed, "and I am old and fat."

"But—" Wendre began, glancing at Horn.

"We can't stand on ceremony," Wu said. "You can trust Horn. Like us, he is dead if he falls in Duchane's hands. Besides— Ah, well. Get in."

Horn caught Wu's quick glance and understood. The wily, old man didn't entirely trust Wendre. Or, perhaps, he did not trust her impulses. Once alone, she might decide to try something else on her own. Surprisingly, Horn trusted her, without reason, and he was a man who had trusted no one.

Wendre had appealed to Horn as no woman ever had. She had a man's mind and a woman's heart. She was self-reliant, proud, courageous. She grasped the situation quickly, accepted the odds, and did what had to be done without complaining. This was no spoiled child of empire, no sheltered darling of an all-powerful father; this was a woman fit to stand and fight beside any barbarian from the restless marches, made for love and ready to battle for it.

Horn grimaced, and told himself to stop thinking about her. He was probably reading more into her character than was there. In any case, it was hopeless folly. Even if she was capable of great love, it couldn't be for him. He was not only a barbarian; he had killed her father.

Wendre was looking at him curiously. "All right," she said.

Horn climbed into the car, sank into the seat, and fastened the belt around his legs. He motioned for Wendre to sit on his lap. She hesitated, but it was obviously the best arrangement. She sat down stiffly, warily. Horn reached out for the door handle.

"The north cap," he said to Wu.

"I'll follow immediately," Wu assured him.

As the doors closed, Horn slipped an arm around Wendre's slim waist and reached for the upper white disk to the left. The car fell from under them. In the darkness, the arm tightened around Wendre's waist. The touch made Horn cold; he couldn't control a shiver.

"Did you find the prospect of riding with me distasteful?" Wendre asked suddenly.

So Wendre had seen the face he had made. "Not at all. A private thought."

"I see. You don't have to hold me so tight," Wendre said curtly.

"Your pardon, Director." Horn started to withdraw his arm.

Wendre floated upward, weightless. Quickly Horn pulled her back. This time, when he held her close, she didn't object.

Only the single red eye of the emergency disk relieved the darkness. Slowly Wendre relaxed.

"I can't believe that my steward would betray me," she said finally. "He was more than a servant; he was a friend."

"When the world is rotten," Horn said, "it needs a strong man to resist corruption."

"Like you?" Wendre asked scornfully.

"No," Horn answered. "Not like me."

"Rotten?" Wendre repeated. "Eron?"

"When a race stops fighting its own battles, it begins to die," Horn said. "Where are your learners, your doers, your workers, your fighters? You won't find them among the Golden Folk. There you will find effeminate dandies with padded bosoms and shapely legs, concerned only with their eternal search for pleasure and relief from boredom. It leads them to such places as the one we just left. There you will find back-stabbers and traitors. Where can you find a man you can trust to act for Eron first and himself second?"

"I don't know," Wendre said. And then, quickly, "My father was such a man."

"Garth Kohlnar was Eron. What he did for Eron he did for

himself. He was a strong man and wise enough to realize that beyond power itself is the power of using it wisely."

"That's true," Wendre said.

"But not wise enough to see that he was preserving a fossil."

"That fossil defeated the Cluster!" Wendre snapped.

"Even a fossil can be dangerous if it is as big as Eron. But the interesting question is: why did Eron attack?"

"The Cluster was a constant threat, a—"

"The nearest outpost of the Empire was ten light years away. What threat was that? Eron itself was almost three hundred light years from the Cluster. Where was the danger to Eron? The only threat was the insidious propaganda that there was freedom in the galaxy, that outside the Empire was a vigorous new civilization where men were free. The only danger was internal: rebellion."

"The Empire is greater than it has ever been. How can it be rotten? I haven't seen any of these things—"

"You haven't been down to the lower levels and seen them there," Horn said, "the brute animals who shuffle from birth to death in the eternal twilight, never having seen a star. You've never seen the food plantations on the conquered worlds, where Eron's food is grown by slaves lashed on by overseers. You didn't see the ravaged worlds of the Cluster, the slaughtered billions, the shattered cities, the starving survivors—"

"I saw that," Wendre said quietly.

"For slaves there is only a thin line between life and death. Give them hope, give them the faintest glimpse of a star, and they will explode like a nova into all-destroying violence."

"And leave interstellar civilization in ruins. Is that preferable to empire?"

"Perhaps. To slaves. And yet it doesn't have to happen. One man could control them. One man could save civilization from total destruction."

"Who?"

"The Liberator."

"Peter Sair? But he's dead."

"So I've heard. If it's true, it's humanity's loss."

"I wish I were a man," Wendre said fiercely. Under his hand, Horn could feel her waist move as she breathed quickly. "I could save the Empire and make it a better thing. It doesn't have to be like this. I tried to tell Garth— But he laughed."

"Perhaps Duchane was right," Horn said.

"How!" She stiffened.

"That you didn't love your father."

Wendre relaxed a little. "In that, perhaps. I respected him but we weren't close. There were reasons. Some of them Duchane mentioned; some of them he could never guess. I should have been born a man. I've always wished that."

"Hasn't anyone ever made you glad you weren't?" Horn asked.

"What do you mean?"

"Like this." His right hand reached up and pulled her down against him. In the darkness, his lips sought hers and found them, and they were soft and curious and sweet. Horn's breath came fast. His mind whirled. Into it, like a dark intruder, crept a chilling thought. If only Wendre and her father knew about the Dedication at the time he was hired, Wendre had to be the one who had hired him—

Horn's stomach turned over. His lips stiffened. He pulled away.

After a moment, Wendre said, "Why did you do that?"

"Do what?" Horn asked harshly.

"Draw back?"

"Maybe I suddenly remembered," Horn said, "that you are a Director, and I'm a guard. Aren't you angry?"

"I should be, shouldn't I?" Wendre said wonderingly. "There's something strange about you. I don't think of you as a guard. I keep feeling that we've met before, that I've talked to you in the darkness, like this— But it's impossible. We've never met—"

"You're revealing a maiden's secrets," Horn said harshly.

Wendre sat up straight. "Perhaps I am," she said distantly.

The car jolted to a stop. The door swung open. Outside was the circular room Horn had left less than twenty-four hours ago.

"There's a lot to do," Horn said, "and not much time to do it in."

Wendre's face was puzzled and thoughtful as she stood beside him facing the closed cylinder door. Seconds later it opened. Wu stepped out of a car. His face was still Matal. "Lead the way, my dear," he said to Wendre.

Slowly the girl turned and walked to one wall. A panel opened toward her as she touched it. Memorizing the spot was automatic with Horn. The little room behind the panel was an elevator. They crowded into it. Horn stood at the back of the car, frowning.

Why had he doubted Wendre suddenly? Why had nausea swept over him as they were kissing and the meaning of what she had told him become clear? Could it have been his own guilt that had pulled him back? He had killed her father. It was very possible that he had rationalized his guilt as hers. There was no real reason to suspect her.

Horn realized that his guilt was like a weight on his shoulders. It had been there for a long time. It would be a relief to get rid of it, to confess. But there was only one person he could confess to: Wendre. And when she knew she would turn away or—

Horn blinked as the light returned brilliantly. They stepped out of the elevator into a vast circular room, many times the diameter of the room below. Colored spots of light danced and flickered in intricate and meaningless patterns across the distant walls. Chairs and panels circled the walls and made concentric, narrowing circles inside them. Switches, cameras, pickups, communicators. . . .

The room was deserted. The chairs were empty. One ten-meter section of the wall was dark.

Wendre gasped. "Where are the technicians? There's always a full crew on duty."

The room had two wide doors, opposite each other. They were both closed. In the center of the room was a large, gray-walled boxlike structure. Horn circled it cautiously. Wu followed him.

Behind it, they found the first body. It was dressed in gold; the bloodstains didn't quite hide the technician's ensignia.

There were other bodies scattered among the chairs and panels. Some were dressed in orange, some in green, but most of them wore gold. A black pool seeped under one of the doors. Wu opened it. Behind it the bodies were piled thick. Green, orange, gold—and black. Technicians and security guards. All of them were dead.

"The first assault was thrown back," Wu said. "The technicians that survived followed up their advantage. But we haven't got much time. There will be other attacks."

When they turned, there was a door in the gray box. It stood open. It was at least thirty centimeters thick. That was thicker than the heaviest ship plate. Wendre stood beside the door, waiting for them. Horn stopped and looked inside the vault. Set into one wall was a large switch. It was without any distinction, a completely ordinary switch. It was closed.

"That's it," Wendre said. "The master switch. Do we have to open it?" She looked at Horn and then at Wu. "It hasn't been touched since the first Tube was set up."

"How can you be sure?" Horn asked.

"Only the Directors can open this vault."

"How else can we isolate Eron?" Wu asked. "How else can we defeat Duchane?"

"What's the use of talking?" Horn said impatiently. "I'll do it."

He took two steps into the vault and pulled the switch open with an easy sweep of his arm. "There," he said. "That's done." It was a moment of unparalleled power.

Wendre laughed mockingly. She pointed to the walls. The spots of color flickered unchecked across them.

"It didn't work," Horn said.

"Of course not," Wendre said scornfully. "If anyone could do it, Eron would have been destroyed centuries ago. A Director must be present to activate a new Tube, and a Director must cut them off. To be eligible for the position of Director, a person must be of pure golden blood. You've probably scoffed at the Great Mutation, but it has kept the secret of the Tubes for a thousand years."

She sighed. "If it must be done, let me do it."

She pushed the switch back into place, hesitated, and pulled it down, her face frozen, her eyes distant. Horn turned to look at the walls. When he heard her gasp behind him, he knew that she had seen. The walls hadn't changed.

"Should they be dark?" he asked quietly.

"Yes," Wendre whispered. "I can't understand— It's—" She stopped. There were no words to express the terrible disillusion of that moment.

"A fake," Wu said. "A dummy."

Horn slipped an arm around Wendre's shoulder and led her out of the vault. She leaned against Horn's chest, accepting the comfort automatically. "All false, then," she said. "Everything I was told. Everything I believed."

"A wise man," Wu said softly, "never believes anything completely until he has tested it for himself."

"There must be truth somewhere among the lies," Horn said. "The Tubes are real."

"Maybe they're an illusion, too," Wendre said wildly, "and the Empire is an illusion, and we're an illusion, and—"

She was shaking violently. Horn drew her in tight and held her. "Stop it, Wendre," he said softly. "Stop." He didn't notice that he had spoken to her with the familiarity of an equal; neither did she, or she didn't care. "There's a secret; someone must have it. Who? Think, Wendre! Think!"

She stopped shaking. Her head lifted; she looked into his intent face. "That's right," she said softly. "Someone must have it."

"Who?" Horn repeated. "New Tubes have been activated ever since this switch was installed. The secret couldn't have been lost."

"Men all over the galaxy have tried to find it," Wu said. "They had all the technical information available to Eron. They always failed. They couldn't activate the Tube. The secret always eluded them."

"At the Dedication," Horn said, his eyes distant, remembering, "there were six of you on the platform: Duchane, Matal, you, your father, Fenelon, and Ronholm. You all touched the switch. It must have been one of you."

"Unless that was a sham, too," Wendre said.

"It couldn't be anyone else," Horn said. "The secret couldn't pass through the hands of any other group for a thousand years without being discovered by the Directors."

"We were all there," Wendre agreed, "but that wasn't significant. We've been at other activations one at a time." She shook her head bewilderedly. "It couldn't have been Father. He would have told me. Or someone. Something as precious as that you can't take chances with. One other person should have known in case of accidental death. For safety, it should have been all of us."

"Perhaps he only trusted one other person," Horn said.

"It should have been me."

"But you didn't love him."

"He loved me. He made me a Director."

"Who else could he have trusted?" Horn asked.

Wendre shook her head again. "Not Duchane; he knew his ambition. Not Ronholm. Father wanted us to marry, but he thought he was too young yet, too hot-headed. Fenelon? Perhaps. Or you." She turned to Wu. "You had the longest service, next to Father."

The Matal-face looked discouraged. "Not me. And if it was Fenelon or Ronholm, I'm afraid the secret is lost. That gunfire when we left Duchane's sounded like their requiem."

"Look! Could it have been Duchane?" Horn asked. "He seemed so confident. Your father was ambitious once; he might have understood that in Duchane."

"No, no," she said frantically. "That was one of the things

Duchane kept asking me. He kept saying, 'Tell me the secret and I'll let you go.' I thought he was going mad. We all knew the secret."

"Then he was up here, too," Horn mused. "He tried the switch. He knew it didn't work."

"Perhaps there is a secret," Wu said softly, "that even the Directors do not know."

Wendre moved in Horn's arms. "Help me, Matal," she pleaded. "You've been a Director longer than anyone. Surely you—"

"It's time the situation was clarified," Wu said. "Things are not always what they seem." He turned his back to them; his voice sounded oddly muffled. "I want you to remember that we rescued you from Duchane at considerable risk to ourselves."

Horn had a premonition of disaster. "Wait!" he began.

"I am not Matal," Wu was saying. "I'm only an old man with a penchant for lost causes, a talent for disguise, and a thirst as big as the Empire."

He turned back. Wu faced them, his wrinkled face screwed up apologetically. With sudden and surprising strength Wendre pushed herself out of Horn's arms. Her narrowed eyes shifted without understanding from Wu to the bedraggled parrot sitting, head cocked, on the old man's shoulder.

"I don't understand," she said breathlessly. She took several steps away. "If you're not Matal, who are you? Where did that bird come from? What—"

"Friends," Lil said in her cracked voice.

"Friends," Wu echoed.

"And you!" She whirled to face Horn. "If he's not Matal, you're no guard. What are you? Why have you brought me here?"

She turned away frantically and started across the room.

"Wendre!" Horn shouted. "Wait! Let me—" He was going to tell her then; he was going to say that he had killed her father, and all the rest. But she turned back, and it was too late.

Her eyes were wide and stricken. "You! Of course I recognized that voice! You're the assassin!"

She turned and fled toward the elevator door.

"Wendre!" Horn called again, despairingly.

"Boarders!" Lil screamed.

Horn spun around. It was too late even to reach for his gun. The black uniforms swarmed over him, entering like a flood from the gaping door. In a few seconds Horn was being dragged toward the door. He struggled to free his head, to look around.

Wu was beside him. Lil had disappeared. Horn glanced hopelessly over his shoulder.

A ragged, clay-faced rabble erupted through the other door, swept around Wendre, and waded with suicidal frenzy into the black forces.

THE HISTORY

Vantee. . . .

Prison Terminal. World of the condemned. Purgatory for lost souls, whose release was not suffering but death.

There was no escape from Vantee. Like Eron, the prison planetoid circled the feeble warmth of a dim, red sun. The nearest inhabited world was many light years away. Where in the Empire was Vantee? No one, not even the Warden himself, knew that. There was no help from outside.

There was one entrance to Vantee: the Tube. There was one building on Vantee: the grim, black fortress in which the Terminal was housed. There was no exit. The fortress had a name: Despair.

The fortress kept the prisoners out. They had freedom of a sort. Freedom to roam the barren surface, freedom to kill each other, freedom to die. Twice a day they gathered to eat at the troughs. Their only restraint was to stay on Vantee. It was enough; it was doom.

Not a thousandth part of those eligible for Vantee ever reached there, but it served its purpose. It was more effective in discouraging the prospective criminal, the incipient rebel, than the threat of death itself.

Many of the prisoners sat and looked at the golden Tube that rose from the black fortress and dwindled away into the night. Their thoughts might bridge the gap, but for them the Tube ran only one way. From Eron to Vantee. Vantee was the end.

It had been the end, rumor said, for Peter Sair. But men quickly lost their names.

Like the fortress, they were all named despair. What can bare hands do against walls a meter thick . . . ?

15

DEATH IS THE DOOR

Weaponless, his pistol torn away, Horn was hustled down a wide corridor inlaid with tracks. He tried to pull free, to look back where Wendre had been, but it was futile. A pistol came down sharply against the side of his head. Horn staggered forward, fighting blackness, sagging in the hands that pulled him along.

Wu was sometimes alongside, sometimes behind. The guards took them a long way down the corridor while the sounds of fighting died behind. Horn had a long time to think and all he could think was: *Duchane! Duchane!*

Duchane had them and maybe the control room, too. Struggle was pointless. Wu was suffering his indignities with the resignation of a martyr. Horn decided to save his strength and start thinking again.

A giant door was gaping open at the right. The guards turned, took them into one of the towering Tube rooms. In the cradle was a small transport; a tall escalator was pressed against the dark oval in the ship's side. Wounded men were being helped up into the ship.

Horn and Wu were stopped in front of a hard-faced officer. There was an odd insignia on his shoulder, something black and squat and—

"Matal's men, eh?" he said. "Where's Matal?"

Horn glanced at Wu, but the old man wasn't going to talk. Horn didn't see that it would get them anything but a beating and a quick death.

"He's dead," Horn said.

"Fenelon? Ronholm?"

"I think they're dead, too."

"Wendre Kohlnar?"

Horn shrugged.

"Duchane?"

Horn shrugged again, but behind his impassive face was a mind suddenly alive again. This man might be attached to Duchane's security forces, but he wasn't getting his orders direct from Duchane. Nor from any of the other Directors. The question was: who was he taking orders from?

"Take them away," the officer said. His nod to the guard in charge of their group was barely perceptible.

Horn knew what the nod meant. He tensed his muscles for a final struggle.

Suddenly the officer turned back. "Put them on the ship. Maybe the Warden will have a use for them."

The Warden! Horn stiffened as the guards pulled him toward the escalator. That was where the troops came from. That was where he was being taken. Vantee! Prison Terminal. In the long history of Eron, no prisoner had ever returned from his trip to Vantee. He couldn't go there. He had to find out what had happened to Wendre; she needed his help, and he would help her in spite of herself.

At the foot of the escalator, a convulsive twist tore his arms free. A chop with the hard edge of his palm crumpled one of the guards; a fist in the belly doubled up the other. He started to sprint toward the distant door. It wasn't as foolhardy as it seemed. The guards wouldn't dare shoot while he was dodging among the troops, and before the others became aware that someone was escaping, he would be through the door and away down the corridor.

Once there, his planning ended. He didn't need to think about it. As he passed Wu, he stumbled. Something hit the back of his head. As the darkness spread behind his eyes, he had a dazed moment to wonder: *Wu? Wu?*

Someone was groaning in the blackness. Horn opened his eyes and listened. There was no sound. A feeble light beamed behind a sheet of thick, unbreakable glass in the low ceiling. He was strapped to a bunk. Dull thumps were transmitted to him through the walls.

He unsnapped the belts and sat up. The sudden movement shot bright, jagged pain through his head and down his spine. He groaned. The other groans had been his, too. He felt the lump on the back of his head; it had stopped bleeding.

The ship lurched. Horn grabbed the edge of the bunk to keep from falling. The sounds, the movements were familiar. The ship was settling into a cradle. They had put him on the transport he had tried to escape.

He remembered stumbling. Had Wu tripped him? Someone had, and Wu had been closest. Horn shook his head; pain brought instant regret. If it had been Wu, it was incredible; there was no reason for it.

He glanced around the room. It was a little, square box with four bunks in it. The three others were unoccupied. The door was locked; there was no window in it.

He was on Vantee, then. Escape-proof Vantee. He took a deep breath. That remained to be tested. Peter Sair was here. The only man, he had told Wendre, who could save the Empire from complete destruction. Everyone said that Sair was dead. At least he would have a chance of finding out the truth.

His waist felt unprotected and cold. He patted it and realized what was wrong. The money belt was gone; naturally it would be. Horn shrugged. That was the least of his worries; he would have given it all—all the kellons he had been paid for Kohlnar's assassination—for a gun. He had neither.

He was sitting on the bunk when they came for him. They were good. The door slid aside. Two pistols covered him. The faces behind them were cold and experienced. They wasted no words, no motions; they took no chances. But then they were used to dealing with desperate men.

As Horn came into the narrow corridor, they retreated, keeping a meter or so between them and Horn.

"That way," one of them said, nodding. "Start moving. We'll tell you when to stop."

Horn started moving. He was never close enough to anyone or anything to have a chance at escape. They wouldn't hesitate to shoot him down, and they'd shoot not to kill but to cripple. That, Horn knew, would be worse than death. He had no faith in the promises of Entropy; death would be final and with it would come the end of doubts and torments and regrets. To be alive and yet incapable of acting to change his circumstances was another thing; it was a thing Horn didn't care to face.

They descended from the ship in an escalator. Horn realized that the prison ship was only a shuttle; the cradles at each end were fixed, and the ship never left them. It had no reason to.

They walked through the Tube room, which was only big enough to contain the slow movements of the Terminal mechanism as it followed the apparent movement of Eron. They walked down a long corridor, through a doorway, and into a luxurious office. Horn had no attention for it; he was looking at the man behind the huge, black desk.

The man was a curious contradiction: he was a big man, bigger than Horn by many kilograms and centimeters, and a barbarian; his eyes were hard and calculating; but time seemed to have blurred his outlines. His face and body were those of an athlete after his active days were over; he had grown fat and soft, but inside there was still an iron core.

This could be no one but the Warden, keeper of the Empire's enemies: her criminals, her traitors, her rebels. Of these, only the worst; Vantee received only a real elite.

It was logical that the Warden and his guards would be part of Duchane's Security forces, and the black uniforms supported the logic with data. It was likely, however, that the Warden had received no orders or, if some had slipped through, was ignoring them. Chaos offers every ambitious man a golden opportunity.

The Warden would not be troubled by ideals. As a barbarian, he would never have climbed so high with such a burden. His attempt to seize the north cap and the main control room seemed like his own idea. If Duchane was able to smother the fires of rebellion in blood, the Warden could name a high price for his help. If Duchane fell—well, other barbarians had seized an empire and held it for their own.

The Warden's shrewd, dark eyes sized up Horn. "Watch him! He is a dangerous man."

Behind Horn, the guards shifted, one to each side. Now they could shoot through Horn without endangering their commander.

"So," the Warden rumbled, leaning back in a giant chair, "Matal is dead."

"That's what I was told," Horn said calmly.

"And Fenelon and Ronholm, too."

"It's probable. I didn't see them die."

Horn caught the flicker of the Warden's eyes as he glanced down and back up. Horn shifted his position casually.

"Don't move!" the Warden snapped. "Kohlnar, too," he continued. "They haven't caught the assassin."

Horn realized that he was standing on or in some kind of lie detector. His instinct to tell the truth when a lie wouldn't help had been right; as long as he stuck to literal truth, he gained an advantage. "No," he said.

"Of the original six, only Wendre and Duchane are left. Who is General Manager?"

This one was a question, not a statement to be verified. "Duchane," Horn said.

"That's logical," the Warden said. "But can he keep it?"

"It's doubtful."

"Why not?"

"At the top, they're fighting among themselves. The troops and guards are battling each other. The lower levels are rising. Eron is in flames. Only one man can stop it short of total destruction."

"Who?"

"Peter Sair."

"He's dead."

The statement was quick and flat. For the first time, Horn's stubborn conviction that the Liberator still lived was shaken. This man should know, but then he had no reason to tell the truth. Horn wished he could sneak a glance at the instrument the Warden had behind his disk.

"Do you think my men can take and hold the control room?" the Warden asked.

"Not a chance," Horn said quickly, firmly.

"I should be there," the Warden growled to himself. "How can I trust that— Three hours away! Who was the old man captured with you?"

Horn blinked; the question had caught him by surprise. "Matal's steward," he said hastily.

"That's a lie."

Horn shrugged. "He said his name was Wu."

"Where is he?" the Warden snapped.

Horn looked blank. "Why ask me?"

His innocence was apparent. "He's gone," the Warden grumbled. "Impossible."

No, Horn thought impassively, *even Vantee couldn't hold Wu and Lil. They would have to be taken there, and how could they hold them on the way? They must have escaped on Eron.*

"We've hunted a man of that description for a long time," the

Warden mused, "a fantastically long time." He shrugged. "All right. Throw him out."

Horn leaned forward, caught himself, and obeyed the guard's order to turn around. That didn't sound like a death sentence. He didn't give the guards an excuse to shoot.

Horn led the way down the long corridors, his eyes watchful, cataloging the turns, the doorways, the ventilators, the defensive possibilities. . . . The hall straightened. In the distance, it ended against a blank wall. As they walked toward it, Horn paced off the distance, counting silently.

Ten paces from the end of the corridor, a mounted gun stuck an ugly barrel through a wall slit on each side. The guns pointed at him. The guards were behind him and well back as the wall lifted. Air swept in. It was icy. Beyond the wall was darkness. Horn shivered.

"Out," one of the guards said quietly.

Horn walked forward. The heavy guns turned to follow him. As Horn's eyes adjusted, he saw the bridge. It was barely wide enough for one man. Beneath it was a ditch. The bottom of the ditch was black. Horn started across the bridge to the dark mass of land on the other side.

He shivered in his thin, orange uniform. He faced the unknown darkness without a weapon except the strength of his body, the skill of his hands, and the determination of his mind.

Behind him the light was cut off. The wall clanged down with a terrible sound of finality. The way back was closed.

Horn stepped off the bridge onto cold, hard stone. He waited there while his eyes got their night vision. The ground was slightly uneven nearby, but generally it seemed remarkably level. There were no mountains, no hills; the horizon curved perceptibly. Gravity was light; the air was thin and cold, but it was breathable. There was no one near. There was nothing growing. The prison planetoid seemed lifeless.

Horn swung his head. A dim, red glow was on the horizon. It

was twilight or dawn. He turned around to study the place he had left. It loomed squat and black. Sheer walls rose vertically from the ditch. The only relief from the blackness was the thick, golden cylinder that speared starward from a dome at the top.

Horn's eyes followed it until it dwindled away to a thread in the distance and disappeared. It went to Eron. From Eron a man could go anywhere in the Empire. It went to Wendre. It might as well not have been there.

The Tube was only a tormenting reminder of what was forever lost. Three hours to Eron? Eternity wouldn't get him back. He was cut off forever, here on this frigid satellite of a forgotten sun.

To get to the Tube you had to go through the fortress, and the fortress was impregnable. This entrance would be the only one, and it was an exit. Only the narrow bridge led to that thick, immovable door. There would be guns to protect it and other things. What could bare hands do against those walls?

No one came back from Vantee. Horn was there until he died. Death was the only door.

It was a strange path that had led him to this place. From one end of the Empire to the other, across the star distances, driven. He could face that now: driven. There were forces that drove men, unknown, unknowable, over strange roads to stranger destinations. Once set your foot upon one of them and compulsion drove you, irresistibly, until the end. This was the end. Journey's end, world's end, life's end. Beyond this, there was nothing.

And yet a man had choice. Only omnipotence can pick out the course of every man's life upon the infinite fabric of space and time. And the forces were not omnipotent. They were broad and sweeping, yes, and they swept masses and empires, not individuals. The men in the stream were carried along with it, unaware of the movement because others were moving, too. But let a man escape the stream, let him strike out boldly for the shore and stand there, dripping, to see the flow, and the things he does then can dam the stream and send it reeling backward. Or he can channel it toward another end.

He had accepted money to kill a man. Nothing forced him to take it; having taken it, he hadn't been bound by anything except his own nature to carry out the verbal contract. He could have become discouraged along the way; he could have faltered at the obstacles piled high; he could have held Kohlnar in his sights and let him go.

The forces that said, "Eron shall fall," had not said when. His bullet had speeded Kohlnar's death; it had precipitated crisis into rebellion. If Kohlnar had died a natural death, the orderly processes of empire would have passed on authority without a slip. Certainly Eron would fall; that was inevitable. But when, and how?

The inevitability had come from that. It had been his doing. He had struck the spark of rebellion; his hand had directed the stream that had carried him to Vantee. Anywhere along the way, he could have stopped and said, "Hold! I go no farther!" Perhaps the stream would have rolled unheeding over his head, but for him the inevitability would have ended.

An act of violence had changed the stream. He could not be proud of it, not if it bore sweet fruit for a thousand years, but it was done. Instinct had surrendered him to the stream, and the stream had carried him to Eron. Instinct: the unthinking necessities like survival and food for hunger—they were the tumbling molecules of the stream. They are negative; they are surrender.

But a man could fight the stream; every positive act fights it.

In the Entropy Chapel, he had pitted himself against the stream; the dream had told him that. He had gone with Wu to the meeting at Duchane's because it was, in a sense, rebellion against necessity. And that choice had had its effects. If he had not gone, Wendre would surely be dead or helpless and Wu, if he had gone alone, would have been lost. Perhaps their fates caught up with them later, but that didn't change the importance of the reaction. It had been an act of love—which is positive, too—that had kept him by Wendre's side until her disillusionment and his capture.

He could face it now—that, too—he loved Wendre, and it was hopeless, but a good thing, as well, because it was a positive force and a strong one. It gave him the strength to fight the stream once more, to beat back up the river to the source. If a man can change his fate once, he can change it again. Eron must fall. But how?

The fortress was not impregnable; nothing was. Out of this eddy, where the unseen forces had left him forgotten, he would fight. It might be fatal, but it was important to fight and not be swept along by the unfeeling, inhuman forces that say "rise" and "fall" to empires.

Horn stared again at the tapering, golden Tube, and it was not a mockery but a link with the galaxy. He remembered a moment of defeat in a lonely valley when he had seen the stars connected by a network of nerves, and it was like that again. Not just the stars, it was all mankind, linked together by consequence and compulsion. Intangible, untraceable, almost moral: the smallest event on the most distant edge of the Empire affected everyone in the Empire.

A man could build a philosophy on it, and it might well be better than individualism. It was not exactly these unseen forces, or perhaps the network was a corollary to them, a gentler part. It said: if there is a slave anywhere in the star-flung worlds, no man is free. And it said: while there is a free man anywhere, no man is completely a slave. And so, even the General Manager of Eron was a slave; he could not choose to let the Cluster remain free.

He could not choose because he was a focus of many forces; they would not let him exercise his will. But a free man can choose; in that, individualism is good. In that, all men are free.

There were other things Horn heard: *No man can act alone; he is bound up in humanity. No man suffers alone; humanity suffers with him. Injustice to one is injustice to all; every man should resent it as if it happened to him; it did.*

What was it Wu had said, in effect? When somebody moves, something has pushed. It was a mistake to say it like that, dehumanized. It's better to say: when somebody moves, somebody has pushed.

There was a simple way of saying it all: no matter how far apart people seem, there is a bridge that joins them all.

Horn had learned that. It was a great deal to have learned. It was worth dying for. But even more important, it was a reason for living.

The Tube. Symbol of oppression. Symbol of hope—

The weight landed on his back, bearing him down. Quick, sure hands reached for his throat. Horn stumbled and, stumbling, ducked forward. The weight flew over his shoulder. It was a man, diving into the ditch, dark arms flailing the air like something Horn remembered. But there was no time for memory. The ditch flashed as the man hit the bottom; it was the end of screams and the beginning of the slow stench of cooking flesh.

Before then, Horn had turned, lashing out with hard fists at the shadowy figures that pressed around him. One of them staggered back, but he came in again. These weren't careless, casual guards. They were skilled killers; they had learned to kill with their hands—or be killed.

They closed in, a deadly semicircle. Two of them dived at Horn simultaneously, one for his knees, another for his throat. Horn gave his knee to the man who wanted it. He grunted and fell to the side, rolled quickly to his feet. Horn clubbed the other down with the hard edge of his hand; he fell and lay still.

But they had forced him back. He reached behind with one foot. There was only emptiness there. He was on the edge of the ditch. Below was the death the first one had died. He could retreat no farther.

There was the bridge. If he could find it, he could back along it and take them one at a time. But he didn't dare turn and look, and his foot touched nothing as it swung.

They closed in. Did they want him to die? Did they want to force him back? He was safe as long as they had to come to him; he was sure enough of his own strength for that. But if he went to them, it was a different matter. They would be all over him then, and it would be a miracle for him to get away.

But it was that or give ground, and there was no ground to give. He tensed his legs.

THE HISTORY

Freedom. . . .

How much is it worth? As much as anyone can pay and sometimes a little more. And even then no man can own it clear or bequeath it to his children.

The Cluster had it, and Eron bid. To the Cluster, freedom was worth everything it had. The federated worlds ventured it all, not once but twice. And it wasn't enough.

Eron was shaken by the incredible defeat of the first Quarnon War. A second defeat might have shattered the Empire. But even that risk was worthwhile to erase the insidious propaganda that free worlds existed outside the Empire.

Years passed as black fleets drove toward the Cluster at nearly the speed of light and set up Tube Terminals nearby. From them men and machines poured out within hours of the time they left Eron.

And yet the Cluster fought.

How can you estimate the cost? What is the price of a depopulated world? Of civilizations destroyed? Of billions of human lives?

Here is one figure: the share of the Company's revenue received by every man and woman of pure golden blood was cut in half.

Freedom? Set your price. Somewhere a man will want it bad enough to pay anything. . . .

16

THE KEY

Horn leaped toward the encircling shadows, twisting, dodging, fists smashing. There were too many of them. When one reeled back, another took his place. Fists got through Horn's guard. They battered at his face; they found his body. And then the shadows were all over him, clinging to his arms, his back, trying to take his legs out from under him. Horn swayed like a tree about to topple.

One face reached over his shoulder, teeth bared, seeking his throat. Beyond the enclosing mass of fists and fingers and teeth, a loud voice boomed out, "Enough, you blood-hungry wolves! Enough, I say! I'll have no more of this!"

Horn could feel them being torn away like leeches. At last he stood free. If his legs trembled a little, he controlled them quickly. He looked up at the wild face that loomed above him.

It was not a face to inspire confidence or trust. The features were craggy and big enough to match the better than two-meter height. A mane of violent, red hair fell unruly around the man's broad shoulders. It was matched, below, by a long, bristling, red beard. The dim sun, which had made up its mind to climb over the rocky rim of the planetoid, made the beard even redder.

Horn looked into the deep, joyful blue eyes and took a deep breath. "Thanks," he said simply.

The beard parted. "Nothing!" the giant bellowed. "I like you, little man. You did well against that pack of curs. Even curs get brave when they run together, and a lot of them can bring down the proudest stag. They call me Redblade."

The name was familiar. "The pirate?" Horn asked.

Redblade's eyes sparkled. "You've heard of me?"

Horn nodded. It was a name synonymous with destruction, massacre, rape; also with defiance of authority, which was the Empire.

"It took three cruisers to beat me," the pirate boasted, "and then they caught me asleep."

"I'm Horn. Soldier of fortune."

"Another pirate, eh? But smarter. We'd make a pair." His face darkened. "If there was only a chance of getting off this forgotten rock."

"No chance?" Horn said.

Redblade shook his head despondently. "No one has ever done it; not in all the time Vantee has been a prison."

"There's a key to any door."

"Not this one," Redblade said. "Come along. I'll tell you why. You're just in time for breakfast."

As the pirate led him around the broad ditch, Horn said, "Why did those men want to kill me?"

"After you've eaten breakfast, you'll see."

They came to a cluster of ragged men. They were sitting, squatting, standing, several hundred of them, waiting for something to happen.

"Make way!" Redblade roared. "We have a guest."

He forced his way through the throng with easy movements of his shoulders that sent men flying aside. Those that resisted were staggered by a tap of Redblade's hand. Horn recognized a brutality in the pirate; perhaps it was necessary.

They stopped beside a shallow trench gouged out of the rock. A pipe ran to it from the black wall of the fortress. As they arrived, a sticky, yellowish, viscous stuff began to gush from the pipe into the trench.

"Breakfast," Redblade muttered. "Eat."

He knelt and scooped up a handful; Horn went down beside him and tasted the stuff. It was edible but not much more. Horn couldn't afford to be squeamish; he ate hungrily.

"Mush!" Redblade said with disgust. "Morning and night, mush!"

The pirate was wiping his bearded mouth on a copper-haired forearm. Horn got to his feet. The other men were lining the trench, some of them with their faces half-buried in the mush as they stretched full-length. Men were dragged away by those behind them. Fights started. One man fell into the trench and staggered away, making a meal of what he could scrape off his body.

Horn felt a little sick.

"Pigs!" Redblade said with disgust. "Oh, it's food. They put things in it, someone said, minerals, things. None of us die—from that. It's filling but it isn't satisfying. We get hungry for meat."

Horn shivered. "That was what they wanted."

"Some of us get hungrier than others."

They were walking away from the squatting fortress. In a few minutes it dropped away below the horizon. Horn and Redblade stood at the rim of a large but not deep depression that was shaped like a saucer.

"Understand how we live," Redblade said, "and you'll understand why escape is impossible."

He pointed out the dark holes in the wall that were caves, dug laboriously out of the rock over the years and generations. They were invaluable, Redblade said, as protection against the cold—

"No fire?" Horn asked.

Redblade shook his head. That was the basic thing. Vantee had never been alive. There were no deposited stores of chemical energy: oil, coal, or wood. Nothing on Vantee would burn. The planetoid's only resource was rock, and rock has few uses. Aside from rock, the only things the prisoners had were what they had brought out of the fortress with them. They were valued in this ascending order: bone (implements and poor weapons), rags (warmth), and metal—

"Metal?"

"Shoe nails, pins, belt buckles, buttons, eyelets. . . . It takes a long time to accumulate enough to hammer out something as useful as a knife."

Horn accepted it. Without fire, almost all construction and manufacture was impossible.

For amusement, Redblade continued, they had such things as men without women can have. Such as they were, they supplied a backbone for the prison culture. They were the private indulgences and the contests.

The contests were athletic and usually bloody. Somebody got maimed or killed. A complex system of behavior and social prestige had developed around it. At the present, Redblade was the undisputed champion, having defeated all challengers. It carried certain privileges: a share of all corpses, the right to give as many orders as he could personally enforce—

"You could do that anyway," Horn objected.

"True," Redblade admitted, "but they won't gang up on me unless I overestimate my strength or get unreasonable. The result of all this, though, is that no one will do anything he doesn't want to do or can't be made to do."

"They won't act together, then," Horn mused. "That's individualism with a vengeance."

"So," Redblade said, shrugging his massive shoulders, "it adds up to this: there's no chance of rescue. No one even knows where Vantee is."

Horn remembered the unfamiliarity of the stars; the sky might as well have been that of another galaxy.

"The only way back is through the Tube," Redblade said, "and the only way to the Tube is through the fortress." He looked down at his huge hands, clenched them. "We tried that once. We threw rocks into the ditch until we could reach the walls. We didn't make a dent in them."

"What happened?"

Redblade shrugged. "The Warden cut off the food until we cleared the ditch out. A lot of us died. You see, though, that it's hopeless."

"In ordinary circumstances," Horn agreed. "But conditions have changed. The Empire is breaking apart; it's every man for himself to pick what he can out of the pieces."

Redblade's eyes blazed. "What's happened?"

"Rebellion!" Quickly Horn briefed the pirate on what had happened in the last few days.

Redblade growled deep in his thick chest. "Ahr-r-r! I'd give ten years of this life to dive into a real fight once more, to feel the flesh give and the bone break, to see the blood run." He sighed. "You think Eron's really in trouble?"

Horn nodded. "It's not just the fighting on Eron, though that's dangerous enough. Every conquered world in the Empire will be up in arms. There won't be many troops to spare for Eron itself, and ships are useless against the fighting inside. Guard detachments will be rebelling. The top leadership is gone.

"A few strong men might swing the balance either way, and one name could make all the difference: Peter Sair."

"He's dead," Redblade said casually.

"Did you see him die?"

"He was never out here with the rest of us. They kept him in the fortress. Newcomers brought out the news of his death."

Horn sighed. It was just rumor, then, like the rest; it was something the Empire would deliberately release. Sair had to be alive.

"So we wait," Redblade said disgustedly, "until someone releases us."

"I can't wait," Horn said. "And I'm afraid we might wait forever."

"Then you've got a plan?"

"If you're willing to take a chance."

"Anything," Redblade spat out.

"How many men are there out here?"

Redblade shrugged. "Three or four hundred. Nobody ever counted. Men die. Others come out of the fortress."

"What would you do if you were the Warden?" Horn asked. "You've only got a few men to do a big job: taking over the north cap with its vital control room. You've got no scruples—"

"I'd use the prisoners!" Redblade exclaimed. "I'd put guns in their backs and throw them into the fight. There's lots of times guns are no good anyway. A few hundred real fighting men would swing most battles; they'd get killed, but they'd swing it. But it's dangerous letting us into the fortress."

"Not as dangerous as losing," Horn said. "Remember, this comes as a surprise. We're called in suddenly, jammed into a carefully guarded room, taken out under guard a few at a time—"

"Yeah," Redblade said. "It would work."

"But if we've outguessed him, if we're ready to make a break before he expects it, then we've got a chance. Not a good chance, but a chance."

"Any chance to get off Vantee is a good chance," Redblade muttered and ran his fingers through his thick hair. "What do we need?"

"A handful of men we can trust," Horn began.

"There aren't any. If they were trustful when they reached here, they soon learned better."

"It's freedom, man!" Horn exploded. "Won't any of them take orders for that?"

"They might," Redblade admitted. "But don't trust any of them." He hesitated. "Not even me. You can lure us with freedom and promises or force us with blows, but you can't trust us."

Horn stared fiercely into the pirate's eyes. "Stick with me," he said, "and we'll whip the Empire and get our pick of the pieces. Go off on your own, and you'll get nothing except a quick death."

"I might do it," Redblade muttered. "I might do it. I will do it. But don't trust me."

"I'm going to," Horn said firmly. He had no choice; he had to count on this amoral giant to guard his back. "We need weapons."

"Knives, blackjacks, slings, or bone clubs?"

"Those that can be concealed are all right," Horn said, "but we need something small that will kill from a distance."

"Like this?" Redblade asked. He pulled something metallic out of his rags.

Horn took it and turned it over in his hands. It was a gun, crudely made with a small, rolled barrel, a bone handle, a trigger, and a crank of some kind on the side. "What is it?" he asked dubiously.

Redblade dumped the contents of a small sack into his broad palm. The dim sunlight glowed along slim, pointed darts. "It shoots these. Inside the barrel is a spring. The crank pulls it back until it's caught by the trigger. Drop in one of these"—he dropped a dart into the barrel of the gun, lifted the gun, and aimed at a boulder—"and pull the trigger."

Twang-g-g! S-s-s-s. Ping-ng-ng!

"Not very accurate, but it'll kill a man if you're close enough," Redblade said.

"You didn't make those out of belt buckles."

"There used to be metal troughs where the trench is. We took them out, hammered the metal, rubbed it against the rocks. It took a long time, but we had lots of that."

"With two of those," Horn said reflectively, "we might do it. See if you can round up half a dozen men who are quick and will take orders. Nobody else is to know."

The men came sullenly, herded in front of Redblade like sheep in front of a sheepdog. But as Horn outlined the opportunity and the plan, they caught fire from him. When he asked them if they would take orders, they nodded eagerly.

He gave them the same incentive to follow him that he had given Redblade, and then he added, "And if you don't, we'll kill you, Redblade or I."

The pirate growled agreement, and the ragged prisoners shrugged as if the terms were obvious.

Horn paced off the fortress dimensions, assigned them their roles, and drilled them in the plan until they were able to go through it in unison with their eyes closed. It was uncomplicated, but the simplest plans are the best. Its success depended on surprise and timing.

At last Horn realized that he had done all he could. "Nobody else gets told," he said. "They'd give it away or interfere. There's only one way to keep it to ourselves. Nobody leaves."

They accepted it, not gladly but with resignation to the realities of the situation.

"Now," Horn said, "all we have to do is wait and hope the Warden gets desperate enough to use us."

They were still fired and enthusiastic then. They gathered just out of sight of the footbridge that led to the solid, forbidding black door of the fortress. As the hours passed, Horn watched the unity of the group breaking apart.

Horn stared at the door and turned the plan over and over in his mind. He realized how feeble it was and how feeble were the instruments he had to work with. A ragged handful of treacherous rogues with a few, poor, handmade weapons to throw against a fortress. It was folly, but even folly is preferable to resignation; any chance is better than none.

Once, during the long wait, Redblade pulled him aside. "Look, man," he said. "I've been thinking over what you told me. I'll go along with you."

Horn felt then that he could trust the man—within reason. It was a moment of cheer in a deepening depression.

He tried to keep his conviction that the Warden would call on them for help and that they could succeed, but it faded in front of the grim, black reality of the brooding fortress. There were too many things that could happen, too many reasons the Warden could find for not using the prisoners. He would have to be desperate or careless to let in these doomed, desperate men, unarmed as they were. Horn didn't think that the Warden was a careless man.

Time moved slowly. The sun arched lazily across the dark sky. It reached the horizon. The darkness crept in again. A clamor announced a new flow of food from the pipe into the trough. The men stirred, but Redblade glowered them back. Only he left. He returned quickly with a heavy, cloth bag. They ate moodily, staring at the black barrier that kept them from Eron.

Before they were finished, the silence and the waiting ended. A voice boomed out of the fortress, amplified, urgent:

"Prisoners! You have been condemned to spend the remainder of your lives on Vantee. Now you are given a second chance.

"The Empire is at war. All of you who will fight her enemies will be admitted to the fortress and shipped to Eron. Survivors will be given a pardon and their freedom.

"There will be no chance for escape. You will be heavily guarded at all times. Only those sincere in their repentance need enter. Others will be shot down without warning or mercy.

"In five minutes the door will open. You, who wish to take advantage of this offer, file into the hallway.

"A second warning: violence means death! . . ."

Before the voice had reached the end, Horn and Redblade had shepherded their men toward the footbridge. A crowd had already collected. They forced their way through and stopped at the ditch.

The crowd grew behind them. Tensions grew with it as the minutes passed and the dark door did not lift.

A crack of light became a torrent. The door went up. There were four guns trained on them: the two mounted guns in the wall slits and unitron pistols in the hands of the two guards. It was just as Horn had visualized it, and it was firepower to make even desperation hesitate. The mounted guns could spew projectiles that would cut men down like a scythe, and the pistols weren't much slower.

The mass of men surged forward. Redblade planted his feet at the edge of the ditch, spread his arms wide, and braced his back. "Easy," he bellowed. "One at a time."

Redblade trotted across the bridge. Behind him came Horn. Behind Horn came the men he had drilled so thoroughly. Behind them, hurrying, came the rest. They filed into the hallway, blinking, wary, like long-caged animals.

Horn and Redblade matched strides at the head of the rabble, Horn counting under his breath. They moved toward the two guards. The guards backed away in front of them, guns ready, eyes shifting back and forth cautiously.

Horn walked a little faster. Redblade lengthened his stride. The guards couldn't back up fast enough. The distance closed. Perhaps, at that moment, a premonition struck them. One gave a little lift to his gun; the other opened his mouth. Horn was already diving, feeling Redblade moving beside him, fast and low, and the air was exploding from his lungs in a scream of "Now!"

They hit the guards. A shot echoed and whined through the hall. One of the mounted guns chattered briefly, violently. Horn was too busy to worry about anything else. He shoved his guard's arm straight up. The pistol went off into the ceiling. Horn's fist plowed into the guard's belly. The man grunted, doubled a little, but his own hand came around. Horn took it on the shoulder and swung a chopping backhand at the man's neck. There was a dry, snapping sound. The guard dropped, his head lolling at an impossible angle. As he fell, Horn twisted the gun from his hand.

Horn swung around. The mass of men were still frozen. The action had elapsed in less time than it took them to absorb the meaning of what was happening and move again. A few men were crumpled on the floor, but the wall guns were silent. A man was supporting himself by the muzzle of each of them, peering through the slits, spring guns ready. Below them, two more men were frantically winding little cranks.

Redblade's guard was down and motionless. The pirate had a

gun in his hand, too, and he seemed more complete. He smiled gleefully at Horn.

"Quick!" Horn shouted, without a pause. "There'll be gas. Run." And as he said it, he was turning, running. Behind him began the thunder of feet.

The hall was long and straight, but there were no more guns in the walls. If they could make it to the end, they would be in the barracks area. Beyond that was the Tube room. There were doors in the walls they passed. They were closed. Horn didn't know what they were and didn't stop to investigate. He glanced beside him at Redblade. The pirate was running with long, loping strides, his red mane floating behind him, his teeth bared in a fearsome grimace. Perhaps, Horn thought, it was a smile.

At the end of the hall a door opened. A man stood in the doorway, blinking into the light, looking toward the running men and the noise. He was an old man, small and stout; his white hair glistened like an ice-cap seen from space. Horn's eyes widened. Out of one corner, he saw Redblade's arm lift. There was a gun at the end of it.

Horn's hand swept out and up. The bullet whined off the ceiling.

"That's Sair!" Horn shouted. "That must be Sair!"

Still not a minute had passed. Redblade glanced at Horn and back to the figure at the end of the hall.

Behind them, over the sound of the stampeding feet, the corridor began to hiss. That was gas, Horn knew, and it was quick; but not quite quick enough.

And then, a few meters ahead, a partition began its swift, deadly fall from the ceiling.

THE HISTORY

Crisis. . . .

It comes, inevitably, in the affairs of men and in the affairs of empires. The little decisions pile one atop another until the Big Decision must come. Men must live or die. Empires must rise or fall.

The Big Decision. When it comes, it is only a little thing after all. Among the great sweeps of history, among the massive forces moving races and empires toward success or extinction, one man can make all the difference.

A man is an insignificant thing. But so is a mote of dust. And if the scales are delicate, if they are perfectly balanced, a mote will bear down one pan as certainly as a lump of lead.

A mote or a man. . . .

17

LIVING SYMBOL

As they leaped forward, Horn realized that he and Redblade could get past the falling door without trouble; but few of the men behind would be able to follow. They would be trapped back there with the gas, and two men would be helpless against the fortress guards.

And Redblade was under the door, reaching up to catch it as it descended, cushioning it slowly to a stop. His muscles cracked. His legs trembled under the strain; cloth ripped as his chest expanded and his back tightened. As he held it there, straining, his face reddened to match his beard, and sweat dripped from it to stain the beard darker.

"Fast!" Horn yelled at the runners behind, and they came on, arms and legs working frantically but approaching with fantastic, dreamlike slowness.

But they were streaming under the half-descended door, ducking as Redblade sagged a little, and a little more, and then the only men in the corridor were collapsed far back.

"They're past," Horn said.

Redblade released his tortured grip and threw himself forward. The door thundered against the floor.

As Horn drew close to Sair, he realized how very old and tired the man was. His blue eyes peered dazedly at the men milling around him. His mouth opened and shut, but no sound came out. But Horn recognized him.

This was the Liberator, hope of the Empire's enslaved billions. It would be tragic if age and imprisonment had broken him beyond usefulness. Even broken, Horn told himself, Sair was a symbol, and symbols live on when the reality which fashioned them has disintegrated.

"You and you and you," Horn said, grabbing out of the passing throng three of the men who had helped in the assault. "This is Peter Sair. The Liberator. Guard him. If he's not safe when I come back, I'll kill you."

They stared at him, nodded, and turned toward the doorway. As Horn looked back, he saw them leading the old man into his room again.

Horn sprinted until he was beside Redblade. There were others ahead, fanning out down the corridor that had turned a right angle. There was a doorway open on the left. Men hurled themselves through it—and died. More poured in; bullets whined through the packed bodies, but a few of them lived. The sounds of guns and splintering furniture and the shouts and screams of men were a cacophony of violence from the room. When Redblade and Horn reached the door, the room was quiet. It streamed with blood like an abattoir; the air steamed with still-warm flesh violently torn apart. A dozen ragged men trotted out of the silent barracks with guns in their hands.

Horn tried to split them up into groups of armed and unarmed men, but they were beyond direction. The fighting raged ahead. By the time they reached the end of that corridor, they had lost at least fifty men. In the battle for the Tube room, the original three or four hundred was cut to less than a hundred. They were all armed, all sound except for minor flesh wounds, and all fighters.

Only one scene stood out clearly to Horn in the whole kaleidoscope battle that shifted and blurred with meaningless colors. He saw Redblade throw open the door to the Warden's office. The pirate stood there, feet spread wide, blazing eyes fixed on the Warden's whitening face. Redblade roared, dropped his pistol as if he had forgotten it, and charged toward the Warden. He pawed frantically in a drawer, afraid to take his eyes away from Redblade long enough to find his gun.

Redblade slid across the wide desk and hit him. The gun spun away. The Warden staggered back. He recovered quickly. He was fully as tall as Redblade and perhaps even heavier. It was not all fat, either. They came together like wild bulls. The impact shook the room. Their arms worked for a hold. The Warden's knees came up like pistons, but Redblade twisted his body aside and got one massive arm around the Warden's waist. The other was under the Warden's chin, pushing backward, the outstretched fingers working into the Warden's face, reaching toward the eyes.

The Warden's fists thundered against Redblade's chest and belly for a moment, but the pirate ignored them. He pulled the man close with his arm while he pushed the chin away with the other hand. The Warden grabbed desperately for the hand under his chin, clamped it in two big hands and yanked at it, but he was off-balance now, his back arched, his feet straining to stay on the floor. It was too late. A moment later his neck snapped.

Redblade let the body fall away. It fell like a doll stuffed with rags and poorly stuffed, at that, because it was all crooked. He looked down at it for a moment while his chest heaved once. He looked up and laughed; it was a joyous bellow.

"I've dreamed about that," he shouted. "He always hated a big man. Maybe he was afraid one of them would be bigger and stronger than he was."

The fortress was almost quiet. The sounds of fighting had died away. Quickly Horn explained what had to be done.

"Try to get the men organized. Get as many as you can who will follow us to Eron and take our orders. Any of them who won't, let them stay here. If you have any trouble, shoot straight."

Redblade nodded; Horn whirled and started away.

Sair was sitting in the little room. It was bare of everything except necessities: a metal-framed bed, a chair, a table, toilet facilities starkly in sight. A slot at the bottom of the door provided space for a food tray to be passed through. The Warden had allowed the old man paper and pen; several sheets on the table were covered with hieroglyphics of some kind. As Horn entered, Sair was eyeing the three silent guards with suspicion. He swung toward Horn, grabbed the sheets of paper, folded them, and thrust them away inside his flimsy coat.

The three men were on their feet.

"It's all over," Horn said. "Report to Redblade in the Tube room."

"Damn you, Horn," one of them said bitterly, "you made us miss all the fun."

"Don't complain," Horn told them. "Two of you would be dead by now. Out."

He motioned with the gun. They left quickly, and Horn was alone with Sair. The old man's head was shaking. It looked like a senile tremor.

"Who are you?" Sair asked. His voice was soft, hesitant, and old.

"Alan Horn. A prisoner, like you. We've conquered Vantee. We've taken the fortress."

"I shall write an epic," Sair said. "And now?"

"We're going back to Eron."

"Ah-h-h," Sair sighed. He folded his veined, wrinkled hands across his paunch.

"We want you to come with us."

Sair looked up slowly. "What is there for an old man on Eron?"

"Rebellion," Horn said. "Only you can unite it, make it work, keep it from reducing the Empire to savagery."

Sair shook his head, and it rocked back and forth until Horn thought it would never stop. "My fighting days are over. I'm an old man. Let younger men do what they must. I'm finished, worn-out, half-dead."

"It's a job no one else can do," Horn said grimly. "It's not fighting we want. It's your presence, your mind." *What's left of it*, he thought.

Sair's head continued to rock, but his eyes brightened just a little. "Rebellion, you said? Against Eron? It's hard to believe."

"Kohlnar was assassinated. The Directors began fighting among themselves. When Duchane elected himself General Manager, the lower levels rose against him. What's happened since, I don't know. We've got to get back—quickly."

"Kohlnar dead? He was a great man. It's hard to think of him as dead."

Horn stared at Sair without understanding. *Kohlnar? A great man?* "But he conquered the Cluster and condemned you to Vantee!"

"Still, a great man. He kept the Empire alive long after it should have died. It was our misfortune that he was faithful to a dying dream." Sair's head had stopped rocking. He seemed steadier, more alive.

Horn paced the room impatiently; Sair's faded eyes followed him curiously. Horn had to get back to Eron; every wasted moment was agony. But he had to have Sair, too.

"You know what will happen if Duchane wins," Horn pleaded. "Or if he drowns in his own sea of blood and the leaderless mobs rage through Eron. They'll tear the Empire apart. They'll wreck the Tube system that holds the stars together, tear down the very walls of Eron itself, and die. They must be starving already; no food has come through for days."

"Duchane." Sair nodded, and then he sighed. His head shook decisively. "No. No. All my life I've worried about these things: freedom—starvation. Starvation and freedom. Between those millstones I wore my life away. Now there's only one freedom I want, the final one: death. Let other, younger men battle for their ideals. Let them throw their inexhaustible energy into the struggle and find it useless against the tides and currents that sweep men and empires to their destinies. Let them pawn themselves to causes and discover that they cannot buy themselves back. I have no strength to spare. There is barely enough to draw in one breath after another. I want only peace and time to die. Here is as good a place as another."

"They said you were dead," Horn said quietly. "Many people believed it. And the hopes of uncounted billions died, too. If they discovered that you were alive, it would draw them together; among the chaos of their own wild passions, unleashed for the first time, it would save them. They need you. It's useless to speak of other men; there are no others who can do this job. Even the Empire needs you. Only you can save it, for Duchane will destroy it, win or lose."

Sair looked up, his face alive. "You believe that, don't you?"

Horn nodded.

Sair sighed heavily. "Perhaps it's true. A dying man must be dragged from his grave to serve the living. Is there no peace? No peace anywhere?"

Horn waited, scarcely breathing.

Slowly Sair raised himself to his feet. "What are we waiting for?" he asked. His lips curled wryly. "Let's go free the slaves and save the Empire."

Horn let out his breath and turned to the door. He held it open for the old man. Sair's stride was surprisingly brisk as they walked toward the Tube room. Now that he had made his decision, he was full of questions about the situation on Eron and about how they took the fortress. He nodded shrewdly as Horn described the Warden's need for troops and the way they guessed it and the plans they laid to take advantage of it. By the time he had described the battle, they had reached the Tube room.

"Redblade," Horn said. "This is Peter Sair."

Sair's eyes danced. "The pirate?" He tilted his head back to stare into Redblade's bearded face. "Among other things, I have been called a pirate."

Redblade laughed. "Your men, Liberator." He swept his arm toward the cluster of men who had survived the attack. There were about seventy-five of them now. There were a few bodies on the floor, and a handful of men were gathered sullenly in one corner. The main body were in black uniforms, scavenged from the stores. To identify them from other Security agents, the sleeves of the tunics had been cut off above the elbow. The faces had a strange similarity; they were all hard, thin, and hungry. "Thieves, murderers, traitors," Redblade went on. "Command us—and maybe we'll obey."

Sair chuckled. "This young man has done a good job, even with me. Let him continue."

Horn turned to the men. "Prisoners!" he shouted. "Redblade and I and a few others—we've done what everyone said couldn't be done. We're escaping from Vantee. Alone we wouldn't have a chance; together we can tear Eron apart and take what we want out of the pieces. We need one thing: discipline.

"We'll take you to freedom and give you a chance to live in a world where you can go where you want to go and do what you want to do without asking permission of any master. But you've got to take orders until we've won; those who refuse will be shot down. Redblade has given you one chance; this is your second and last one. Those who will obey my orders or Redblade's or Peter Sair's instantly, without question, step forward and turn around."

The men looked at each other and murmured. Half of them stepped forward and turned, then most of the remainder until only five were left.

"All right," Horn said. "Here's your first order." He shouted, quickly, "Shoot down those men!"

The five died before they could reach their guns. In the corner the bunch of ragged men crouched warily.

"Good," Redblade said admiringly. "Very good!"

"Salutory," Sair agreed.

"Into the ship!" Horn ordered. "Let's go to Eron!"

They swarmed up the escalator into the waiting ship. The

transport was not built to hold so many, but they jammed them in, seventy of them.

Before they followed, Horn turned to Redblade. "I'm going to trust you," he said slowly. "Don't betray me."

Redblade frowned; after a moment his face cleared. "I don't think I will. I think I wouldn't like to have you mad at me."

The three of them took chairs in the ship's control room and strapped themselves in, Horn as pilot, Redblade as copilot, Sair as navigator.

Horn let his hands fall forward on the panel. "Three hours to Eron," he said, "and the ship's clock won't have changed a second when we arrive."

"An interesting detail," Sair said. "How do you explain it?"

"Everything stops in the Tube," Horn said. "No light, heat, sound—no energy at all. It must be connected in some way to how the Tube works."

"You've discovered something generations of scientists have searched for," Sair said intently. "How did you do it?"

Horn shivered. "I went through the Tube conscious. Never again."

"It's too bad we can't do that now," Sair said. "We could put those three hours to good use. But I'm afraid it's some kind of field effect, generated in the gold bands, perhaps. We haven't time to locate it."

"And a shipload of madmen would be little use on Eron," Horn added.

"I must ask you, then, to outline the situation before we depart— and arrive," Sair said.

Horn went through it quickly from the political aspect to the strategic position. "The key, then, is the north cap. Whoever controls that, controls Eron."

"Then we must control the north cap," Redblade said simply.

"True," Sair said. "It won't be an easy job—others will have the same idea—but that will be chiefly a military operation. I won't be much use there. I must make myself felt in Eron."

"And you can't do that until we capture the control room," Horn said. "Let's go!"

He tapped the keys with practiced fingers. The ship slid forward into the lock. Horn waited while the red light on the panel turned to gold. He tapped the keys once more. There was a brief surge of power that pressed them back into their seats—

They blinked. The ship thumped gently into the cradle. Horn glanced at the clock on the panel. It was moving, but no time had elapsed, according to its stiff hands. The cradle was moving with them now; it slid them out of the air lock.

They had returned to Eron.

"No time," Horn said wonderingly. "It is as if within the Tubes wasn't a part of our universe at all."

He hadn't time for any more reflections. Redblade was pointing at the screen. It was directed toward the floor beneath the cradle, and the floor was a battlefield for ants. Masses of them swayed back and forth, became detached, joined back together. Slowly it separated itself into a battle between drab little ants and large green ones.

A few faces had been turned up toward them and then more. It spread, like a white sea, across the floor.

The drab ones were slaves. Somehow they had fought their way here from the lower levels. Battling in from the wide doorway were giant Denebolan lancers in the green uniforms of Transport. That was Fenelon. Did it mean that Fenelon was alive, Horn wondered, or had these mercenaries found another master?

The battle was going against the rabble. The huge Denebolans were mowing the undisciplined horde down like ripe grain, using pistols where there was room, swinging clubs and swords when they were closed in. Many of them were dragged down and swarmed under, but the rabble was doomed. Hundreds of them died for every Denebolan.

Through the hull Horn heard the whine of ricocheting bullets. Shouts came from the rear of the ship. Horn was on his feet and racing toward the port before they started. It was open. The escalator was in front of it, but no one was climbing down. Through the oval door came a rain of bullets.

Several men were huddled against the corridor wall. "We can't get out," one of them shouted. "They've killed two of us already. In a minute they'll be climbing up here."

"Who's shooting?" Horn demanded.

"The damned slaves!"

"We'll have to make them understand that we're trying to help them," Horn said impatiently.

"After ten centuries of betrayal," Sair said softly from behind, "do you expect them to recognize assistance when they see it?"

"I'll have to tell them," Horn said. He started for the deadly opening. "Hold your fire!" he shouted. "We're friends—"

It was useless. The sound would never carry through the clamor below. Sair's gentle hand drew him back.

"Come on, you dead men!" Redblade shouted. "We'll fight our way out!"

"That's not the way either," Sair said. "This is my job: diplomacy. This is why you needed me."

Before anyone could stop him, he had slipped past. He stood unarmed and alone in the empty oval, looking out over the sea of faces, calmly.

A bullet whistled past him. He didn't flinch. Slowly quiet spread out over the faces. Through it came a mutter. The mutter became a shout from a thousand throats.

"SAIR!"

The old man raised his hand toward the distant door. "Let us fight the enemy!" he shouted. His voice was loud and clear and strong.

Horn leaped toward him as a volley of bullets streamed through the door.

THE HISTORY

Creation. . . .

It is its own nemesis. Success is temporary, and idolization will not make the ephemeral permanent. Decay is implicit in the birth of any organism.

An empire is an organism.

Leadership is admired and imitated while it is creative. As a substitute, force is self-defeating. The consequences are inevitable. Outside the organism, resistance to incorporation grows strong; inside, rebellion begins.

Creators are always a minority. Geniuses, saints, supermen, they rise in response to the challenge of conditions. They leave the mass of the people behind them. They must transform the world or perish.

Eron's answer to the rhythmic repetition of challenge and response had become fixed: force. And force must always give way to a greater force. . . .

18

WAR

Horn's momentum carried Sair to one side out of the path of the bullets.

"They shot!" Sair exclaimed softly.

"The Denebolans," Horn said. "That had to be. If one side is your friend, the other is your enemy. Somebody shoots at you all the time." He rolled over and started crawling back. "Redblade! Sharpshooters!"

Three short-sleeved guards came forward on hands and knees. They lay full-length below the level of the port. Their pistols lifted; they sighted toward the wide doorway. In a few seconds bullets were streaming toward the tall lancers.

"Let's go back to the control room," Horn said. "It'll be a few minutes."

In the screen, the change was obvious. The ragged rebels were attacking with a maniac frenzy, and the Denebolans were falling back before it. The wide doorway was being cleared by the sharpshooters' deadly accuracy. The size that made the lancers such dangerous fighters made them easy victims to ambush. They were men and mortal; one bullet was enough. Hundreds died. Those who could not retreat were torn apart.

When the lancers were gone, the rebels turned their white faces to the ship once more.

"Sair!" they shouted.

The fighting men from the naked plains of Vantee raced down the motionless escalator and cleared a semi-circular area at the foot of it. Sair followed, slowly, and the mob grew silent. Behind him came Horn and Redblade. With him the pirate carried a hastily improvised, portable amplifier. He held it under his arm for Sair to use. It thundered the soft voice through the towering room.

"Rebels! Soldiers of freedom! As you recognized, I am Peter Sair, once president of the Quarnon League, most recently a prisoner of Eron on Vantee. Like me, these other men in the captured uniforms of Security agents were prisoners. With courage and desperation, they fought their way to freedom and brought me with them. They are fighters and leaders. We will have need of them.

"You, too, are fighters. But you have no leaders, and leaderless men are weak. There is no time for democratic processes. I ask you to recognize me as your leader and to name me as your leader to all other rebels, wherever you meet them. I do not ask this because I am eager for glory or hungry for power. I have had enough of both; they are fleeting and worthless. I ask this because I am Peter Sair; my name and face are known.

"Eron must fall, but it must fall without breaking apart. That means there must be leadership. I ask your allegiance; I ask your unquestioning obedience."

As the echoes died away, there was silence, and then the room rocked once more with the shout of "SAIR!"

Horn realized, as he had realized above in the ship, what had made Sair great. His talent was people; the thing to do and the thing to say that would move them—that was sure instinct.

"Agreed!" Sair said, and there was a touch of wistfulness in his titan's voice. "I am bound, as you are." His voice grew strong again. "Let us get down to business. My lieutenants are Redblade and Horn. Obey them as you would obey me. Under them will be the men who came with us from Vantee. As experienced fighters, they will lead you; each of them will command fifty men.

"They did the impossible: they escaped from Vantee. With your help they will do the impossible again!"

Redblade took over the amplifier and, holding it easily at mouth level, began barking commands. The men from Vantee moved out and began splitting the mob into groups. It was quick and efficient. Soon there were almost seventy groups being inspected for arms, ammunition, and physical condition. While they were being organized, instructed, and drilled, guards were posted at the door and up and down the corridor.

Redblade called for any of the rebels with information to come forward. Out of the few who made their way slowly across the floor, Horn picked one whose eyes were bright and intelligent. In response to their questions, his story came out in brief spurts of words that they pieced together into coherence.

His group of rebels had seized a ship at the warehouse level. With a fantastic idea of reaching another planet, they had forced the pilot to take them out of Eron. Once in space, they had been helpless and confused; the pilot took advantage of their indecision to slip the freighter into a north cap lock. Instead of help, he found a quick death. The rebels spilled out into the cap, raging back and forth aimlessly as groups attacked them and they attacked others.

Inside Eron rebellion was general. The slaves had poured up into the forbidden upper levels. Sometimes the gray guards fought against them; sometimes they joined the ragged mob. Often they found gray guards fighting with the personal guards of the various Directors; most prevalent were Duchane's black agents. But the golden blood had run thick, and it was red, like that of other men.

The battle had seemed to be going against the rebels when they had fled into space, but it might have been just a local action. There was no pattern to it, no order, no easy victor.

Yes, they were hungry. They hadn't eaten since they left the warehouse level. But it helped to think that the Golden Folk and their guards were hungrier. The warehouses had been the first areas seized by the rebels; they would be the last surrendered.

They had seen other rebel groups during the fighting in the cap, but had been unable to join forces with them. Most recently, these Denebolan giants had charged out of one of the Tube rooms and forced them back into this one. Such reinforcements were coming frequently, but there was no way of predicting from which room they would come or from what world or on whose side they would fight.

No, he hadn't seen Wendre Kohlnar. Some of the golden women had been killed; he had seen it happen in the early hours of the uprising. The madness had wanted to drown itself in blood; they had taken no prisoners. Later they had been too desperate and afraid to do anything but defend themselves.

Horn's eyes were distant and unhappy as he turned to Redblade. "Are we organized?"

"As much as possible. Most of it will have to be done under fire. That'll shake 'em down. So far they've been a mob; now they'll learn what it is to be an army."

"What do you think? Will they have a chance against trained guards?"

Redblade squinted speculatively at the milling men. "These men have something personal to fight for—over and above their lives. The guards are fighting for money. I'll take these, puny lot though they are."

"How many are armed?"

"More than I thought. Over fifty percent."

They went over their plans in the light of the forces they had gained. The chief goal was the control room, which was down the corridor to the left. Twenty groups would be sent in that direction with instructions to take and hold all Tube rooms as they came to them. Five of the fastest men in each group would be designated runners to report new developments to headquarters. No group was to move forward until its sides and rear were protected.

Fifteen groups would start down the corridor to the right, with the same instructions. The rest would stay at headquarters as guards and reserve.

Each group leader would receive instructions to give opponents a chance to join them. Again with any survivors. The battle cry would be "Sair!" All recruits would cut or tear off their sleeves.

Above all, communications. Group leaders would keep in constant touch by runner—

"I'll go with the group to the left," Redblade said, showing his teeth in a ferocious grin.

"You'll stay here!" Horn snapped. "You'll coordinate information from the runners and dispatch assistance and supervise organization of new—"

"But the control room," Redblade pleaded; "we can't hope to take the cap and hold it unless we can isolate it. We need the communications. We need to cut individual Tubes and close air locks and—"

"That battle, like all the rest of them, will be won and lost here," Horn said firmly. "A staff operation may not be glamorous, but it's vital."

Like all staff operations, this was blind; like most, this was confusion. Horn fought for eyes and after that for order; he never got either one satisfactorily. There was never time to do anything thoroughly or well. Impressions swarmed about him; decisions pressed in on him. He snapped off answers and orders by instinct and impulse and a vague sort of pattern that grew unconsciously at the back of his mind.

While Redblade bellowed commands through the amplifier, calling off names and assignments, Horn turned to the floor. As the room cleared, he drafted a group to begin laying out a map of the north cap. When the runners began streaming back, Horn was ready. Slowly the map was clarified and filled in. This room was taken; that one clear. Here a desperate battle with Denebolan lancers or gray guards or blue guards or green guards. . . . So many casualties. Send more men. Send more guns. Send more ammunition. Send—

The groups that had been drilling under their black-uniformed leaders began to thin out. Soon there were only ten groups left to run and throw themselves flat, dry-fire, and take cover. Horn glanced around worriedly. In a few minutes, there would be too few for safety.

A mass of ragged recruits streamed through the door and went wild at the sight of Sair. When they were quieted, they began to drill. Leaders for them came from the remnants of previous groups.

Perhaps that was the turning point. Horn was never able to pin it down. It might have been earlier when Sair appeared at the ship's lock and the ragged mob shouted his name. But if anything was the key to victory, it was Sair and the name of Sair.

As the word spread that Sair was alive and on Eron, their forces grew. Sair himself, sitting wearily on an empty crate, spoke briefly through the amplifier to each new throng and passed them on dedicated and malleable.

Impressions assailed them, demanding, relentless: reports, consultations, orders, alarms, successes, failures, garbled messages, lost runners. . . . But the area under their control grew and the map grew with it. Here was a ship; cargo—packaged food. There was a store of weapons, dynode cells, bullet clips. . . .

The room became jammed again. Casualties were heavy, but reinforcements were greater. Most of the new recruits were slaves but some of them were rebellious guards and service troops, and there was one bunch of Tube technicians in gold uniforms.

Horn drew them aside and asked, as he had asked dozens of times already, if they had seen Wendre or heard from her. They shook their heads. They had been in the control room when the first attack came; they were all who were left.

Horn turned aside and back to the ever-increasing demands of organization. Nearby rooms were commandeered for assembly and training areas. The first one became headquarters alone. Squads were detailed as arsenal workers, locating and centralizing weapons and ammunition, passing them out. The service troops became cooks and mess-attendants. One kitchen cooked countless liters of soup; it was distributed with condensed emergency rations.

Horn gulped down lukewarm soup and swallowed a few pellets. It was poor stuff, but it was food and food was strength.

As men became proficient in the use of the map, Horn placed them in charge with instructions to report to him as decisions became necessary. Redblade assumed the burden of sending reserves where they were needed, and his amplified bull's bellow echoed through the tall rooms and corridors.

Horn tore himself away from the barely ordered confusion and tried to think. After so long in the middle of it, he needed a perspective. He rubbed his eyes and stared at the map. At last he saw what he had been missing.

He hunted down the bellow; he fought his way to the pirate's side. "What happened to those groups we sent toward the control room?"

"Some of them reported back," Redblade said, surprised.

"I know. The corridor to the left is in our hands for a kilometer, but not the control room. Reports stopped coming in. How's it going otherwise?"

"We're not getting so many calls for reinforcements. Now I'm wondering what to do about the new men who keep coming in. We're running out of room."

"Spread out," Horn said, shrugging. "We seem to have most of the corridors and over half the Tube rooms. But it's no good without the control room. Is there anyone you can trust to leave in charge?"

"No," Redblade said frankly. "But I think they'll be too busy for a while to do any mischief, and I don't think they can move a mob like this. Only one thing is holding them together. Sair. So there's a few of our fellow prisoners from Vantee who can take over."

"Good," Horn snapped. "I've got one on the map. Deputize them. We've done as much as we can do here. It's time we saw some action. We'll take two groups. More would get in the way."

Redblade's shoulders straightened and he seemed to grow taller as he turned away.

Horn assembled the gold-uniformed technicians and turned to lead them into the corridor.

"I think," said a soft voice at his elbow, "that it is time for me to act also."

It was Sair. Horn studied him for a moment and nodded. "Let's go."

They moved quickly down the corridor. The Tube rooms they passed were securely in the hands of their forces. After a kilometer they discovered why there had been no reports. The corridor ended against a solid wall.

Horn turned to one of the technicians. "What's this?"

"Safety barrier. It's air tight. There's hundreds of these. They can be lowered from the control room."

"Can we get through it?"

"Eventually, I suppose. With unitronic torches."

"We can't waste that much time." Horn turned away. "Let's go in the back door."

As he led the groups back through the corridor to the first ramp to the lower levels, Horn thought about the safety barrier that had been lowered and the barriers that could have been lowered but weren't. Someone was in the control room, and he wasn't taking advantage of his opportunities. He seemed to be interested only in defense.

Horn and Redblade were in front of the party with Sair just a little behind. They were followed by the dozen technicians and two, well-disciplined, fifty-man groups. They met squads coming and going, trotting outward, fresh and confident, or trudging back with their wounded, weary and bloodstained. Even the latter looked up and shouted "Sair!" when they caught sight of the old man.

Runners tried to deliver their message to Horn or Redblade, but Horn waved them on. As they came out into the throbbing, dark, bottom level, bullets whined close to them. Horn quickly deployed his groups. In a minute, they moved out into the corridor and the disorganized remnants of a gray guard detachment scattered and ran.

At the end of the narrow corridor, the door stopped them only for a moment. It gave easily, and Horn decided that it was not the one he had used before. The circular room with its cylindrical pillar was empty.

Horn stood under the ladder and stared up at the plate covering the opening. It had not been screwed back down. Horn climbed to the top rung of the ladder and hesitated. Redblade moved under him. Horn put one foot on Redblade's shoulder, one foot on the ladder, and shoved the plate open.

As it clattered against the floor above, Horn was through the opening, his pistol in his hand. There were guards in the room, but they were careless. They were helping two men scramble through the open door of the central tube into the room. The guards were dressed in gold uniforms, but some of the others were ragged laborers from the lower levels.

"Don't move!" Horn said briskly, and they were too surprised to think of disobedience.

Then Redblade was beside Horn, and men were pouring through the circular opening after him. By the time the guards had made up their minds to resist, the odds were impossible. One of them started to move toward the wall that hid the elevator, but Horn waggled his pistol suggestively.

When Peter Sair was boosted and lifted into the room, many of the laborers gasped.

"This is Peter Sair," Horn said. "Didn't you know he was back?"

"Thought I heard that name," one of the slaves muttered. "It was a fight up there. Thought it was a trick."

"How many of you would like to fight for Sair and freedom?" Horn asked.

All of the slaves stepped forward eagerly. A few of the uniformed guards glanced at their officer and then settled back.

Gold, Horn thought. *Gold for Communications. Gold for Wendre.* It seemed incredible that they could still be working for her. How could she have got away from the men who grabbed her above? How could she have contacted her guards, found the loyal ones, and dispatched them here?

"Who sent you here?" Horn asked.

The guards were silent. Horn glanced at the slaves.

"The Entropy Cult," said the slave who had spoken before. "They sent us through that thing to fight for freedom."

Horn shook his head bewilderedly. Now the Cult. Where did it come in? Unless Wu had got away and thrown the Cult's forces, whatever they were, to the side to rebellion—

He turned to the wall and pressed the spot on it that Wendre had pressed. The wall slid silently aside. He motioned to the leader of one of his groups. He put the man's hand over the concealed latch.

"Count five and press this. Send up three men. After them three more. Stop when there's just enough left to guard the prisoners."

He stepped into the elevator. Redblade was close behind. Sair crowded in as the third man. Horn frowned and shrugged. Although Sair would be useless in a fight, his face was worth a dozen guns. It would be disastrous if he were killed, but violence was everywhere. No place was safe.

The door slid shut in front of him. Beside it was a lighted disk. Horn palmed it. The elevator started up. When the car stopped and the door opened, pistols were in the hands of Horn and Redblade. They stepped quickly out of the car and to opposite sides.

The room was the same as Horn remembered it: the panels, the chairs, the walls with their flickering dots of color. . . . But it was busy now. Technicians were at the panels, sitting in the chairs, moving around the room. It had an air of purpose and efficiency.

Everything stopped. Everyone turned to stare at the three men standing in front of the closed elevator doors. Horn's orange uniform was tattered; Redblade had almost no clothing at all to hide his massive body. Between them was a man with a familiar face who wore a torn prison coat and trousers.

"Peter Sair!" one of them muttered, and the name worked its way around the room.

In the middle of the room the vault door hung open like an admission of Eron's poverty, a reminder of a long-lived secret that was a better secret than Eron suspected. Beside it was an officer with a golden, pure-blood face and an air of command. He stepped forward, his eyes fixed on Horn.

"Horn?" There was a note of curiosity and expectancy in his voice.

Horn's gun lifted in warning. Behind him, the elevator door slid open. Three more armed men stepped into the room.

"I'm Horn," he said slowly.

"We've been waiting for you," the officer said. He waved his hand at the control room. "If you returned, the Director said that we should turn this over to you."

THE HISTORY

Knowledge. . . .

For some, it is an end in itself. For most, it is a tool, the greatest tool, archetype of all tools. Knowledge is basic. With it, man's puny strength can be multiplied infinitely.

One of the peculiarities of knowledge is that it always overflows its container. New containers must be built to hold it. Books supplanted the human brain and were themselves superseded by films, which gave way to tapes. . . . At the end of the sequence was the Index.

Its inventor was trying to discover the secret of the Tube. He built a bigger container. Its capacity was unlimited, because additional units could be attached as needed.

Each unit contained billions of floating, microscopic crystals. Each crystal, coated with a monomolecular metal film, was a dynode cell capable of receiving, storing, and discharging energy on its own wavelength.

The inventor filled it with knowledge and asked it the vital question. The Index answered: "The invention described is impossible."

The knowledge it called on was, of course, human knowledge.

To Duchane, on the other hand, the Index was invaluable. It grew until it occupied mile after square mile of precious Eron floor space. Into it were fed the

complete files of every Company office, the immense
volumes of police reports, intimate data on every individual within the limits of the Empire. . . .

Duchane didn't ask the impossible. The questions
he asked were simple. But, sometimes, the answers
were a little strange. . . .

19

DANGER BELOW

"The Director?" Horn asked shakily.

"Wendre Kohlnar," the officer said. His face was puzzled and a trifle condescending. "Don't ask me why. I'm just obeying orders."

"Where is she?" Horn asked quickly. His eyes searched the room.

The officer shrugged. "Somewhere in Eron. I suspect that she's mad, but then everyone seems to be these days."

The elevator doors kept opening and closing behind Horn; armed men spread out around the room.

"The last time I saw her," Horn said, "she had just been captured by rebels—"

"Slaves," the man amended. "They seemed to have some connection with the Entropy Cult. They gave the Director a chance to talk, and she said she wanted to help. Oddly enough, they believed her. Even odder, they were right."

Half of the workers in the room, Horn had noticed, were dressed in the drab rags of the lower levels. "And you don't know where she's gone?"

The officer shrugged again as if the whims of the insane were beyond him. "She contacted me from here, gave me instructions to gather what loyal guards and technicians I could find, and told me how to get here through the Directors' private tubeway. When I arrived, she left by the same means."

Horn was silent. He felt Redblade and Sair staring at him curiously. "All right," he said quickly. "We're taking over. You'll tell your men that they'll take orders from us, Sair, Redblade, or myself. So will you. Let's get busy."

With the dozen technicians Horn had brought, the control room had close to a complete complement. Horn had the barriers raised and the doors opened. In a few minutes he was reunited with the main body of rebel troops. The control room, with its myriad circuits, indicators, communication facilities, and controls, became central command. Reports steamed in.

Ninety percent of the north cap was in the hands of the rebels. Only a few strong points of resistance remained. With the control room's flexibility, they would soon be reduced. Communication devices of several kinds brought coherence out of confusion. Barriers began to drop throughout the cap. In a few minutes, the opposition was isolated. Ventilators were closed, and firefighting gases were released. As the effectiveness of these measures became apparent, ideas for turning facilities into weapons occurred on every side.

But new forces kept arriving, and it was impractical to keep guards in every Tube room.

"Can't we stop them from coming?" Horn asked the casually efficient officer.

"We can't cut off the Tubes," he said. "Only a Director can do that with the main switch. But we can cut the power to the Tube rooms. The ships won't come out of the lock. The troops will have to climb through the personnel lock in spacesuits. We can lock all doors, flood them with gas—"

"Good," Horn said quickly, cutting him off as his enthusiasm threatened to get out of hand. "As soon as our troops are out of the way, do everything you can think of. What about the south cap?"

"We cut off power to there as soon as I took over. Duchane's men were in control, but now we haven't been able to raise anyone for hours."

In half an hour, the north cap was in their hands as securely as it would ever be. Horn turned to Sair. "Eron's isolated. Now it's only a matter of dealing with the forces already here."

Horn felt a great weariness. After so long they had only taken the first step, important though it was.

Sair took a deep breath and turned to the gold-uniformed officer. "You said you were in touch with the south cap. Could you make a general hookup from here to broadcast to every receiver in Eron?"

He shrugged. "Of course. It will go out to every screen, public or private. But I can't guarantee how many are still in operation."

"Set it up," Sair said. "Let me speak to Eron."

In a few minutes, it was ready. Sair stood in a small cubicle surrounded by the round, blank, staring eyes of camera lenses.

"Yes," he began quietly. "You recognize me. I am Peter Sair, who has been called the Liberator. I am alive. I am on Eron. Forces under my command have just taken over the north Terminal cap and the control room. Eron is isolated. The Empire is doomed.

"It is right. It is just. It is past time. Once more, throughout the five-hundred-light-year radius of the Empire, men will be free to live as they wish, to choose their own paths, and to follow them to their own goals. It is not a simple thing, or an easy one, to be free. And it isn't simple or easy to break the power of an Empire without shattering that Empire to pieces.

"But it must be done. The framework of the Empire must not be destroyed; the Tubes are vital to the interstellar civilization that man must have if he is to be free and strong. Destroy Eron and the Tubes, and every world in the Empire will be isolated as Eron is now. Into this isolation, this power vacuum, will rush men greedy for power. If freedom survives at all, it will be an oddity, unstable and short-lived. Humanity will become not one race but many.

"That need not be. It must not be. Do not exchange one set of chains for many. You can have, instead, a loose union of free worlds held together by the Tubes. You can pass mutually agreeable regulations through elected representatives. You can trade freely with each other in what one world overproduces and another needs. You can exchange information, knowledge, and art, growing strong and wise together.

"It is a noble dream. We had it, in the Cluster— A dream? No. Its realization is before us. If only we are wise now, strong now. Now is the time to strike a blow for freedom and strike it well. You are not alone. All over the Empire men are fighting for the things you fight for now. But here, on Eron, the real decision will be made. Free men are counting on you.

"I call upon you then—all you who love freedom—to fight for it. But I call upon you, too, to fight wisely. Obey the commands of your leaders. If you have none, go where you can find them. Do not kill without reason; do not destroy wantonly. You have many blows to repay, but they are not the ones you should strike now. They are pointless; the future is yours. Eron is yours. Do not destroy what belongs to you.

"And you who still fight for the Empire—I call upon you to surrender. Lay down your arms. Your cause is lost. The Empire is dead. Your former allegiance will not be held against you. This is a new day. We are all born again, alike in heritage, alike in freedom. The galaxy is ours.

"For now—farewell. I will be with you soon."

He had stepped into the cubicle an old man. He had stood in front of the cameras, his head lifted, ageless, a symbol of man, free and unconquerable. He stepped out of it rejuvenated, his stride brisk and purposeful.

"What did you mean by that last sentence?" Horn asked.

"I'm going into Eron now. I'm needed there."

"How? Where? You—"

"How? By that private tubeway I saw below. Where? It doesn't matter much. I'll soon work myself to the place where I'm needed."

Horn saw that the old man's decision was unshakeable. "I'm going with you," he said firmly.

"Your place is here," Sair objected. "We can't afford to lose the north cap."

"You've forgotten one thing," Horn said quietly. "We don't know the secret of the Tubes. Without that—"

"We'll struggle along," Sair interrupted. "The Tubes won't fail. We can still use them. The Directors of Eron used them for centuries without knowing the secret. You said so yourself."

"I did," Horn said, "but did they? I keep remembering things. Tubes were activated all the time. Someone had the secret. Someone had to have it."

"SAIR!" The word thundered across the room.

Everyone turned. A screen had come to life on a distant panel. On it was the face of a middle-aged man, lined and worn but firm; over his head was a dark hood. Behind him was a scene of confusion: men shouting, running, talking, arguing, crossing the screen. It was familiar; it was a command center.

Beside the screen, a gold-uniformed technician was shocked. "I didn't do anything!" he blurted out. "It just started coming in."

The officer's eyebrows climbed toward his hairline. "Someone," he said, "has some unorthodox equipment."

Sair was already in front of the screen. "Turn down your volume," he said wryly. "It's a little loud."

The man turned to someone out of view and said something. He turned back. "Sair?" His voice was normal. "Sorry. Had to be sure I broke in. This is Entropy Cult headquarters. We've been coordinating the rebellion from here."

Sair did something with his fingers up close to his chest. On the screen, the man's eyes widened momentarily.

"Good!" he said. "We've been doing what we could. With the preparations we've made, that's been quite a bit. We've got duplicates of the controls over Eron that are in the control room you've captured. We've been closing fire doors, releasing extinguishers, cutting off water. The mobs have been the big problem, and they've calmed down since you spoke to them. I think we're over the hump."

"What's Duchane been doing?" Sair asked.

"The last we heard, he had his men in spacesuits and was blasting holes in the skin. That's effective only in the top few levels, but it slowed us down. We lost touch with him a while ago. How soon can you reach here with your staff to take over?"

"I'm leaving now," Sair said. "How shall I come?"

"Directors' tubeway. Sixth emergency stop. Count the flickers. Palm the red spot after the fifth flicker."

Horn stepped in front of the screen. "Is Wendre Kohlnar there?"

"Yes," said the man; "somewhere."

"Where is she?"

The man in the hood glanced helplessly over his shoulder. "I don't know. There isn't time." He stared at something far to the left. "What?" he shouted. "Who's that—?"

The screen went blank.

"What's happened?" Sair said, alarmed.

"Try to get that connection reestablished," Horn told the officer. He turned to Sair. "I don't like it. That could have been an attack. If Duchane should get hold of the controls in the area, he might swing the battle yet."

"What can we do?" Sair asked.

"Act on the assumption that Duchane has captured it, get there as fast as we can with the best chance to retake it, and pray he didn't use poison gas." Horn turned to the officer. "What luck?"

"The screen was unlisted. If we've managed to trace it correctly, it's dead."

"Are there any air suits handy?" Horn asked.

The officer shook his head thoughtfully.

Horn turned to Redblade. "Get as many spacesuits as possible out of the nearest personnel locks. And find me men who have fought in them."

As Redblade turned away quickly, Horn paused. Who could he leave in charge here? He looked toward Sair, but the old man shook his head, as if he had read Horn's mind.

"I'm going along," he said.

"We need fighters," Horn pointed out.

"You'd be surprised what I've learned and done in a long lifetime. I'm going."

There was no use arguing with him, and that left only one person to choose. "Redblade," Horn said. "You're in charge when I leave."

"Oh, no!" the pirate protested, shaking his bearded head defiantly. "I'm not missing out on—"

"You're the only one I can trust," Horn said quietly. The giant subsided. "Pick a dispatcher. As soon as I've left by the tubeway below, have him signal another car and send another man off. The men will press the gold disk, then watch five flickers of the red disk and press it. There'll be room for only one man at a time dressed in a suit. Understand?"

Redblade nodded. Horn turned and picked out a heavy suit from the growing pile on the floor. Redblade held it for him easily as he slipped into it. Just before Horn slipped on the left gauntlet, he slipped his unitron pistol into the slot provided in the right gauntlet. Horn wiggled his fingers to see if they worked easily. They did. The gun was ready. He was ready.

Five minutes later, the tube car slid to a stop. The door swung out. The corridor was stone and dimly lit. Horn stepped out quickly into the catacombs; he closed the stone door behind him. There was no one in sight.

To the right, the corridor darkened. Horn turned to the left. The corridor turned right within a few meters. There Horn found the first bodies; they were as ragged as the clothes they wore. Horn paused, held his breath, and brushed the intercom control on the front of his suit.

". . . and how long we wear these things—" someone was protesting.

"Silence!" The inside of Horn's helmet roared. "Only orders and reports will be given. When the gas is dissipated—"

Horn cut it off and let out his breath. That was Duchane. Cautiously, he moved to another corner. Beyond it was the back of a spacesuit. Horn ducked back quickly, breathing hard. A sentry. But he hadn't seen, and he couldn't hear.

Horn walked around the corner. This time the sentry was looking toward him. Through the helmet, his face was surprised. His mouth started to open; his right hand started up. Horn's hands were already against the suit's breastplate. One hand brushed the intercom off; the other shot the gun.

There was no noise. The man collapsed, his face still surprised. Horn felt the distant vibration of his fall. He flicked on his own intercom again. It was silent. He flicked it off.

Something tapped him on the back. Horn swung around, his gun pointing like an elongated index finger, and restrained himself from pulling the trigger. Sair's white hair gleamed through the helmet that faced him.

Horn looked to see if Sair's intercom switch was off; it was. He leaned forward and pressed his helmet against Sair's. "Stay here!" he ordered. "Wait until you've got a body of men. Then attack!"

"What are you going to do?"

"If the gas wasn't poisonous, I might be able to stop a slaughter."

"And Wendre is there, eh?"

"Yes," Horn admitted. "Now wait!"

He moved forward toward where the light slowly brightened. There was another guard. Horn caught him from behind, but he died the same way, silently. There were more of the ragged men on the floor; some of them had no marks on them, and others had their heads caved in.

Horn looked down at the man he had killed. The foot of his right boot was covered with blood and brains. Horn was glad he had killed him.

There was a wide doorway now and no more guards. Horn

turned on his intercom again. There was a sighing, background noise; it was the breathing of many men.

"Bring them out here," Duchane was saying. "We'll need some of them to show us the controls. Tie them up. . . ."

They would revive, Horn thought with vast relief as he slipped through the doorway into the large, rock-walled room. All around it, stone panels had opened outward. Behind them were indicators, gauges, switches, screens. Doors opened off the room into other lighted rooms. The room was filled with plastic and metal-clothed men. They were busy. He was one among many; he was unnoticed.

"Kill that one and that one," Duchane said casually. "They won't be useful. . . ."

Horn looked around trying to locate the man. He noticed that the unconscious men were being dragged toward a distant part of the room. Horn circled toward it, threading his way among over-turned tables and chairs and Duchane's own men. He located Duchane at last, saw the heavy, dominant face within the plastic bubble, and slipped closer.

Duchane glanced at him curiously as Horn approached and looked away as another man came up with a burden in his arms.

"Ah-h-h!" he breathed. "Wendre!" He looked down into the peaceful, golden face; the red-gold hair dripped like blood over the metal arm of the man who held her. "Treat her with care! I'll have use . . ."

Horn was behind Duchane now. His gun was a metal finger in Duchane's back, but the new General Manager of Eron could not feel it.

"You'll have use for nothing," Horn broke in. "I'm behind you, Duchane. Don't move! Not if you want to live."

"I knew that face," Duchane said wonderingly.

"Put her down," Horn said slowly. "Put her down carefully. If anyone moves, your master dies—and you know how long you will last then."

They stood like metal statues, all but the man who held Wendre. He started to bend toward the floor.

"Kill her!" Duchane screamed, throwing himself forward and to one side. "Kill him! We can't stop—"

He was twisting in the air, trying to bring his gun around, but the man who held Wendre was tilting his right hand under her body, bringing up the muzzle of the gun.

Horn's left hand cut off Duchane's screams by smashing the helmet. He was taking a breath; his face went blank and limp. The crash in the helmet was thunderous, but other thunder followed it so quickly that it was like a continuous roll. A hole appeared suddenly in the helmet of the man holding Wendre and was duplicated in his forehead, blackly. He kept on bending and fell slowly over the unconscious girl.

Horn never had time to watch the results. His gun was sweeping the room in an arc, spitting projectiles, and then he was diving through the air toward the protection of an overturned table, which was no protection at all, but concealment at least. And there was someone in the distant doorway, more than one, but the one in front was white-haired Sair, and his index finger was spraying bullets with incredible accuracy. Men were toppling, and the intercom was deafening.

And the room suddenly went black.

THE HISTORY

The unpredictable. . . .

There are always pebbles to make us stumble, sudden winds to chill our hopes or shred our fears, earthquakes to tumble our plans down around us. . . . Even the most careful analyses of the shrewdest historians go awry.

No one can predict the unpredictable.

Perhaps it is for the best. When life becomes predictable, it will be life no longer. Only the inanimate repeats itself. And even there, if one digs deep enough, one reaches a level where the principle of uncertainty makes prediction futile.

No one could have predicted longevity. No one, predicting it, could have calculated its effects. It was outside experience. Historians strive for the long view, but they ignore it in their extrapolations.

A man who could plan in terms of centuries and cultures and races—and live to see those plans reach fruition—would be an incalculable force. . . .

20

PRIME MOVER

Horn opened his eyes. The light was gentle and golden. It shifted. He felt something cool on his face, cool and wet. And then he realized that the light wasn't golden; it was only a reflection. There was a face above him; the face was golden. He should know that face. Even tired and without makeup it was beautiful.

He sat up quickly. His head reeled. Pain stabbed through it. He leaned back against the rough wall and closed his eyes. When he opened them again, she was still there.

"You'll be all right in a moment," Wendre said. "The pain goes away."

"What happened?" Horn asked dully.

"Duchane's forces were wiped out, but you had your helmet punctured by a stray bullet. You breathed some gas."

Horn looked down the corridor. There were men lying along the walls, some dead, some wounded, some unconscious. "Sair?" he asked.

"He's fine. They're working now to clean up the last of the resistance. He's a wonderful old man."

Horn remembered him standing in the doorway, throwing bullets into the armored bodies of Duchane's men, not missing a shot. "You don't know the half of it," he said wryly.

"There'll still be sporadic fighting and rioting for days, he says, but he thinks the organized resistance will be finished shortly."

"Duchane?" Horn asked.

"He's alive. They've put him in a cell." She nodded toward the far end of the corridor. It was straight until it faded in darkness.

"I was taken to Vantee," Horn said.

Wendre seemed to understand that he was explaining his absence. "I know. Sair told me. He told me how you escaped, too. It was brilliant, daring—"

"A man does what he has to do," Horn said, shrugging.

"Why did you have to do it?"

Horn looked up at her face, looked into her eyes staring at him curiously. This time he had no urge to look away. Whatever men mean by "love," he felt for Wendre. It wasn't just the desire to possess, though that was part of it. It was a need to see that no sorrow ever touched her. "I thought you might need me," he said steadily.

Her eyes fell away. "Do you expect me to believe that? When you killed my father?"

"I didn't know you then."

"Why did you do it?" she said suddenly.

"For money," Horn said.

"I was afraid of that. It might have been different if you had done it for revenge or an ideal or any passion—"

She was turning away. Horn caught her hand impetuously. "Wait! I'm not asking for anything except understanding." She stopped and turned back. "Your father was not a man except to the few people who knew him personally. To everyone else he was, at the most, a symbol, at the least, an institution. Symbols and institutions don't bleed or suffer; they are things to be shaped, changed, shattered as the need arises. By becoming General Manager of Eron, your father gave up his humanity.

"That's part of it," Horn continued, "but only a small part. To understand the rest, you have to understand my past." Slowly at first and then more rapidly as the words came to him, he told

Wendre about the Cluster and his life there, about the way he had been hired to assassinate her father, about his difficulties in reaching Earth and then in reaching the mesa, about Wu and Lil, about his arrival on Eron and what had happened afterward. She listened attentively, soberly, her head turned away a little.

"But why I did it," he finished, "I really can't explain because I don't understand it myself. There was the money, but that wasn't important in itself. It was only a symbol of what a man can take from the universe if he is strong enough and clever enough. All my life I'd done that and now I had a chance to do something that would really prove to myself and everyone that I was stronger and smarter. . . . It wasn't the shooting, you see, it was the getting there and outwitting the people who tried to stop me and overcoming the obstacles, and then when I had him, there in my sights, I had to shoot, because I'd taken money to do it.

"But don't ask me why. I don't know. It was another man, and I can't understand him. Men change, of course. That's axiomatic: a man is never the same two seconds in a row. And when a man lives hard and lives through what I've lived through these last days, he changes fast and he changes a lot. I'm not trying to absolve myself. This hand did it; this finger pulled the trigger."

She shook her head as if she couldn't understand. "To kill an unarmed man, cold-bloodedly, without warning—"

"Unarmed!" Horn exclaimed. "With thousands of guards, dozens of ships, and the firepower concentrated there! And what of the billions of people your father killed, cold-bloodedly, without warning— No! I don't mean that. When a man lives by his wits, you see, it's him against the universe, and he gets to thinking that he's all alone; everyone's all alone, working against the rest like dogs fighting for a bone. But it isn't true. We're linked together, all of us, just as the worlds are linked together by the Tubes of Eron."

"It's no use, don't you see?" she said passionately. "I've got to hate you. Nothing can change the fact that you killed my father."

"Then why did you leave instructions to turn the control room over to me?"

"Because you were right—about Eron being rotten. Once, perhaps, the Empire was worthwhile; once it had something to give to humanity. Now it was only taking. The only way I could save anything that was good about Eron was to help pull it down; you said that only Sair could save it. I thought Sair was dead, and I thought perhaps I could make up for that, a little. If you were right about that I thought you might be right about other things."

"I see," Horn said. He pushed himself up slowly. His head had stopped aching. He started walking down the corridor and bent to scoop up a pistol that a dead man would never use again.

"Where are you going?" Wendre asked.

He looked around to see her walking beside him. "I'm going to talk to Duchane."

"Why?"

"There are two things I want to find out: who hired me and who has the secret of the Tubes."

"And the person who hired you had to know my father's plans at the time of the surrender on Quarnon Four. I told you I was the only person who knew them. Why didn't you suspect me?"

"I did," Horn said, "for a moment."

"Why don't you suspect me now?"

He glanced at her quickly and away. "I believe you."

"I'll go with you," she said hurriedly. "Maybe I can help."

"You don't have to."

"I owe you something. You saved my life three times."

"The first two don't count. One was by instinct, the other by strategy."

They stopped talking as they approached the cells. Horn recognized them; he had been behind one of these barred doors not many days ago. Behind one of them was Duchane, one-time Director of Security, one-time General Manager of Eron, prisoner. He leaned against the back wall, his face dark and thoughtful, his arms folded across his chest. He looked up as Wendre approached the door and Horn stayed back beyond recognition in the shadows. Duchane's lip curled.

"The only thing worse than a renegade is a civilized woman who has gone native," he said. "I hope you have pleasant memories of the way you survived the downfall of the greatest empire man has ever known—and how you helped bring it down."

"I won't argue with you," Wendre said quietly. "You wouldn't understand actions not motivated by self-interest."

"With what I've seen of fear and cowardice and treachery in the last few days," Duchane said bitterly, "I'm glad for the first time that I'm not of the pure golden blood."

"You're not?" Wendre exclaimed. "Then that explains—"

"What?" Duchane asked violently.

"Your methods," Wendre murmured.

"Do you know what it's like to be all Eronian except a minute fraction and have that imperceptible dilution bar you from all you want? Do you know what it is to have strength and ability and courage and be forbidden to use them because a remote ancestor was careless? Do you know what it is to try to pass and wonder, always, when the truth may spring upon you and tear away everything you have won?

"Methods!" Duchane exclaimed. "Yes, I had my methods, and they worked. They should; I learned them from your father. Nothing is important but success; means are only stepping stones to goals. You can't imagine what I had to do to get where I wanted." His face darkened, remembering. "I ordered my mother's death; she was a dangerous link to my past. But it didn't matter. It made me General Manager of Eron."

"For a few days," Wendre said. "Your methods made the downfall of the Empire inevitable. More than anyone else, you were the one who destroyed it. Was it worthwhile—for a few days?"

"Better to rule for a few days," Duchane said proudly, "than to serve for a lifetime."

"You wouldn't have ruled long in any case," Horn said, speaking for the first time, "without the secret of the Tubes."

Duchane peered futilely into the shadows. "That's true," he said slowly. He looked back at Wendre. "But you would have given it to me. You would have fought me and suffered but in the end you would have told."

"I couldn't. I didn't know it."

"You had to," Duchane said bewilderedly. "You were pure blood; it would have worked for you. And Kohlnar must have told you—"

"It didn't work for me," Wendre said slowly, "and he told me nothing more than you were told. Perhaps he didn't know either. Perhaps nobody knew. It was a joke, a joke on the Empire, but a bigger joke on the Golden Folk. We were so proud and secure in our secret, and we never had it."

"It's a lie!" Duchane protested. "Kohlnar knew. He had to know—"

"It was a mistake then," Horn said quickly, recognizing that Duchane was telling the truth, "having the old man killed."

"I didn't!" Duchane came forward, grabbed the bars, peered between them. "Oh, I thought of it. But it was too dangerous. I was bound to be suspected— *Who are you!*"

"The assassin," Horn said softly.

"Then you know I didn't do it!" Duchane said violently, pulling on the bars that separated them. "You know who hired you—"

"But I don't." Horn stepped forward so that the light fell across his face.

Recognition was instantaneous. Duchane fell back several paces. "You! The assassin. The man who sneaked behind me a little while ago. The guard who was with Matal. That's fantastic. And it wasn't Matal. Matal was dead. It looked like Matal, but it couldn't have been. Dead men don't walk. Fantastic!" His eyes slitted thoughtfully; they opened again. "You were with him; who was he?"

"I don't know that, either," Horn said. "What about Fenelon and Ronholm?"

"Oh, they're dead; they're dead," Duchane tossed off absently. "I asked the Index that question. It gave me some very interesting data. Reports of dead men walking and two living men being in two places at the same time. All of the men were of the same general build: short and fat.

"The prototype was a thief, a ragged old man seen frequently with animal companions. He appeared here and there, all over the Empire. He has been imprisoned countless times, and he has always escaped immediately. The record goes back a long way"—Duchane was coming forward, his right hand moving toward the inside of his packet—"right to the beginning of—"

"Look out!" someone shouted. "He's got a gun!"

The pistol in Horn's hand reacted almost with a life of its own. It jerked up and spat silently. Duchane gasped. His eyes looked past them, wide and staring, as his hand slowly slipped away from his jacket. He folded quietly to the floor beside the bars.

"Killing," Wendre said dully, "killing. Do you always have to be killing?" She turned, her head bent, and walked quickly away.

"It seems like it," Horn said. He swung around. Wu was standing behind him. He was in his space breeches once more, the single suspender, the green synsilk shirt, and the skullcap. Lil, perched on his shoulder, stared one-eyed at Duchane's crumpled body.

"Such," Lil said sadly, "is the end of all ambition."

"You seem to make a habit of saving me," Horn said, letting the cord pull his gun up to his chest.

Wu shrugged. "It is a pleasure to lengthen the years of one who has so few to spare."

"Where have you been? The last I saw of you, you were being taken to Vantee with me."

"The prison has not yet been built that will hold us, eh, Lil? Since then we have been here and there, as whim and fortune dictate. It is a good time for picking up diamonds."

Horn knelt beside the bars and reached through them to Duchane's jacket. He felt inside it. When he pulled back his hand, it held a sheaf of papers. "I didn't understand how they could miss a gun," Horn said. "He was unarmed."

Horn opened the pages and scanned them, his eyes flicking back and forth, the pages turning. When he looked up, his eyes were distant. "It's a report on you," he said. "You've been at almost every Tube activation."

"So?" Wu said. "I had not thought we attended so many. But they are times of ceremony, where even the hours are jeweled."

"The Directors didn't know the secret of the Tube," Horn said slowly. "And yet the Tubes were activated. Someone else had to know the secret, and yet—I said it once—the secret couldn't pass down through the hands of any other group without the Directors discovering it. But if a man lived for fifteen hundred years—"

"I!" Wu chuckled. "If we had known the secret, Lil, we wouldn't have needed to steal diamonds, eh? We would have sat us down somewhere, and the worlds would have brought them to us."

"There were six people on the platform at the Dedication," Horn went on inexorably, unheeding. "I kept thinking that one of them had to know the secret. But they were at other activations singly. Wendre told me that. It couldn't be any one of them. It had to be all of them. But it wasn't. It wasn't any of them. But you were there. You were closer to the platform than anyone else. It has to be you, Wu. It has to be you."

"Reductio ad absurdum," Lil said pontifically.

"But logical, dear friend," Wu said. "Very logical." His voice had changed. It was firmer, colder, harder.

"You made me shoot Duchane," Horn went on. "He was going to tell me something about you, and you made me shoot him. Not you. You didn't shoot him. You got someone else to do it for you. *Somebody has pushed*," he muttered. "There's a pattern in that. Someone who thinks like that might readily hire an assassin."

"A pretty argument," Wu said. "But it doesn't quite hold true. You see, I have no objection to doing my own killing."

It should not have surprised Horn to see the pistol in the yellow hand that Wu thrust forward out of his ragged green sleeve. It did; he had been unable to believe what logic proved. He stared at the gun and looked back at Wu's lined face. He could not remember now why he had thought the face was harmless and benign. This was a face that had been weathered by a millennium and a half; these were eyes that had seen too much. The face was old and wise and evil.

"It's true then," Horn said dazedly.

"Should I tell you?" Wu asked. "Of course. What difference does it make? You've come too close to the truth, about me and about the Tubes, and so you must die. I hope you will let me explain before I kill you. You want to know the meaning behind all this. And it is a vast relief for me to speak. You can't know the immense burden of keeping a secret for a thousand years. There was Lil, of course, but, as fine a companion as she is, she isn't human."

"And are you?" Horn asked sharply.

"I'm not at all sure I am," Wu said carefully.

"You did hire me then?"

"Yes, I hired you to kill Kohlnar. I hired many men, but you were the only one who even reached the foot of the mesa where Sunport once stood. But the story begins a long time before that."

"A thousand years before?"

"Exactly. Eron did not rise haphazardly. It was the only empire that was built, and the tools we used were challenge and response and a little subtle guidance. I choose Eron as my instrument of empire because it had bred a strong, hungry race. Humanity needed the Tube, and it needed Eron to force it upon them. Listen carefully, Horn, and you will be enlightened before you die; you will hear a strange story of human emotions and how they benefit humanity and of good intentions and how they change."

"I'm listening," Horn said grimly, judging the distance between them, estimating his chances. The distance was too great and the chances too slim. He forced himself to wait.

"The Tube, then. Man needed it if he was to develop an interstellar civilization instead of isolated, divergent, spatially determined cultures which could contribute almost nothing to the race. With the best of motives, then, we gave man the Tube, Lil and I. If mankind were to continue as a single, functioning race, we had to abolish that deadly limitation: the speed of light."

"Since the speed of light is a limitation in our universe," Horn said, moving a little, "then the Tubes enclose a space that is not in our universe."

Wu shook his head appreciatively. "I was afraid your experience in the Tube might lead you to that conclusion, and a scientist, with that clue, might be able to activate a Tube. But it isn't likely. It has been recognized, for longer than I have lived, that gravity is a consequence of the geometry of physical space, which is determined by matter. In other words, it is the matter in the universe that curves space around itself, which effect we recognize as gravity. But it is another thing to build a space not of this universe."

Horn nodded and edged a little closer.

"Light," Wu went on, "is affected by this curvature of space. It, too, is curved. And in this universe of matter and curved space, speed is restricted to that of light. But outside this universe, this isn't true. Lil and her people knew this a long time ago. When the uranium in their cavern was gone, they were forced to learn the nature of energy and matter and space and time. They became the greatest mathematicians the universe has ever known."

"Go on," Horn said, sliding one foot forward imperceptibly.

Wu wiggled his gun. "No, my friend. Do not move. Not if you wish to hear the rest. Our problem, you see, was to provide within this universe a space which was not of this universe. A star was our power source; Lil's mind was the matrix. Inside the energy cylinder of the Tube was created something never before known: space shielded from the warping effect of matter, shielded from gravity, if you like. Inside the Tube, the universe shaped by matter doesn't exist; the unnatural limitation set upon velocity by this matter-determined universe does not exist. All our terms are meaningless there: light, sound, energy, matter, velocity, distance. Anything in the Tube exists, if at all, as an anomaly in its own miniature universe with its own space folded around itself; the Tube, by its nature, must reject it."

"Then only you and Lil can activate a Tube."

"Only Lil," Wu corrected. "And it has kept us busy. But I get ahead of my story. This fact, though, influenced our choice of Eron as the instrument through which humanity would be reunited. It would have been physically impossible for Lil to have activated Tubes in two or more civilizations. That wasn't desirable for other reasons; it would have meant conflict, disunion, destruction. We chose Eron."

"Ah, those were days to live in," Lil croaked reminiscently.

"They were indeed," Wu agreed. "With the best of intentions, we gave Eron the Tube and built around it a myth of secrecy and greatness; the Golden Folk were quick to believe and go on to build their own myths. At crucial points we helped the Empire continue its growth until only the Pleiades Cluster remained outside. You, my short-lived friend, won't understand how we began to change. Power is habit-forming. We grew addicted to it. Few things survive the centuries' slow decay: senses grow dull; passions grow weak; and ideals die. Only the taste for power lives on as an excuse for survival."

"You began to meddle then," Horn said grimly, "for the sake of meddling." He couldn't move toward Wu; he could never get close enough to hit him or knock the gun aside before Wu fired. His own gun, nestled under his left arm, would be quick to his hand, but Wu's finger would be quicker. *Wait!* Horn told himself. *Wait!*

"True," Wu said. "We meddled, but not in the amateurish connotations of the word. We were skillful. Kohlnar needed little help in conquering the Cluster; his own fiery determination carried him on. But this was only postponing the slowly approaching crisis, and the longer it was delayed, the more dangerous it became. Eron was decaying; revolt was inevitable. The only chance to save it was to precipitate the crisis. Against a premature rebellion, Eron might win and gain a second chance."

"So you hired me to assassinate Kohlnar," Horn said. His right hand was inching across his waistband toward the pistol butt hanging above it.

"I was wrong," Wu said. "Even the experience of fifteen hundred years can be wrong; even Lil's fantastic mathematical ability can't balance the billions of terms implicit in the star-flung problem. We miscalculated. Eron lost."

"And you've lost, too," Horn said.

"We?" Wu chuckled. "Oh, no. We never lose. There will be more strings to pull, more puppets to dance. We will transplant ourselves to the new focal center of power, the Cluster. It is disorganized now, but it will soon grow strong. It will shape the Empire into something new and dynamic, and we will shape the Cluster."

"Haven't you done enough?" Horn asked. "Isn't it time for men to work out their own destinies?"

"And remove my one reason for existence?" Wu asked mockingly. "No, my idealistic friend, I can't permit that. And it is time for you to die. Kohlnar is dead. Duchane is dead. Now you."

Horn's eyes widened briefly. Behind Wu something had moved.

"An old trick," Wu said, smiling. "Subtly done. But it won't work." His hand tightened on the gun.

Horn tensed himself. The flicker of movement came again. Red-gold. Wendre! What was she doing? She hated him. She had said so herself.

Wendre threw herself toward Wu's back.

"No trick! No trick!" Lil screamed, glancing behind.

Wu twisted away instinctively. Horn threw himself to one side, his pistol jumping into his hand. For a moment he couldn't shoot for fear that the bullet would pass through Wu into Wendre.

Wendre missed. She slipped past, and Horn's response was instantaneous. He did not miss.

THE HISTORY

Giver of gifts. . . .

The galactic frontier: new worlds without end, virgin planets lying fertile for the human sperm, a million unspoiled continents rich with every treasure, black soil and mountain dawns and mysterious shores of a million seas. But the greatest gift was freedom.

With the coming of the Empire, the frontier became the marches.

The influence of great civilizations have always reached beyond their immediate borders. Around them, like armor, they created protective states which kept at bay the alien hordes. And when the civilizations began to decay, the marches turned their martial talents inward against their creators.

Eron created the Cluster by the challenge of its power and crushed it when it refused to be absorbed.

But Eron was rotten. The Empire could not last. Its response to challenge was not leadership but force.

Eron was a fossil. Its continued existence was a deadly threat to all humanity. . . .

21

CHALLENGE

Horn sat in the exotic luxury of the golden room and squirmed. Under him, the chair was too soft and slick; he sank down into it so far that it would take him minutes to get out. Around him, the colors were too indefinite; the pictures glowing in the wall were too meaningless. There was nothing to look at.

He had been waiting for half an hour and he wished he hadn't come.

What did Wendre Kohlnar have to say to him that she had not said before?

Soaked, scrubbed, trimmed, shaved, Horn felt like a different person. He had stared into the mirror at a lean, dark-faced stranger. He hadn't recognized the suggestion of understanding in the once-hard eyes, the lines of suffering and compassion around the once-immobile mouth. He had grown old and wise in the last few months.

He was glad that he had turned down the rich synsilks and furs. It was good to be back in the sober, durable, woven cords of the Cluster.

Horn shifted again. Whatever Wendre had to say, he wished she would come and say it. There had been seven days since he had seen her, seven days in which she could have summoned him and he would have come, seven days since the major fighting had ended. Now, long after he had stopped hoping, only hours before he was due at the ship that would take him back to the Cluster, she had asked him here to wait—and wait.

He remembered the last time he had seen her. He remembered how Wu had collapsed, tiredly, almost gratefully. He had cheated death for the last time.

Horn's gun had followed the swooping, screaming thing called Lil. His finger had tightened on the trigger and relaxed. He couldn't shoot her. What had she done except befriend a man? She hadn't sought vengeance against the race that had exterminated her own. She had attached herself to one of them and served him, too well. . . .

And then it had been too late. Lil was gone.

"Why didn't you shoot it?" Wendre asked. She had picked herself up from the floor.

"You heard?"

"Enough to know that she was dangerous. Why didn't you shoot?"

"I couldn't."

"Think what she could do if we don't find her!"

"How can we find her?" Horn asked helplessly. "She might be anything, anywhere. And if we found her, how could we hold her? I wonder if a bullet would have done any damage. I wonder, too, if the master switch—the one that would cut off the Tubes—is Lil's life."

"But it could be important. She might—"

"I wonder. Wu was the human. Without him, what could that alien thing do? The damage would be insignificant compared with the chance of destroying the Tubes. The damage Wu did was subtle and all-pervading; Lil doesn't know enough about people for that."

Horn knelt beside Wu's body. A red stain spread darkly over the torn green shirt from the hole in the chest. The heartbeat was still; the breath was stopped. Wu was dead. There was something strangely pitiful about the limp body in the tattered clothes. It was so small and weak to have done so much, so finally dead after having evaded death so long.

It was irony that the man who had preached the social theory of history to him had been the greatest proof of the personal theory. Wu had been the somebody who pushed. He had stood outside the river and guided its course. He had guided Horn, too. He, more than Horn, had pulled the trigger that fired the bullet that killed Kohlnar. He had wielded the forces that shape empires and men's destinies. But Horn had escaped and been himself a shaper; perhaps Wu's death had been implicit in that moment.

Horn had been bred on individualism and independence; events had forced him to recognize the truths of interrelation and interdependence. He recognized now that there was no sharp division between them. They were not a dichotomy; they blended together inseparably. They could not be equated with good and bad abstractly. Circumstances dictated which one should predominate, which one should be stressed, which one should be desired.

Horn had looked up. Wendre had been standing beside him still. "Why did you save me?"

For a moment her eyes had flashed. "You saved me," she said. "Now we are even." And she walked away.

Horn had stared after her with eyes that burned, but he did not follow. He went to get Sair and found him gone. In the moment of victory he had slipped away. They searched for him; it was like locating one ant in a city-sized anthill. He returned, as he had gone, alone, unnoticed.

He had been sitting in a chapel, he said; he had been thinking. Although he was not a religious man, he had been forced to recognize occasionally a power greater than a man or the sum of men. It was incredible that a few men should have defeated the greatness of Eron. Surely they owed it to something or someone else, whatever it was called. A man can sometimes be stronger or wiser than he is; sometimes he can reach his dreams.

"But not too often," Horn had said. "The fulfillment of dreams can become an obsession. A man may be tempted to play god, and there is only one end to that—tragedy for his creation, destruction for himself."

He had taken Sair to see the body—and the body had been gone. "What did Duchane say about dead men walking?" Horn asked, incredulous.

"Duchane?"

Horn had rushed to the bars. The door swung open. "He's gone, too! They were both dead. I'm sure of it."

"Of course they were," Sair said, chuckling. "The bodies have been collected; they're probably burnt by now. It doesn't matter. I'd have liked to have seen the man who built Eron and the Empire, but it is only a fancy. That era is ended, and he is ended with it. All men must die, even demigods. Death is Nature's way of canceling her mistakes, of making room for the new and the different—"

The little noise the door made as it slid aside broke into Horn's thoughts. He looked up. Wendre was standing in the room. He was surprised at her appearance. She was beautiful, true, and rest and care had made her young again. But he had expected, unconsciously, that she would wear something as lovely and revealing as the gown she had worn at the Dedication. Instead her suit was blue, tailored, and practical.

So much for vanity, Horn thought wryly as he struggled to his feet.

"Have you been waiting long?" Wendre asked.

"Long enough."

She flushed. "You have a talent for saying the wrong thing."

"Would you like me to lie and flatter?"

"Oh, be as blunt and tactless as you like. I could endure it if you would only say the right thing occasionally."

"The right thing?" Horn repeated.

Wendre shook her head wearily. "You don't understand women at all. I kept you waiting so long because I couldn't decide whether to wear a beautiful gown or a sensible suit. Now I'm being frank."

"And you're wearing the suit," Horn said gravely. "That should mean something, but I don't understand women."

Wendre sighed. "Yes. It means I'm being frank. Let me give you three examples of why you don't understand women. First, you don't ask the right questions. Second, you don't say the right words. Third, you—"

"Wait a minute," Horn interrupted. "What is the right question?"

Wendre took a deep breath. "You asked me: 'Why did you save me?' You should have said: 'Why did you come back?'"

"Why did you?" Horn asked.

"The right question's no good unless it's at the right time."

"Well, what are the right words?"

She hesitated and then said swiftly, "Words with 'love' among them. You said a lot of words, but that wasn't one of them."

"But I thought you knew," Horn stammered. "I mean—I thought I—"

"A woman wants to hear it."

"But you said you hated me," Horn protested.

"I said I had to hate you. There's a difference. And anyway, that's the third thing. A woman doesn't want to be taken at her word, not her first word anyway. Don't you know that a woman wants to be talked into something?" She paused for breath.

"I love you, Wendre," Horn said steadily. "Why did you come back?"

"I just told you," Wendre said softly.

"You can forget that I killed your father?"

She winced. "No. And neither can you. But you've told me how it happened. I believe you and understand. We can live with it, I think. Nobody else knows and nobody else matters. It's just us. You see, I happen to love you—"

Without quite knowing how it happened, Horn found her in his arms. After a moment, Horn lifted his head and asked, "Why me? Why a barbarian?"

Wendre shrugged. "Maybe a woman loves a man who makes her feel like a woman. You're the only one who has ever done that."

"You could leave all this," Horn asked, "and go with me to the Cluster?"

"Yes," she said. "You see—"

"You see, she has no choice," someone said behind them.

Horn whirled around. It was Sair, white-haired but stout and hearty in cords like Horn's. "What do you mean?"

"Wendre can't stay here. I told her that several days ago. Rebellion often has its sentimental reaction. We can't afford to let a tender remnant of the Empire remain behind as a nucleus for a new tyranny."

Horn's arms had dropped away from Wendre. He stepped back, looking between Sair and Wendre. "She wouldn't do that."

"Of course she wouldn't. Not the woman she is now. But people change. The memories of an older Wendre might enhance the glories of empire and forget its deformities. Or, if she does not change, her children would be dangerous. No, she must go to the Cluster and marry a barbarian."

"I see," Horn said heavily.

"What do you see?" Wendre demanded.

"I see why you sent for me."

"You don't see anything," Wendre said fiercely. "You think I only wanted you because I couldn't stay here, because I didn't want to go to the Cluster alone. You're wrong. I only learned today that you were leaving. I hoped that you would come to me, that I wouldn't have to go to you."

She looked at him proudly, demanding belief. Horn waited.

She moistened her lips. "I was just about to tell you when Sair came in. That's why I was wearing this suit; I was trying to be honest with you. Oh, I admit it makes a difference, my having to go to the Cluster. It adds need to my love, and it becomes a part of it. Here a woman doesn't need the qualities in a man that she needs in a less civilized culture. In the Cluster, she needs strength and courage and skill in a man, for her children as well as herself. And her recognition of that is just as instinctive and valid as love—"

"You'd better believe her, boy," Sair said softly. "You'll never find another woman like her."

"Oh, I believe her," Horn said. "I was just wondering how I could live with a former Director of Eron."

"Whatever a woman is," Wendre said, "she's that second and a woman first."

After a few minutes, Sair coughed. "I only wish to remind you," he said, as they drew apart, "that you have just two hours before the ship leaves for Quarnon Four."

"Aren't you coming with us?" Wendre asked.

"Not now but shortly. I must wait for the interim governor of Eron."

"Where is he coming from?" Horn asked.

"From the Cluster."

"Are you sure you can trust him?"

"No," Sair answered. "I'm not sure of anyone. But he has the proper background of democratic government; he was once chief executive of Merope Three. He is passionately attached to his home. He won't be happy here."

Wendre looked puzzled. "Is that good?"

"He can leave only when the Empire is prepared to govern itself. He will work hard for that day so that he can go home. He will die before then; this isn't an overnight job. But he won't know that. And there are other safeguards."

"The Cult?" Horn said.

"For one. Through its part in the rebellion, it has won the popularity of a fighting religion. It must, necessarily, have much to say about future decisions. The Cult head will be an adviser to the governor. In addition, there are the troops and their commanders, the technicians, the laborers, and many other classes. All of them have different desires and different ideas about how to gain them. Multiply this by the number of worlds in the Empire and you have a conflict of interests which can never be reconciled."

"But isn't that inefficient?" Wendre asked.

"It is indeed. But inefficiency is one of the penalties of freedom. You can't be efficient unless you can force people into channels and make them go where they don't want to go. There was enough of that under the Empire. These are different times. Inefficiency and freedom are vital. The governor's prime responsibility is to preserve Eron as the hub of an interstellar civilization. When power is diffuse, no one can gather enough to take over Eron and levy toll on the shipments passing through."

"And no one can attack the Cluster," Horn added.

"True," Sair agreed, "although there is little chance of that in any case. As a unit, the Empire is finished, and nothing less than total power could make an impression on the resurgent Cluster. It lost its freedom once, lost it bitterly; it will never lose it again until it gives it up as something outworn and useless. No, Eron is unimportant; the future lies with the Cluster and the newer cultures that will rise beyond the Cluster. As a Tube center Eron must be preserved, at least until scientists, working from the clues Horn has gathered, can duplicate the Tube or find a substitute. But the Cluster will be the dominant human culture for many centuries to come."

"You said that the Cluster would give up its freedom," Horn said, his voice puzzled. "I don't understand."

"The love of freedom dies as the memory of its alternative fades. Oh, it's not a sudden thing. It takes generations, centuries. But gradually it slips away. And it's more than that. There is a time for freedom, just as there is a time for empire. Only Eron, with its dynamic hunger for empire and its efficiency, could have unified human civilization and kept it united with the Tubes against the forces that sought to scatter it through the stars. Then, when its job is done, empire disappears, and it is freedom's turn to revive the human spirit by the challenge of the infinite horizon. And then, when men begin to grow too far apart, empire will return to unite them again."

"That's a cynical viewpoint," Horn said slowly.

"I'm an old man. I can afford no longer the luxury of ideals. If I am to achieve results recognizable within my few remaining years, I must be practical. So I set up checks and balances on Eron, and I admit that it is faulty but necessary. I see that the freedom we have won is good, but I admit that it is impermanent and not always the best thing for humanity. I think I can even see a good aspect to your Mr. Wu; it is possible that he made a great contribution to the human race."

"How?" Wendre asked quickly.

"Empire and freedom have seldom been exchanged so efficiently. Always before there have been interregnums of chaos. Sometimes they lasted for centuries. We enter this new period of expansion with the backbone of empire to give us strength, its communication facilities to give us the ability to react quickly. It may be because of him that this is so, and we may need both of these things badly before the job of freedom is done."

"And what is that," Horn asked, "aside from this business of reviving the human spirit?"

"Who knows?" Sair said. He shrugged. "There will be something that only freedom can do, that would have broken the Empire and with it the human race. I can think of any number of possible threats. The natural threats, in which the metal of a race is tempered or shattered: perhaps our part of the galaxy may sweep into an area of cosmic dust. The external competitions: we've never met a competitive alien race at our stage of technology; it's time our luck ran out. The internal competitions: mutations. . . . I've been dreaming lately about the Silent Stars."

"The Silent Stars?" Wendre repeated.

"Beyond the Cluster," Horn explained. "Some of the worlds sent colonists out to them over one hundred years ago. They haven't been heard from since; other ships have gone out to trade and haven't come back. It isn't exactly sinister yet; they might have had to go on farther than expected or been delayed in building their technology to a level capable of supporting space flight. But people have begun to speculate."

"I wonder," Sair said, his eyes distant. "I wonder which it will be."

"Who knows?" Horn repeated. "Wu might have," he added suddenly.

"That's a strange thing to say." Sair looked at Horn with narrowed eyes.

Horn nodded. "I guess it was. I got to thinking about what you said, the possibility that Wu helped the human race. He had many eyes and a long time to grow wise. He could have been a great force for good. To the blind, historical forces he could have been eyes and a purpose. Sure, when something moves, somebody has pushed, but that isn't good or bad in itself. It depends on the situation and the pusher."

"You're learning wisdom," Sair said. "Only the circumstances determine good and evil. And only the future can say what the circumstances actually were."

"Then there is no firm basis for acting at all," Wendre objected. "What you do for the best of motives may be the worst thing to do."

"Exactly," Sair said dryly. "It is a commonplace that more harm is done by well-intentioned fools than by the most unscrupulous villains. A wise man learns not to judge. He may set himself certain standards, but he recognizes that they are only a personal pattern to guide his own conduct and that other standards have the same validity. Some men are interested only in means; some work for immediate goals like freedom; a few are concerned with results far in the future."

"But that would take a wisdom beyond humanity," Horn said seriously.

"Perhaps." Sair nodded, smiling. "Only the future can judge. You'd better go now; you'll miss the ship."

They turned and started for the ship that would take them to the Cluster where the future would be shaped. There, events were moving toward decision.

THE HISTORY

Challenge. . . .

Six months after the fall of the Eron Empire, it arrived. It came from the far edge of the Cluster, from the world nearest the Silent Stars. It was a scream, a cry, a plea.

Its coming was predictable.

The Quarnon Wars had built a magnificent, deadly armada of fighting ships and trained a generation of fighting men to use them. But the decaying culture of Eron had to be destroyed; it would have collapsed before the first assault.

Only a people in the first vigor of a new culture could rise to meet that challenge.

On ten thousand worlds, man looked up into the night sky with sober eyes and laid aside his tools and picked up his weapons. The long battle of man's survival had already begun.

An enemy was coming. And this time it was not human.

Response: hopeful. . . .

EPILOGUE

The Historian sighed and put down his brush. He rubbed his hand down through the snowy hair and over the face of Peter Sair. The hair darkened. The face rippled and began to flow. It dripped to the table, and it was a parrot. Lil stared up at the Historian with one fierce eye.

"Sometimes," the parrot said, "I wish I had left you in the catacombs of Eron with a hole through your black heart."

"I wish you had," Wu said slowly.

A millennium and a half. Personal desires were dead; even the instinct to survive was gone. But a man cannot die while the survival of his race depends on him.

"I don't see the necessity of this mummery—"

"Necessity?" Wu said. "Free will is a necessity. And the illusion is more important than the reality."

He picked up the top sheet of manuscript. The ancient Chinese characters marched in columns across the page from right to left. He read the last sentence once more, picked up the brush, and added a final character.

The end. But it was only the end of a long, long chapter. Another had already begun.

AFTERWORD

Some creations take on a life of their own. That's the way it was with *Star Bridge*.

Gerald Jonas reviewed a reprint edition of *Star Bridge* in 1977, twenty-two years after the first publication as a Gnome Press hardcover followed by an Ace Books paperback. Jonas wrote: "The book is not a recognized 'classic' of that period. . . . It stirred no controversy, won no awards, added nothing to the reputation of its authors. Not only had I never read it before, I had not even heard of it. I mention these facts only to help the reader understand my astonishment at discovering that this obscure collaboration between Williamson and Gunn reads more like a collaboration between Heinlein and Asimov. The concept is pure, classic science fiction. A vast empire spans the galaxy, controlled from the planet Eron which alone holds the secret to faster-than-light travel."

Neither Jack Williamson nor I had any idea we were up to anything like that. It was an accident it happened at all. I was working as an editor for Western Printing & Lithographing Company (which selected, edited, and printed Dell's paperback books) in Racine, Wisconsin, and talked the editor-in-chief into sending me to Chicago to attend my very first Science Fiction World Convention in late August of 1952. I'd been writing SF stories for four years and having them published for three, but it was my first encounter with other writers and editors and agents. I met some of my heroes, including John Campbell, Tony Boucher, Bob Bloch, Clifford Simak, and many others, including Fred Pohl (my agent at that time), who told me he'd sold four stories that I didn't know about and on the strength of that I went back and told my boss that I was resigning to go back to full-time writing.

But the biggest event was standing in line at registration and turning to find behind me a face I recognized from the backs of some of my favorite novels. "You're Jack Williamson," I said, and he admitted that he was. It was the beginning of a long friendship that ended only with his death at the age of ninety-eight. We met again in early 1953 when Jack and his wife, Blanche, visited Kansas City, where her sister lived, and at that time Jack mentioned that he'd had writer's block for the past decade and would I be interested in working on a novel he'd started and couldn't continue. I was writing my first novel, *This Fortress World,* but I would finish that soon and I agreed to look at his manuscript.

Jack sent me the first fifty pages (the opening chapter as I rewrote it) and 150 pages of notes about the background and the characters. I developed an outline that Jack approved and then wrote the novel (and rewrote it once) in three months, and Jack approved that. Our mutual agent (Fred again) sold it to Marty Greenberg of Gnome Press, a small specialty press that was publishing more science fiction than anyone. Gnome published *Star Bridge* and *This Fortress World* in 1955. He paid us a $500 advance for each book, but since I shared the royalties for *Star Bridge* with Jack, that amounted to a total of $750 for six months' writing. Even in the early 1950s when my wife and I were living in my parents' home rent free (they had moved in with my physician brother a couple of miles away, and I was using a basement room as an office) and my brother was providing free health care, that wasn't a living wage. I decided to give up space epics and collaborations, and focus on near-future issues, and to break up future novels into novelettes or novellas publishable individually in magazines. That's when I derived my later motto "Sell it twice." Most of my later novels were written that way.

Marty Greenberg was a good publisher but not so good at paying his authors. Jack and I never got any share of the paperback royalties, and it was only some years later, when Gnome Press went out of business and *Star Bridge* and *This Fortress World* and my other novels began to be reprinted in the United States and overseas, that we got some financial return. Actually, the three years I spent as a freelance writer selling almost everything I wrote but never earning more than $3,000 a year provided the basis for a literary career and financial return as reprints continued. *Star Bridge* has been in print, somewhere in the world, almost continuously.

But I had no idea that *Star Bridge* had any claims to classic status until writer Ed Bryant showed up in Missoula, Montana, where the Science Fiction Research Association met in 1976. Ed had just attended a convention in Washington and he told an audience that a novel named *Star Bridge* had turned him into a science fiction writer, and he added, turning to Jack and me in the audience, "I'm not sure I thanked you."

A month later I was having breakfast in New York City with John Brunner and Samuel R. Delany, and I mentioned the incident. Delany said, "The same thing happened to me." And we put Delany's comment on the cover of the Berkeley reprint that Jonas reviewed.

Since then Bryant wrote, in an introduction to volume #4 of *The Collected Stories of Jack Williamson*: "I think I was about twelve, probably in the sixth grade, when the TAB Book Club delivered a paperback of *Star Bridge* by Jack Williamson and James E. Gunn. To this day, I refuse to understand why this novel is not accorded the same classic status as *The Stars My Destination* or *The Moon Is a Harsh Mistress*."

I don't know that I can really take any credit for it. Oh, I wrote it. I know that because it has my name on the cover, along with Jack's. But that was more than fifty years ago, and I read it now as if they were someone else's words. No doubt Jack's vision had a lot to do with it. He was always young in spirit and his imagination soared.

A number of years ago I was having lunch with David Hartwell in New York City, when he was editor of Timescape Books, and he said that he wanted to reprint *Star Bridge*. "I seem to reprint it whenever I move to another publisher," he said. "It has the ideal combination of Jack's experience and your youthful energy."

"You've got it wrong," I said. "It was my experience and Jack's youthful energy!"

James Gunn

ABOUT THE AUTHORS

JACK WILLIAMSON (1908–2006) was born in Arizona and sold his first story at the age of twenty. He was the second author to be named a Grand Master of Science Fiction by SFWA and is often credited with inventing the terms "terraforming" and "genetic engineering."

JAMES GUNN is the Hugo Award–winning science fiction author of *The Joy Makers, The Immortals,* and *The Listeners.* He lives in Lawrence, Kansas.